The Crunchy, Munchy Christmas Tree

A Harry & Emily Adventure

Karen Gray Ruelle

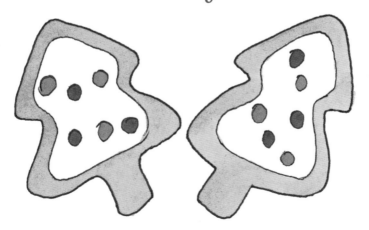

Holiday House / New York

**For Nina
and Lee
for bringing
me joy
and Christmas
trees**

Library of Congress Cataloging-in-Publication Data
Ruelle, Karen Gray.
The crunchy, munchy Christmas tree / Karen Gray Ruelle.— 1st ed.
p. cm.
Summary: When a heavy snow falls, Emily and Harry
must postpone taking a Christmas tree to their grandparents' house
for Christmas Eve, but their parents know how
to celebrate in the meantime.
ISBN 0-8234-1787-5 (hardcover)
ISBN 0-8234-1799-9 (paperback)
[1. Christmas trees—Fiction. 2. Christmas—Fiction.
3. Snow—Fiction.] I. Title.
PZ7.R88525Cr 2003
[E]—dc21
2002192198

Contents

1.
The Perfect Tree

"I like that tree," said Harry.

He pointed to a short, thick tree.

"That tree is too fat,"

said his little sister, Emily.

"Grandma will not like it."

They were shopping for a

Christmas tree for their grandparents.

It was hard to find the right tree.

"How about this one?"
asked Harry.
He pointed to a tall tree.
"It is too tall," said Emily.
"Grandma cannot
reach the top."
"You don't like any
trees," said Harry.
"I do so," said Emily.
"I just don't like
these trees."

Just then, Harry and Emily's
mother said,
"This is the perfect tree."
She was standing in front of a tree.
It was not too tall.
It was not too fat.
It was just right.

"Grandma and Grandpa will love it,"
she said.
"It does not look Christmasy
enough," said Emily.
She frowned.
But she helped carry
the tree anyway.

2.
Getting Ready to Go

Harry and Emily helped their mother.

They found the Christmas box.

Emily took out lights.

"We will not need these.

Grandma and Grandpa have lights,"

said their mother.

Harry took out their

Christmas stockings.

"We will not need those.
Grandma and Grandpa have
stockings for us," said their father.
Emily took out a glass globe
with a snowflake inside.

"Grandma and Grandpa have
ornaments," said their mother.
"But you can each bring
one for the tree."
Harry picked a polar bear on skis.
Emily picked the glass globe
and a prancing reindeer.
"Pick one, Emily," said her mother.
Emily put them back.
She picked an angel instead.
They put the ornaments
in the trunk of the car.

There was a big bag in the trunk.

Harry peeked in the bag.

It was filled with presents.

"Who are these for?" asked Harry.

"They are for Grandma and Grandpa,"
said his mother.

"Where are our presents?"
asked Harry.

DEAR SANTA,
PLESE BRING
OUR PREZNTS
TO GRMA AND
GRMPS HOWS
I WANT A PONY
AND A SKATEBORD
AND A LOT OF CDS
AND HARRY
WANTS ONE TWO.
FROM EMILY

"Don't worry,"
said Emily.
"I wrote
a letter to Santa.
He will bring
our presents
to Grandma
and Grandpa's."

"We will leave first thing
in the morning.
We want to decorate the tree
for Christmas Eve," said their mother.
"I want to make Christmas cookies
with Grandma," said Emily.
"I want to sing Christmas carols
with Grandpa," said Harry.
They went inside just as
it started to snow.

When they
went to bed,
it was still snowing.
All night, Harry and Emily
had Christmas dreams.
All night it snowed and snowed.

3.
Too Much Snow!

The next morning,
it was still snowing.
"We cannot drive in this storm,"
said their father.

"If we stay home, Grandma
   and Grandpa will not have
   a Christmas tree,"
   said Harry.
"You can't have Christmas
   without a tree."
"We will bring the tree
   when it stops snowing.

But we cannot drive
in this blizzard," said their father.
"If we stay home, we will not
get any presents," said Emily.
"I will call Grandma and Grandpa,"
said their mother.
Harry and Emily got on the phone.
They said, "Merry Christmas!"

Their grandparents told them,
"We will wait to celebrate Christmas.
We miss you!"
Their father promised they would
come as soon as they could.

Harry and Emily went outside.

But it was so cold and snowy.

Soon, their noses were frozen.

Their toes were frozen, too.

They came in for hot cocoa.

It was very cozy.

But it did not feel like Christmas Eve.

4.
Merry Christmas
After All

The next day, the snow stopped.

"Merry Christmas!"
said Harry and Emily's parents.

"Some Christmas," Emily said.

"Can we go to Grandma and
Grandpa's now?" asked Harry.

"We have to shovel the driveway,"
said their father.

"Then we have to wait
for the snowplow.
When the roads are clear, we can go."

"How can it be Christmas
with no presents?
How can it be Christmas
with no tree?" said Emily.
She looked out the window.
She saw a tree.

It was covered in snow.

There were icicles hanging from it.

They sparkled in the sunlight.

It looked so pretty.

"I have an idea," Emily said.

"Let's make a Christmas tree outside."

"You can decorate it with popcorn
and cranberries," said their mother.

"Yum," said Emily.

"A crunchy, munchy Christmas tree."
They made strings of
cranberries and popcorn.

While their father shoveled,
they decorated the tree.
It looked beautiful!
"If it had presents under it,"
said Emily,
"it would be perfect."
Harry and Emily went inside
to warm up.

"I wish Santa could see our tree,"
said Emily.

She looked out the window.

"Look!" she said. "I see reindeer!
Santa must be here."

Harry and Emily ran outside.

Under the tree were two presents.

"Are those for us?" asked Emily.

"I think so," said their mother.

They opened the presents.

They were cameras.

"We can take pictures of our tree
to show Grandma and Grandpa!"
said Harry.

Then they heard a loud noise.

"What is that?" asked Harry.

"It sounds like a snowplow,"
said their mother.

"Hooray!" said Harry and Emily.

As they got in the car, Emily said,
"I like crunchy, munchy
    Christmas trees."
"So do I," said Harry.
"Look at the tree!"

The deer were back.
They were eating cranberries
right off the tree.
"You are not the only ones
who like crunchy, munchy
Christmas trees!" said their father.

HIGH
SOCIETY

HIGH SOCIETY

Legal and Illegal Drugs in Canada

NEIL BOYD

KEY PORTER BOOKS

CANADIAN CATALOGUING IN PUBLICATION DATA
Boyd, Neil, 1951-
   High society

ISBN 1-55013-288-1

1. Drug abuse — Canada.   2. Drug utilization —
Canada.   I. Title.

HV5840.C3B68 1991   364.1'77'0971   C91-094510-1

Key Porter Books Limited
70 The Esplanade
Toronto, Ontario
Canada   M5E 1R2

Typesetting: Computer Composition of Canada Inc.

Printed on acid-free paper
Printed and bound in Canada by John Deyell Company

91 92 93 94 95 96 6 5 4 3 2 1

To the memory of Virginia Franklin,
my Auntie Mame

CONTENTS

ACKNOWLEDGEMENTS

There are many people and organizations to thank for making this book possible. For the past twelve years Simon Fraser University's School of Criminology has been a highly supportive working environment. For their advice and assistance on this project, I'd like to thank, particularly, John Lowman, Joan Brockman, Paul Brantingham, and Bill Glackman. Toronto's Osgoode Society provided me with an initial grant to facilitate archival research. Correctional Services Canada was consistently helpful in granting access for interviews. Liz Elliott helped with a number of the early interviews and with the transcription of many more. Petra Accipiter was also helpful with later transcriptions; her editorial comments on the subjects of my interviews were always enjoyable and thoughtful.

I owe intellectual debts to the many academics, lawyers, police officers, and policy makers who work in the field of drug use and drug control in Canada and elsewhere. Their articles and books are, in many senses, the base upon which this book is built. Specifically, thanks to Bruce Alexander, Barry Beyerstein, Pat Erickson, Eric Single, the late Chet Mitchell, Judith Blackwell, Mel Green, Robert Solomon, Rod Stamler, Bruce MacFarlane, Robert Fahlman, Marc Eliany, Arnold Trebach, Ethan Nadelmann, Andrew Weil, and the late Norman Zinberg. I also want to thank those who consented to be interviewed; their frankness was very much appreciated.

I am very grateful to Denise Bukowski for the thoughtful way in which she pursued this project. Charis Wahl has been a delightful editor, helping me to transform the manuscript with insight and candour. There are a number of others who have assisted the development of this book in a variety of ways: René Gantzert, Arlene Elvin, Maggie Davidson, Kim Rossmo, Sharon Rynders, Chris Otter, Mimi Ajzenstadt, Byron Rogers, Rob Roy, Les Rose, Rob Hocking, Nancy Keithly, and Gord Cross. And finally, thanks to Isabel Otter. For her editorial advice, encouragement, and love, I cannot be thankful enough.

CAN WE JUST SAY NO
TO A WAR AGAINST DRUGS?

Human beings have been using drugs for thousands of years, eating opium and marijuana, chewing the coca leaf, consuming the potions of various "medicine men," drinking alcohol, and inhaling tobacco smoke. There is no culture on earth that has abstained from intoxicants, with the possible exception of the Inuit. Unable to grow the plants that produce drugs, the people of the Arctic Circle had to wait until we brought them alcohol, tobacco, and the others.

We take drugs to provide pleasure, to relieve pain, to increase productivity, to alter mood, and very occasionally, to allow for the possibility of spiritual or emotional insight. We drink our morning coffee, a little kickstart for the morning rush hour. We light our cigarettes, the relaxing complement to our stimulants. And, later in the day, maybe at lunch and probably at dinner, we drink a little or a lot of alcohol.

We are a country of drug takers. About 80 per cent of adult Canadians drink alcohol, about 70 per cent drink coffee, and about 30 per cent smoke tobacco. About 10 per cent of us, mostly women, are prescribed tranquillizers, and about 10 per cent smoke marijuana. Cocaine is used by about 2 per cent of Canadians; amphetamines, hallucinogens, and opiates are regularly consumed by less than 1 per cent of the population.

These patterns of use vary as we travel around the globe.

In most Muslim countries, coffee, tobacco, marijuana, and opium are, in that order, the most popular of mind-active drugs. In most of the Persian Gulf, alcohol is the least culturally acceptable of consciousness-altering experiences, the subject of Islamic prohibition. In Japan, tobacco consumption is almost twice as popular as it is in Canada, marijuana use is relatively rare, and intravenous use of amphetamines is significant, accounting for more than 50,000 criminal-court appearances each year. Almost half of those in Japanese jails are serving time for amphetamine offences. Almost 50 per cent of French women and almost 20 per cent of French men are prescribed tranquillizers and other sedatives for use on a daily basis. The French also drink about twice as much alcohol per capita as Canadians or Americans, and slightly more than most of their European neighbours; they are the world's most practised consumers of wine.

Drug use and drug control vary across time and geography, products of specific nations and communities operating in specific historical contexts. "The drug problem" is usually conceived by government and industry as a blend of public-health and criminal enforcement, but it is rarely understood as a cultural phenomenon.

However, similar drugs have different meanings in different cultures. What a drug actually does to you isn't nearly as important as the social context in which it is used and distributed. In many parts of sixteenth-century Europe, after the introduction of tobacco from the New World, tobacco users and distributors were imprisoned, and even executed. In seventeenth-century Europe, shortly after the introduction of coffee, the Catholic church forbade its consumption, promoting wine as a more appropriate sacrament. Over the last one thousand years of human history, at different times and in different places, tobacco, caffeine, alcohol, marijuana, cocaine, and opium have all been prohibited, and their users and distributors tortured, imprisoned, or executed.

In the current era, cultural scripts have also taken precedence over public-health concerns. While marijuana is a less toxic drug than either tobacco or alcohol, its consumption in Western industrial culture has been tied to dissident youth and a rejection of dominant values. Although amphetamines are more potent stimulants than cocaine, and have longer-lasting effects, they are not the object of criminal prohibition. Amphetamines are produced by first world pharmaceutical companies, cocaine by the Indians of various South American mountain ranges.

I first learned of the significance of cultural context in Grade 8. My entry in the local Legion's public-speaking contest the previous year was a stirring tribute to Winston Churchill, and had been enthusiastically received. In my senior year of elementary school I decided to deliver a speech entitled "LSD — The Potential Medical and Social Benefits."

It was not well received. In 1965, LSD was virtually unknown, at least in my small town of Deep River, Ontario, but the concept of profoundly altering consciousness was disturbing to the Legionnaires and others. And the suggestion that this drug might be usefully integrated into our culture was threatening, even coming from a thirteen-year-old boy who hadn't the faintest idea what he was talking about.

Taking issue with these cultural norms as an adult can also be seen as an act of economic and political heresy. *Out of Control* was a documentary about drugs, prepared in 1990 for the CTV national network by Stornoway Productions, a Toronto-based company with a reputation for thoughtful work on complex political issues. The documentary was a substantial commitment, signed by outgoing CTV president Murray Chercover as one of his last decisions before his departure. *Out of Control* was to be two hours in length and to air in prime time, with a budget of several hundred thousand dollars. I was hired by Stornoway to arrange and assist with interviews with convicted drug dealers, and to be interviewed for the program.

When a rough cut of *Out of Control* was shown to the new directors of the network, including President John Cassaday, they had few concerns about the production values, but a lot to say about the message. Illegal drug dealers and drug users, informers, and police had not been portrayed as they had wanted them to be. My appearance had not helped. I had argued that the real drug pushers are not those who sell illegal drugs, but those who have the right to advertise their drugs, the purveyors of alcohol and tobacco.

In retrospect, it was probably not surprising that John Cassaday would have found this premise upsetting. Between 1972 and 1976, he had worked in marketing and sales promotion for the Canadian subsidiary of the RJR-Macdonald tobacco company, selling what he likely believed was a legitimate commodity, rather than a dangerous drug.

The final product was cut to one hour and rightly criticized in the media for its "trite conclusions" and "predictable images." The original rough cut had not advocated the legalization of drugs, or anything else particularly extreme. It had, however, presented differing points of view on drug control and some of the quirky contradictions of the business. The mistake that the filmmakers made was to believe that they could discuss legal drugs like tobacco and alcohol with the illegal drugs — marijuana, cocaine, and heroin.

That is not to say that most drugs are pharmacologically similar or that they pose similar physical and social risks. There are profound and important public health differences, but they are overshadowed by cultural beliefs and by existing forms of social and economic organization. The legality or illegality of drugs has shaped the way in which we understand pharmacological consequences. Tobacco, alcohol, and pharmaceuticals are all billion-dollar industries, approved by the state and occasionally subsidized. Heroin, cocaine, and marijuana are also billion-dollar industries, prohibited by the state; the eradication of these industries has consistently been subsidized.

Tobacco, for example, is a multibillion-dollar revenue producer for government and the industry. The drug rose to prominence in Canada during the 1920s with mechanization and cigarette-package production. Before 1920, tobacco was consumed more sporadically, smoked in pipes, cigars, and hand-rolled cigarettes.

Opium, a gummy solid derived from the opium poppy, is also a multibillion-dollar revenue producer. The drug rose to prominence in Canada in the late nineteenth century, imported by Chinese immigrants and typically smoked. Since the late 1940s, morphine and heroin, more potent derivatives of opium, have emerged, typically injected intravenously.

What links opiates to tobacco is the user's irresistible craving for the drug. In the absence of these two drugs, physical and psychological symptoms of withdrawal typically develop. Some clinicians refer to this as drug dependence, and others would define it as drug addiction.

Clinicians usually apply the word "addiction" to continued heroin use and the word "dependence" to continued tobacco use. In large measure, this is because heroin users tend to be more socially desperate than tobacco users. A heroin habit costs about $100 per day and a tobacco habit about $7 a day — both prices artificial creations of government. The real cost of manufacturing two packs of cigarettes is about seventy-five cents, and the real cost of manufacturing a day's supply of opiates is similarly insignificant.

We do know that daily use of tobacco is ultimately much more damaging than daily use of opiates. If opiate use is relatively stable, the most deleterious effects are typically constipation and a somewhat reduced sex drive. These intrusions may be irritating or disappointing, but they cannot compare to the lung cancer, heart disease, and emphysema that tobacco can produce.

Unlike tobacco, however, the intravenous injection of heroin can kill a user at a single sitting. This typically happens when the person injecting is misinformed or uninformed about the dose, forgetful of the amount taken, or suicidal. A lifelong dependence on heroin can, however, be as consistent with social productivity and physical well-being as a lifelong dependence on tea or coffee.

In those societies in which opium smoking or eating is tolerated, it does not appear to be a major cause of premature death. In the industrialized world, however, an epidemic of lung cancer and heart disease has followed the mass production and promotion of the modern cigarette.

The division between legal and illegal drugs was created in Canada in 1908, but the story really begins with the second Opium War in the 1850s. Britain had gone to war in order to impose the opium traffic on China. The Chinese government fought the introduction of the drug into their country, but the Empire was ultimately successful, and by the late nineteenth century opium smoking was a popular pastime in China.

When Canadian industrialists came looking for cheap labour to build the industries of western Canada, they came to China, offering labourers about ten times the amount they could earn for comparable work at home. Thousands of Chinese came to Vancouver annually to work on the construction of the Canadian Pacific Railway and to build other segments of the industrial infrastructure. They were paid about half what white workers received.

Between 1870 and 1908, a number of Chinese merchants operated opium factories in the B.C. cities of Vancouver, Victoria, and New Westminster; each paid a municipal licensing fee. The factories, seldom the object of public concern, produced a black tar opium that was purchased equally by white and Chinese customers, and typically smoked.

The white pharmacies of the day also sold opiated tonics, elixirs, and analgesics to their customers, as patent medicines. The medical profession and the burgeoning patent-medicine industry were hailing opium as a panacea; cocaine and alcohol were also active ingredients in many of the industry's products.

In the late nineteenth century, these concoctions of opium, alcohol, and cocaine were the physician's preferred remedies for emotional or psychological distress. But, by the early twentieth century, this alliance of doctors and entrepreneurs began to falter. In their advertisements the patent-medicine makers urged Americans and Canadians to medicate themselves, in order to avoid the expense and unnecessary intrusion of physicians and pharmacists.

The patent-medicine industry was becoming an economic threat to physicians. Medicine was transforming itself from an art to a science, and into professional associations with both economic and social objectives. By the early twentieth century, the Canadian Medical Association and the Canadian Pharmaceutical Association were becoming politically powerful organizations, opposed to what they called "the quackery" of the patent-medicine companies.

The realities of opiate dependence and cocaine abuse were gradually being recognized, just as medicine was dramatically extending human longevity. While most of this was accomplished through a fairly basic understanding of the importance of personal hygiene in the transmission of disease, there were also increasing successes in surgical intervention and, later in our century, in the development of antibiotics and other drugs.

In 1908, Canada experienced a profound shift in drug-control policy. The sale or manufacture of smoking opium was prohibited: for the first time in our history we had criminalized a psychoactive drug. Only one form of the drug was criminalized, however. Chinese smoking-opium manufacturers were to be put out of business through criminal penalties, but the patent-medicine industry could continue to dispense opiated liquids to its white customers, provided that the ingredients of the various elixirs or analgesics were set out on each bottle.

Mackenzie King was the architect of the policy of criminalization, urging this kind of legislation in the aftermath of Vancouver's anti-Asiatic riot of September 1907. A rally to support a ban on Chinese immigration had turned into a rampage into the Chinese and Japanese quarters of Vancouver. Businesses were damaged and destroyed by the angry crowd.

King, the deputy minister of labour, was sent to Vancouver to compensate the Chinese for their damages. "It should be made impossible to manufacture this drug anywhere in the Dominion," he said of smoking opium while in Vancouver, and added, "We will get some good out of this riot yet." Within two months, the federal government criminally prohibited the manufacture and sale of smoking opium.

In 1911, Mackenzie King went back to the House of Commons as the government's minister of labour. He had two requests to make of Parliament. First, King wanted to add cocaine to the schedule of prohibited drugs. He told the Commons that "the medical men" had told him cocaine was more dangerous than morphine, and he argued that use of the drug would facilitate "the seduction of our daughters and the demoralization of our young men." King had been informed by the Montreal police that cocaine was, among other things, most popular among young black men.

King also told the House of Commons that police across the country were having difficulty in obtaining convictions for sale or manufacture of opium. A new offence, "illegal drug possession," was necessary, if these battles against opium and cocaine were to succeed.

When facing questions about his new drug legislation in the House, King was asked by a member of the Conservative opposition why tobacco was not being added to the list of prohibited substances. "Tobacco has not yet been considered a drug," King, a non-smoker, shot back. He knew that tobacco was a much of a drug as opium, but was not prepared to admit publicly that opium could be taken "in much the same way that an Englishman might use a cigar, or spirits."

In 1923, marijuana was criminalized with a simple declaration in the House of Commons: "There is a new drug in the schedule." There was unanimous passage of this addition and no debate. Marijuana had been associated with Mexican migrants and black jazz musicians, and was said to be connected with madness and promiscuity.

Alcohol was also a much discussed and debated drug during this period of history. Temperance unions were formed, spurred on, at least in part, by women who had experienced drunken beatings at the hands of husbands. In a national referendum on prohibition in 1898, a slender majority of Canadians endorsed the principle of an alcohol-free society; Wilfrid Laurier, a proponent of a "wet" Canada, declined to transform this majority view into legislation. While the temperance movement was ultimately successful in accomplishing a short-lived national prohibition in 1918, as a part of the war effort, it was never really as powerful as anti-opium, -cocaine, or -marijuana organizations. By the late 1920s, each province had repealed its prohibition legislation, and the popularity of alcohol began to climb, along with the power of the industry and the power of government to raise revenue from sales.

Possession of the drug was never criminalized, and legal initiatives generally allowed alcohol producers and distributors, even during Prohibition, to continue with both interprovincial shipments of their products and out-of-country transactions.

By the end of the roaring 'twenties, the way in which Canadians came to understand drug taking had been transformed. As Toronto lawyer Mel Green has noted, what was regarded in 1900 as a matter of private indulgence was, by 1930, a matter of public evil. There were now "good" and "bad" drugs. The drugs of the blacks and the Chinese had been targeted as bad, but white European uses of alcohol and tobacco were acceptable recreations. Marijuana, opium, and cocaine had been elevated to the status of a social problem, their use deserving of severe penalty.

The construction of this moral fault line was assisted by police, increasingly harsh government legislation, and various propagandists. The writing of Edmonton magistrate and suffragette Emily Murphy, also known as Janey Canuck, played a critical role. Ms. Murphy's analyses of the drug problem were serialized in *Maclean's*, and printed in book form as *The Black Candle*. She feared that white women might be seduced by black men using cocaine, or by Oriental men smoking opium. Opium was described as "an attempt to injure the bright browed races of the world." "Persons using marijuana," she wrote, "smoke the dried leaves of the plant, which has the effect of driving them completely insane. The addict loses all sense of moral responsibility. Addicts to this drug, while under its influence, are immune to pain, become raving maniacs, and are liable to kill or indulge in any forms of violence to other persons."

But the late 1960s and early 1970s have again changed the way in which we understand drugs in our culture. From the 1920s to the 1960s, there was sporadic use of marijuana, cocaine, and opium by a small and typically socially and economically marginal population: jazz musicians in the 1930s and the beatniks and the beat generation in the 1950s. But it was not until the late 1960s that illegal drug use began to cut across all social classes and political alliances. Ultimately, a hundred million young Canadians and Americans made the conscious decision to commit the criminal offence of possession of marijuana. Like the Chinese opium smokers of British Columbia, marijuana users were originally economically marginal men and women who were resented and feared. Marijuana was the drug of the hippies, the young, those who questioned the values of materialist success, and those opposed to the Vietnam war.

The young were challenging the moral validity of the line between legal and illegal drugs, and the state responded by budgeting one million dollars to study the problem. In Canada, the federal government appointed the Le Dain Commission, "An Inquiry into the Non-Medical Use of Drugs." The Le Dain Commission issued a final report in 1973, urging very cautious movement towards the wise exercise of freedom of choice. Specifically, they urged that possession of marijuana no longer be a criminal offence, and that heroin maintenance programs be encouraged on a closely monitored and experimental basis.

Their recommendations have been largely ignored. No government wants to be remembered as "soft on drugs" or to concede that the line between legal and illegal drugs is a rather arbitrary by-product of our social history, rather than a matter of moral consequence.

For as long as Canada has been a nation, we have been writing moral, economic, and political scripts about drugs. Amphetamines and cocaine may be pharmacologically similar, but they have different scripts attached. The image of a capitalist pharmaceutical is pitted against the image of a pagan South American powder. Taking a drug thought to be designed to restore an individual to economic productivity is, in political terms, quite a different act from taking a drug in order to obtain pleasure. When we add caffeine, alcohol, heroin, tobacco, marijuana, and other pharmaceuticals to the mix, these cultural scripts and preferences only become more complex and more convoluted.

The war against drugs has very little to do with public health. It is a moral battle about the appropriate methods and reasons for alteration of consciousness, pitting the "le-gitimate" drugs of affluent Western culture — tobacco, alcohol, and pharmaceuticals — against the "bad" drugs of the developing third world — the opium poppy, the coca plant, and cannabis and its derivatives.

The war on drugs serves various political agendas, and most pointedly those of covert military operations. The Central Intelligence Agency of the United States has been implicated in several instances; the governments of Colombia and Panama, and the freedom fighters of Afghanistan, and various participants in the Gulf conflict have also been said to be involved in trading guns for illegal drugs.

By condoning and occasionally participating in the traffic, these organizations accomplish a number of contradictory objectives. They reap millions of dollars from the distribution of illegal drugs, they circumvent government-imposed financial limitations on strategies of political intervention, and they, perhaps inadvertently, line the coffers of international arms dealers. When I asked Rod Stamler, head of the RCMP's drug branch from 1980 to 1989, about the role of the CIA in the business of illegal drugs, he responded, "Well, they're involved in politics, and organized criminals are involved in politics, and drugs are profit, and profits are needed to sometimes tip the balance here and there in various parts of the world."

In Canada, the war on drugs has not been closely tied to foreign policy, but it has been conscripted for political purposes, with limited success. In 1986 Prime Minister Brian Mulroney announced that there was a drug epidemic in Canada, and was promptly contradicted in the national press. There was no evidence to suggest that there had actually been increases in the use of most illegal drugs and the prime minister hadn't mentioned alcohol and tobacco.

Substance abuse, whether legal or illegal, is most fairly cast as an issue of public health, not a moral question. Ultimately, drugs are symbols of a potentially unhealthy lifestyle, and drug use is one more variable to throw into the hopper of what some people call "wellness." Drug use is relevant to health in the way that regular exercise, good nutrition, and stress management are relevant to health.

The drugs that are actually killing us are the legal ones, which are rarely described as drugs. Those who operate these distribution schemes for legal drugs are typically described as captains of commerce rather than drug dealers. There is an Orwellian cant to our rhetoric. We worry about the demonic pushers of marijuana, cocaine, and heroin, while we sit comfortably viewing sophisticated and costly advertisements that link beer consumption with a glamorous and exciting lifestyle. And we leaf through magazine images that link tobacco consumption to healthy and attractive men and women in pristine wilderness settings. In reality, it is the legal drugs that are pushed upon the consumer.

The intention of users — to alter ordinary waking consciousness — does not change as we move from legal to illegal drugs. In every instance, we ingest a chemical and experience a change in our minds, our bodies, or both. What counts in taking drugs is the substance, the dose taken, the mental and emotional attitude of the user, and the social setting in which consumption takes place. Less refined (and, hence, less potent) drugs are better for public health than more potent and refined drugs; smoking or injecting a drug has been shown to greatly increase the risk of dependence.

When we criminalize a particular substance, we pay attention to only a small part of this picture. Criminalization is a metaphor for war, a battle in which the domestic military are asked to arrest and convict those who possess certain psychoactives. And this war on drugs, like all other wars, is a statement of human failure. There aren't so much good or bad drugs as there are good and bad relationships with drugs.

Some drugs are more dangerous than others, however, both in terms of their effects and in terms of the way in which they have been integrated into our culture. And this is what this book is about: the drugs that we use, the people who distribute them, and the people who use them.

What we're doing now isn't working. High rates of premature death are more closely tied to legal drugs than they are to illegal drugs, even when differences in rates of use are taken into account. Moreover, death is less likely from illegal-drug use than from illegal-drug distribution and its control. We are at war with ourselves, and if we can better understand the dimensions of these battles, we might be able to find more peaceful resolutions of our conflict.

THE MOST POTENT PAINKILLER

I consider myself an addict because I was able to
afford what I did. I consider a junkie a person
who has to rob, cheat and steal for his next fix.
Heroin's a rich man's drug. If you can afford it,
everything's fine.

— LES PODOLSKI

Prince Rupert is a small city on the northern coast of British Columbia. Rain, cloud, and drizzle are the dominant themes. Like most other Canadian cities, this little port offers tobacco, alcohol, marijuana, cocaine, and heroin. The major industries are commercial fishing and logging, the bounty of the north extracted to fuel the wealth of the south. According to Les Podolski, there is a "work hard, play hard" ethic among the men who work in the bush, and on the boats.

Les Podolski is a logger in his early thirties, tall, attractive, and physically fit. "I try to treat my body like a temple," he told me. He started to use heroin regularly during the early 1980s, at first sniffing it or smoking it, and then moving to daily injections and distribution.

Opiates are the world's most powerful painkillers, taken by millions of people in pursuit of pleasure and for relief from pain. Generally grown in Asia and the Middle East, opium is extracted from ripening poppy pods, after the flower has withered. A milky liquid oozes from knife cuts in the pod and is collected and dried. This is crude opium, from which morphine, codeine, and heroin are extracted.

In North American culture, heroin, the most potent of the opiates, is usually injected intravenously, though occasionally smoked or sniffed. The drug is sold in capsules, usually containing less than one-tenth of a gram of the product. The heroin distributor typically takes an ounce of heroin, spreads it over a table top, and mixes in four ounces of milk sugar as thoroughly as possible. Because of the lack of regulation in this industry, some consumers are vulnerable to the carelessness and ignorance of some distributors. When the mix isn't very good, the street receives "hot caps," with three or four times the anticipated load. A hot cap can lead to overdose and death.

Self-injection is an important ritual for many heroin dependents, and often critical to the experience of consumption. Those who inject their drugs enjoy the "rush" that follows, an intensely pleasurable sensation heroin users describe as "better than sex," "saxophones begin to play," and "the top of your head gets blown off."

This rush also contributes significantly to heroin dependence. (As more than one doctor has counselled, "If you ever try a narcotic intravenously and feel overwhelming pleasure, never repeat it.") Injection is the fastest method of getting a drug to the brain, and is accordingly crucial for many drug dependents.

When the typical heroin user opens his capsule, he places the white powder in a spoon. With a syringe, he adds about 0.5 cubic centimetres of water, whisky, or vodka; the alcohol adds an extra tiny kick. When the spoon is heated with a match or lighter, the powder dissolves into a clear liquid, and is drawn into the syringe. If contaminants such as chalk are suspected, the liquid is drawn through a small ball of cotton batting. The mix is injected into a vein, usually in the forearm.

Heroin is not the only opiate that can be injected. Demerol, Dilaudid, and many others issued in chalk-based tablet form can be crushed and mixed with water. The chalk drops to the bottom of a glass or jar, and the remaining

THE MOST POTENT PAINKILLER 17

liquid is an injectable supply that typically does not need to be heated.

It is usually not difficult for the heroin user to obtain syringes. One syringe might provide five or six injections, or more; the rubber stopper inside the plastic cylinder usually wears first, the effectiveness of the vacuum weakened with use. Since the late 1980s, syringes have become easier to obtain. The risk of contracting AIDS through sharing needles has produced government-sanctioned needle-exchange programs that trade a used needle for a clean, new one, with few questions asked. The other risks of intravenous injection — serious infections, abcesses, inflammation, and hepatitis — persist, nonetheless.

The RCMP estimates that there are currently about 25,000 heroin users in Canada, men and women who are committed to continued use of the drug. Those who appear before the courts to face heroin trafficking and possession charges are usually economically and socially marginal. The majority are working class or poorer, and usually have an unstable family history, other drug dependencies, and little education. While there is some use of the drug by professional men and women, consumption does seem to be concentrated among the urban poor. More affluent and socially skilled heroin users are also less likely to be arrested: they make their acquisitions in a more careful manner, and their arrests require substantial police resources.

Recruitment into the heroin trade occurs among peers. There are a few distributors who are not users, and a few users who are not distributors; but most of those who occupy the time of our criminal courts are user/distributors, dealing in amounts that do not make them wealthy, but will permit them to continue their habits. The RCMP report that Chinese and Vietnamese organizations operate in Vancouver, and Iranian, Pakistani, Lebanese, and Italian organizations in Toronto and Montreal.

For most people, heroin is not a very enjoyable drug. In experiments in America during the 1950s, psychologist H.K. Beecher and his colleagues randomly injected twenty young, healthy, male white subjects on successive days with a placebo, heroin, morphine, or an amphetamine. The study employed a double blind: neither the person administering the drug nor the person injected with the drug knew what the substance was. Fourteen of the subjects indicated that they would like to receive another injection of what turned out to be amphetamines, but only four were interested in receiving another injection of heroin or morphine. And while only two of the subjects said that they definitely would not want to receive another injection of the placebo or an amphetamine, nine of the subjects indicated that they would never like to repeat the injection of morphine or heroin. Other research has determined that, in China in 1906, with smoking opium freely available, about 3 per cent of the population of 400 million were daily users.

Joseph Westermeyer, an American physician, conducted an on-site analysis of opium use in Laos over several years during the 1970s. He wrote of one experience: "Of my eight Caucasian fellow visitors, six did try smoking opium. None had ever used opium before, and to the best of my knowledge, none has ever used it again. They inhaled relatively small doses, apparently more from curiosity and to say 'I smoked opium' than from any fervent wish to make this ritual part of their regular lives. . . . A few felt nothing, a few more experienced some nausea and lethargy after finishing a pipe or two. None of them reported anything resembling pleasure or euphoria. One man having a bout of diarrhea at the time found that two pipefuls greatly relieved this condition."

For Les Podolski, however, heroin was not only pleasurable, it was also economically rewarding. His partner in heroin distribution was an elderly Chinese man who was able to deliver high-potency heroin at a relatively cheap price. "He supplied it, I distributed it, we split the profit down the middle, and we both reinvested. I could cut it five and a half, six times, and I'd come up with a 10 per cent product. . . . We'd really be talking about a $15,000 to $20,000 investment, and we'd gross over $100,000. There's an enormous appetite for the products in Prince Rupert. You could probably turn that over in a couple of months . . . $200,000 to $300,000 a year, easy, without trying.''

But Les Podolski began to consume larger amounts of his product, and its profits.

"It got to a point where I needed it to function. I wouldn't look on it as getting high — it was getting straight. I had to fix every eight hours, three times a day. I was doing a high grade, uncut. I would do enough to kill three or four normal people and I would get high long enough to smoke a couple of cigarettes. I would feel it for about half an hour, and we could sit here like this and you wouldn't know that I just did $300 to $400 worth of stuff. I'd be totally straight.''

The first time that a person uses heroin or other opiates, there may well be some unpleasant consequences, depending on the dose ingested and the manner of ingestion. Like the first-time user of tobacco, the first-time user of heroin may experience nausea or vomiting. But, unlike tobacco or alcohol, once a tolerance is created, the drug's effects are relatively minimal. Though cellular pathology appears to follow the consumption of tobacco and alcohol, there is no such after-effect with heroin or other opiates.

For Les Podolski, the high-risk business of felling large firs and cedars was not inconsistent with being under the influence of heroin. "Once your system gets accustomed to it, you get an energy off it. You go, and sometimes you don't stop for lunch, you just keep working. You get a motivation, and production.''

It seems odd that a narcotic would have this effect, but some users find the change of consciousness provided by the drug stimulating, rather than sedating, at least temporarily.

The greatest difficulty with heroin begins when a user tries to break a pattern of dependence.

"It's a wild addiction," Podolski concludes of his experiences, "As soon as it put the smile on my face, it was out of control. Some people can control themselves. I had it together for a long time. . . . The majority of my friends didn't know that I was wired to it. I lived properly, I lived well, and I kept it together. They didn't know that I was doing over $500 worth a day to be normal. It went on for about three years."

His enjoyment from the drug started to wane. "I wasn't getting high any more, and I wasn't feeling that good on it any more. For me to sit down in the evening and actually get high, I was on the borderline of ODING. I wouldn't do it alone. I'd need somebody there, cause I'd need so much of it to catch a buzz."

Most of us don't like, want, or need heroin or other opiates, unless we are in severe pain. But for men and women who enjoy the experience of these drugs, dependence is a real possibility. Like other forms of drug dependence, it is more social than pharmacological. One study of American veterans of the Vietnam war found that only about 10 per cent of those who were regular heroin users in Vietnam continued with any consumption of the drug within three years of their return to the United States. The potency of the heroin injected in Vietnam was much greater than that on American streets and though many men went through unpleasant withdrawal, few were interested in returning to the drug. In the stress of combat, heroin must have offered some relief to some soldiers. Dependence tended to disappear in the more friendly and supportive environment of home and family. America was also less tolerant of the drug: any continuation of use generally required association with unpredictable criminal networks.

Among current users of heroin, there is a substantial range of consumption, from occasional recreational injection or inhalation to injections daily, at no more than eight-hour intervals. Policy researcher Arnold Trebach has concluded that there are about 3.5 million occasional users of heroin in the United States, and about 0.5 million addicts. In Canada, RCMP figures suggest that there are about 25,000 addicts, committed to daily consumption. We have no estimates of the population of occasional "chippers," though it seems likely, given experiences elsewhere, that it is many times larger.

Les Podolski was an unlikely heroin user, neither desperate nor disadvantaged. But quitting was a problem, particularly given the extent of his habit. "It was a vicious cycle of quitting, and each time I quit — it's not like a junkie on the corner snivelling that he's doing two or three caps a day, and he knows he's sick. He doesn't know what fucking sick is.

"I was taking six Percodan and four Valium, crushed up, and wolfing them down with beer, and I probably got relief from the pain in my joints for maybe ten minutes. .... I couldn't get off the ground for two days, lying there crying."

This portrait of heroin withdrawal is not universal. Some of those who inject this drug describe withdrawal as similar to a mild cold, some report chills and fever; others, depression and muscular pains. Intense discomfort of the kind described by Les Podolski is less common, and may be, to some extent, a function of the dose he was injecting.

Unlike withdrawal from alcohol, withdrawal from opiates does not involve the possibility of convulsions or death. "The confusion about the severity of opiate withdrawal," psychologist Bruce Alexander has concluded, "may result from ambiguity over whether mental anguish without tissue pathology constitutes withdrawal." The trauma of leaving the drug appears to be more psychological than physical.

The beginning of the end of Les Podolski's heroin dependence began in the bathroom of his Prince Rupert home in

1987. He was in the middle of a deal involving an ounce of heroin, worth about $10,000. "This was the first time I ever came home with anything so big.

"And so, of course, we were going to indulge," Podolski continued. "My partner and I opened the bag up, put it on the table, and I said, 'Help yourself.' I went to fix in the can and I put everything away. I heard somebody come up the stairs. I opened the washroom door, and this shotgun came in the door. This was an awful surprise to me."

Les Podolski's initial reaction was that he was being robbed. He took his ounce of heroin and placed it between some towels in the bathroom. "And then, right away, I heard, 'RCMP.' He's got the shotgun in there, weaseling the door open. And then he was on top of me, boom, boom, boom, you're under arrest. They handcuffed me, and they tore the house apart, but they didn't find the ounce for six hours." He laughed. "They were ripping insulation out of the walls before they actually found it."

Podolski was not particularly concerned about this arrest. He figured that he would be out on bail in a few days, and that he would be convicted of nothing more than possession. "I was thinking, sitting there in jail that night, it's no problem. We get a doctor to say I'm wired to the nuts on this stuff. A cap in Prince Rupert goes for $60. Once you get a habit you're going to need six, ten caps a day. So why not go buy an ounce at a time."

What Les Podolski didn't realize was that he and his associates had been the subject of police surveillance for about two years, and the charge was going to be conspiracy to traffic in heroin. The RCMP had tied him to the president of a local motorcycle club, whom they suspected of cocaine distribution. Podolski had nothing to do with cocaine, but he had gone herring fishing for this man. His legitimate wages, $8,000, had been sent to his bank in Prince Rupert. The police had apparently stumbled across him because of his acquaintances.

"For a week we are in and out of court from the city bucket," Podolski continued, "and they wouldn't give us bail. We couldn't figure out why. A week later the warrants went out, putting the conspiracy together right down to Vancouver, right down to the seventy-two-year-old Chinaman."

This elderly Chinese man was the key to a conviction for conspiracy to import heroin, but he died of cancer before the trial concluded. "I think if he wouldn't have died," Podolski said, "they would've hooked us into the conspiracy to import, and the shit would've really hit the fan. . . . I'd be looking at seven to twelve years right now."

Les Podolski received four years' imprisonment in 1989 for his part in a conspiracy to distribute heroin; he is now out on parole. By the time he left prison, he was no longer using heroin. "My lifestyle doesn't centre around heroin anymore . . . while I was on bail I made steps myself to go to NA. Hearing the stories at those meetings, I just gave my head a shake and realized what the fuck's going on.

"I couldn't hit that street level. Each person has got his own bottom," he went on. "My bottom is the addiction itself, not having to hang around downtown all night long, fixing beside fucking dumpsters. I consider myself an addict because I was able to afford what I did. I consider a junkie a person who had to rob, cheat, steal for his next fix. Heroin's a rich man's drug. If you can afford it, everything's fine. Pure heroin does not fuck you up physically. It's what you do to yourself.

"I was fortunate," he concluded. "It wasn't something I'd been messing with since I'd been fifteen or sixteen. So, there was life before drugs and there'll be life after drugs. This was just a brief interlude."

Les Podolski can work in British Columbia's forests, earning more than $60,000 in a good year, and he seems to have put heroin dependence behind him. But he admits that doing without the thrill of the game will be more difficult.

"You get hooked up in the lifestyle. The adrenalin buzz, this underground aspect. Viva, bandito. I'd pick up the phone on Monday morning and say I want to be on a beach by Saturday. Then I'd phone a girl from out in Vancouver or somewhere, and she'd take a few weeks off and we'd go to Hawaii, rent the condo — one particular time there it was $15,000 U.S. for the condo, for two weeks.

"I like it. And I think I'm going to channel my talents now into doing legitimate business. I have several close friends that are jewellers . . . and I've got contacts now in Bangkok. It's the gem capital. And what I'm going to do now is get my gemology papers, and become a certified gemologist, get a little capital together, and it's the same thing as dealing dope. You just middle it. Who's got it? You know who wants it. Yeah . . . I think I'm going to get down to some serious business here, and get my life together, and get things on track, legitimately."

Eddie Burns and his brothers, like Les Podolski, distanced themselves from the desperate life of the junkie. In the late 1950s and early 1960s, Eddie and his brothers Kenny and Tommy were major players in the Canadian trade, distributing millions of dollars worth of heroin annually in the large West Coast market. Eddie was the key organizer, connected to Vic Cotroni and the Montreal mob, and later making trips to India to acquire the product. Kenny Burns was the delivery man, taking ounces to Vancouver's mid-level dealers. All the brothers used heroin.

They saw the transition from morphine and opium to heroin in Canada during the late 1940s. "As more people tried the heroin," Eddie Burns recalled, "they quit looking for morphine. And in three months there were no morphine users anymore. The guys that had morphine couldn't sell it."

Ken Burns spent most of his adult life in Canada's penitentiaries. He was sentenced twice to nine-year terms, once to seven years, and once to six, and, on many other occasions, to an assortment of other lengths of time. His sentences were received for elaborate conspiracies to distribute heroin, typically with his brothers Eddie and Tommy.

"He done a lot of time, Kenny, you know," Eddie said. "He got more time than me and Tommy, because Kenny was too easy going. He would do things for people, step out for people, and take the heat for people. I don't know how he handled it all, but he still had a sense of humour. That's all that saves your life, I think, is a sense of humour."

Kenny's final nine-year sentence for trafficking in heroin was based on the testimony of a police informant named Owens. Eddie had brushed off Owens's request for a couple of ounces of heroin, and then tried to warn his brother. "I went directly to Kenny and I says, 'that Owens came on to me with a proposition and it stinks. If he comes anywhere near you, don't have nothing to do with him.' " But Ken Burns had already sold Owens two ounces of heroin.

Kenny was never regarded by his fellow prisoners or prison authorities as a violent or dangerous man, although he had been convicted of robbery — Ken sat in the getaway car while his partners robbed a local business — and assaulting police, in an age when heroin addicts were likely to be confronted aggressively. "Kenny took some terrible, terrible beatings from the police," Eddie Burns said, chuckling. "If a policeman threw a punch at him, Kenny would counterpunch. He just wouldn't lie down."

Ken Burns died of liver cancer in 1989, two weeks after the disease was diagnosed. Though heroin had a significant role in his life, it had no role in his death. In the fall of 1985, while serving his final nine-year sentence for trafficking in heroin, he was in good humour. "I am not a criminal," he said, grinning. "I haven't done a lot of things in my life that I'm proud of, but I haven't done a lot of things that I'm ashamed of, either."

During the 1950s Eddie was apparently making about two to three million dollars annually, his brothers between half a million and a million annually. "It just goes," Eddie said of this money. "Racetracks and parties and bad stock investments." He laughed. "I don't have any debts and I have a few assets. A lot of people think I'm a millionaire. They fantasize."

Eddie Burns doesn't think much of the heroin market in Canada in the 1990s. The purity of the drug sold on the street has decreased dramatically. "Now in the 1950s and early 1960s, it went down from about 85 to about 45 or 50 per cent, and then it took a nosedive down to 10, then 5, then 3. One cap from the 1940s or 1950s, you could take that and make eight caps out of it and sell it on the streets today, and no one would complain. They'd say it was good stuff."

Eddie Burns argues that the greed of street distributors is responsible for the decline. "I always wanted to put good stuff on the street. You'd have some guy and you'd give him this material and you'd tell him, don't step on this too many times. Don't cut it too much.

"Now he would cut it, maybe twice, and make three ounces out of one. Well, now he's saying, I can make five ounces, and then I've got two ounces, straight profit, for me. It was never a direct plan to weaken the stuff, or cut it at the higher level. People backed away from heroin. I told them, guys, you're killing your whole market by making it look so weak and so bad . . . they're looking for alternate drugs.

"Heroin users, at one time, were respected people. They weren't the trash they are today. They were qualified thieves, safecrackers, wheelmen, all guys with talent. They all had ways of making money. None of them were bums or beggars. They were well dressed, they were articulate."

Opium smoking had become a popular recreation in China during the 1860s. Somerset Maugham wrote of his visit to a Chinese opium den of this era, "an elderly gentleman, with a grey head and very beautiful hands, was quietly reading a newspaper, with his long pipe by his side

. . . two coolies were lying, with a pipe between them, which they alternately prepared and smoked. They were young men, of a hearty appearance, and they smiled at me in a friendly way. One of them offered me a smoke . . . it was a cheerful spot, comfortable, home-like, and cosy. It reminded me somewhat of the little intimate beer houses of Berlin, where the tired working man could go in the evening and spend a peaceful hour."

The first Canadians to indulge in the recreational use and distribution of opiates were Chinese immigrants who produced smoking opium in factories in Vancouver, Victoria, and New Westminster, during the 1870s. Each business paid an annual licensing fee to its respective municipality.

The opium business was initially of little concern to the residents of British Columbia. For almost forty years, there were no indications of disapproval in the local press, and by the early twentieth century as much smoking opium was sold to whites as to Chinese.

But tolerance for the habit of smoking opium lasted only as long as British Columbia's tolerance for the Chinese. In the early years of the twentieth century, both a labour surplus and anti-Asian resentment developed. The Asiatic Exclusion League was formed, supported by an amalgamation of the Vancouver Trades and Labour Council and federal Conservative politicians. Opposed to the Liberals' immigration policies, the league demanded an end to immigration from Asia, claiming that the "yellow peril" was about to "swallow" a white British Columbia.

The anti-Asiatic riot of 1907, and the federal government's response — compensation to the Japanese and Chinese — were the culmination of these sentiments. The Liberal government of Wilfrid Laurier could not afford, in international terms, such treatment of recent immigrants. Mackenzie King, as deputy minister of labour, was sent to Vancouver to settle the claims, among them a request for damages from the Lee Yuen Opium Company.

The *Vancouver Province* reported that King was initially startled by the presence of the opium industry. "I will look into this drug business," King said. "It is very important that if Chinese merchants are going to carry on such a business, they should do so in a strictly legal way."

At this point King had no interest in making any form of opiate use illegal. But three days later, after receiving a deputation of Chinese Christian clergymen and merchants interested in anti-opium legislation, he told the claims commission of his intention to urge the prohibition of its manufacture and sale. Opium, forcefully imposed upon China by the British Empire, was to be derailed by another British import, Christianity. Salvation would not be achieved through the pipe dreams of the opium den.

In early July 1908, the federal government followed King's advice and, for the first time in Canadian history, criminalized a psychoactive substance — or more precisely, certain forms of a psychoactive substance. The Opium Act was introduced in the House of Commons by Rodolphe Lemieux, the minister of labour, three weeks after Mackenzie King had urged a country-wide ban on manufacture. This initiative was not responding to public-health concerns. It was simple political opportunism — "getting some good out of this riot." The maximum penalty provided for sale or manufacture of smoking opium was three months in prison. Merchants were given six months to sell off their existing stocks.

There was an international backdrop to the criminalization of smoking opium. Britain and China first agreed to limit opium production and trade in 1908. Britain was to cut its exports from India to China by 10 per cent and China to cut its production by 10 per cent. In each successive year a similar amount would be cut by the two partners, and, accordingly, in a decade the problem would disappear. This so-called 10 per cent solution coincided with attempts to organize a strategy of opium criminalization at home. The

Hague Convention of 1912 permitted, among other things, international agreement on this agenda.

For the British in India, a gradual prohibition was economically advantageous. Indian opium was much more valuable than Chinese opium, and reductions in supply dramatically boosted prices, as Chinese supplies diminished. A British government representative wrote from Peking in 1908, "There can be no doubt that foreign opium is superior both in quality and strength to the native product, consequently a great stimulus will be given to smuggling in a country where people attach more importance to quality than to price."

The smuggling has never stopped, whether into China in 1908, or into Canada and the United States in the 1990s. But in the years since 1908 there has been a major transformation in the views of Canadians about the moral legitimacy of opiate use. As Toronto lawyer and social historian Mel Green has observed, the social shift of opium from private indulgence to public evil was accomplished in less than thirty years. Few Canadians, outside of a small population in British Columbia, used smoking opium at the turn of the century. During the next twenty years, Canadians were told of the great social danger that the drug represented.

Provincial court judge Emily Murphy, wrote in *Maclean's* magazine of an international drug conspiracy. "Naturally, the aliens are silent on the subject, but an addict who died this year in British Columbia told how he was frequently jeered at as 'a white man accounted for'. . . . Some of the Negroes coming into Canada — and they are no fiddle-faddle fellows either — have similar ideas, and one of their greatest writers has boasted how ultimately they will control the white men. Many of these Negroes are law-abiding and altogether estimable, but contrariwise, many are obstinately wicked persons, earning their livelihood as free-ranging pedlars of poisonous drugs."

In the absence of scientific knowledge of the pharmacological consequences of the drug, and with credence given to the depiction of opium as a cultural poison, it was socially acceptable for penalties for both possession and trafficking to escalate dramatically. The criteria for amendments to criminal law are to be found in a mix of racism and economic insecurity. Public-health concerns were not relevant to this campaign. By the end of the 1920s, those convicted of trafficking could be sentenced to seven years' imprisonment, and those convicted of possession to a minimum of two months in prison, with flogging.

Mackenzie King has often been described as a "moral entrepreneur" who successfully marketed a new morality with respect to drug use, using his presumed expertise in psychoactive drugs as a springboard to the nation's highest office. But King was more entrepreneur than moralist. His 1909 diaries, written while travelling through India, reveal his expediency:

"Some persons were of the opinion that opium was used by many of the Sikhs in the same way that Lord Morley was using the cigar which he smoked; that it did not appear to harm them in that climate when used in moderation; that if taken from them it might lead to other drugs being used. Lord Morley would give me the names of one or two gentlemen to whom I could speak freely as to conditions in India. They would give me a true statement of conditions, not to be given, for example, to the people in North Waterloo [King's constituency], but which I might impart privately to Sir Wilfrid [Laurier]. I would be informed on the real conditions so that the Government of Canada might be made fully aware of them."

With prohibition and the beginnings of the cat-and-mouse manoeuvring between police and drug dealers, opium smoking declined. Just as Lord Morley had warned Mackenzie King in 1909, taking opium out of legitimate circulation ultimately led to the use of other illegal drugs. More refined products — first, morphine and, then, heroin

— had less bulk, more potency, and greater profit per unit volume. Understandably, therefore, distributors dropped smoking opium from their product line.

More potent opiates reached Canadian consumers, at least in part, because of the criminalization of distribution. Harvard-trained physician and author Andrew Weil has written of the medical consequences of this legal change. "Opium forms a relatively harmless habit in that a high percentage of users can smoke it for years without developing troublesome problems with tolerance. Dependence on opium, if stable, can be as consistent with social productivity as dependence on coffee or tobacco. But when morphine, the active principle of opium, is isolated and made available, problems do appear. In particular, a significant percentage of users (though possibly still a minority) finds it impossible to achieve equilibrium with habitual use of morphine, or with the still more potent derivative, heroin."

In 1960, the Narcotic Control Act was passed in the House of Commons. The Diefenbaker Conservatives dramatically raised existing penalties for importing, trafficking, and possession of "narcotics" — the opiates, cocaine and marijuana. Fourteen years in prison, which had been the maximum sentence since 1954, was replaced by a new maximum: life imprisonment. After a lengthy debate, the House ultimately rejected an amendment that would have permitted capital punishment for drug trafficking, although the trafficker in heroin was said by many members of the House to be worse than a murderer.

"A murderer kills and that is it," said NDP member Harold Winch, "but one who traffics in drugs, who brings a person to addiction, to that insatiable craziness, makes an absolute hourly and daily hell for life for the addict. I, therefore, have no sympathy for him." The members of all three parties condemned the users and distributors of illegal drugs, differing only in their preference for the penalties of life imprisonment or capital punishment.

In Canada today a capsule of heroin costs about $35 and has a purity level of about 5 per cent. The heroin has its origin in Southeast and Southwest Asia; the most common source countries are Thailand, Laos, Myanmar (formerly Burma), Pakistan, and Afghanistan. The opium-poppy farmers of the indigenous hill tribes of northern Thailand receive about $1,000 for ten kilograms of opium. These ten kilos are processed in Bangkok into one kilogram of pure heroin. It is then sold to an exporter for about $5,000.

When the drug arrives in Canada, the price escalates rapidly, to about $125,000 a kilo. And as the kilo is subsequently broken into ounces, grams, and finally capsules of ever-decreasing potency, that ten kilograms of opium cultivated by a tribesman in the hills of northern Thailand for about $1,000 is sold on Canadian streets for well over $1,000,000.

There seems to be very little that law-enforcement authorities can do to decrease significantly either the amount of opium production globally or the profitability of the trade; for it is, of course, enforcement that has made the trade so lucrative. More important, intractable political conflicts in most source countries have fuelled the viability of the business. The RCMP have noted, for example, that "civil strife in Myanmar, which heightened during the latter part of 1988, saw the suspension of their annual aerial opium eradication program. Narcotic enforcement and eradication efforts were virtually non-existent during the active period of unrest, with law enforcement focussing instead on controlling the resistance and demonstrations directed at the current regime."

Although the same report noted increased Laotian support for international efforts to suppress heroin, it added, "Nonetheless, longstanding political conditions, tradition, geography, and dire poverty continued to contribute to increased opium production. [In Afghanistan], the predominantly agrarian economy has been severely damaged by the hostilities. Opium has served as the ideal cash crop for subsistence farmers, when traditional agriculture has been disrupted. Generations of Afghan people have produced opium poppy, which has traditionally been used for medicinal purposes, particularly by the elderly.''

Rod Stamler, responsible for directing the RCMP's drug branch during the 1980s, agrees that the political problems of Southeast Asia make any significant change in heroin control almost impossible. ''The Thais have been in control of their country for a long time and they've blended in with a lot of different regimes over many years. They can deal with the Americans, they can deal with the hill tribes . . . and they just take it easy. They say they're going to comply with the United Nations, but the drugs keep moving . . . they know there's nothing they can do to force the people not to produce the commodity that is so valuable to them.''

The control of heroin is, like the control of other illegal drugs, a game. The police try to ''keep a lid'' on the problem, while the distributors look for a way to make a simple living, or for thousands or millions of dollars' return on a small investment. On the international stage, illegal opiates become the source of money for arms purchases and non-democratic political objectives.

In Canada, as around the globe, opiate prohibition has produced an alienated underclass, the junkies whose lives are more desperate than those of Les Podolski or Eddie Burns.

In 1980, Hugh Ford was convicted of second-degree murder for stabbing a clerk to death in a downtown Vancouver hotel. ''When I stole $150, I did not see that as $150. I saw that as five caps of heroin.''

Ford began to use heroin in high school during the late 1960s, but gradually the price doubled and the potency was cut in half. ''Instead of paying $15 for a cap, you were paying $30 for a cap, but the cap was only half a cap. It was like a 400 per cent increase. I really didn't have any money. For the habit I'd acquired over six years, I turned to illegal activities."

One warm May night in 1980, Hugh Ford had had a lot to drink and had taken some pills when he spotted a young man in a second-floor window on Vancouver's Robson Street, counting business receipts. He picked up a brick from a nearby construction site and walked into the Pacific Palisades Hotel.

"I thought, well, I'll just hit him and knock him unconscious. He'll wake up in half an hour and I'll have the money and I'll be gone, and he'll have a headache, but that's all."

The robbery did not work out that way. The clerk was not knocked out by the brick; staggering to his feet, he began to struggle with Ford, trying to subdue him. "He had a hold of my hair. I just go black when somebody starts hanging on to my hair and pulling. At that point I pulled the knife out. It was a paring knife . . . it went in, and it happened to slip between the rib cage and unfortunately hit his heart. I thought right up to the time of trial that I had stabbed him once. I found out later at the trial that he had been stabbed four times, twice in the chest, twice in the neck."

Hugh Ford ran from the hotel. In order to cope with the knowledge of his crime, he increased his intake of drugs. "I was daily going out and breaking into a drug store or a doctor's office. I was not concerned about going downtown and getting heroin, I was just eating barbiturates, Valiums, whatever pill I could eat that would take it out of my memory and I could forget about it. Until tomorrow, then wake up and eat more."

He was arrested and charged within a few weeks of the crime. He continued his drug use through his trial. "I stayed, again, as high as possible. I just did not want to face reality, the reality of what I'd done. Staying high was the only way I'd ever really learned to deal with pressures like that."

In 1980 he was sentenced to a minimum term of ten years' imprisonment. During his first five years inside, he continued his involvement with drugs and became involved in the prison's drug trade. "I picked up a number of charges, five or six for a syringe, for being under the influence. The last one, they caught me in the kitchen and I had about thirty Valiums in my pocket and a hundred down my shirt. I was trafficking Valiums."

This offence led to his return to a maximum-security penitentiary, and soon afterward, he began to question the way in which he was living his life. He stopped using drugs as part of his daily routine, and tried to face the effect that the murder of their son had upon his victim's mother and father. "If I could, I'd try to explain to them that my past led up to my attitude, which led to the ultimate crime and what I've done since." Hugh Ford didn't intend to kill, but he was willing to take property by force, pushed in part by a desperation for opiates.

As Hugh Ford returns to civilian life, he knows that drugs, particularly opiates, will present a temptation to him. He has already had his plans for parole set back by a positive urine test for cannabis. He can make no easy promises about his future use of illegal or legal drugs, but he does make promises about violence. "I can't change what happened, but I can ensure that nothing like that ever, ever happens again . . . that's all I can do."

The lives of most opiate dependents — the junkies of popular culture — are desperate and often tragic, but their difficulties rarely escalate to the kind of violence that Hugh Ford was involved in. They may steal or distribute drugs in order to continue with opiates, but most are unlikely to be violent. Canada's criminal courts process a few hundred of these people every year, and the descriptions of their lives are remarkably similar. They are involved in crime, in poor health, purposeless, psychologically damaged, and unhappy. Wealthy or more privileged distributors such as Eddie Burns and Les Podolski only occasionally appear in criminal courts.

What most people see in a heroin addict is less the effects

of a lifetime of heroin than the effects of criminal prohibition of a highly addictive drug. It might be that, if heroin was made available, most of those who would use it would still be in poor health, purposeless, and psychologically damaged, but there is no reason to believe that this would be true. Opiate consumption has relatively negligible health consequences, particularly when the practice of self-injection is abandoned.

A relatively modest heroin habit will cost the user about $100 each day, or $36,500 per year. Obviously, such an economic regimen is usually difficult. For all but the very affluent, food, shelter, and companionship may have to be sacrificed to heroin.

The real cost of producing opiates for daily consumption is no greater than the real cost of producing tobacco or alcohol. Criminalization has created a false scarcity of the product and artificially inflated its economic value. The costs of this policy are disproportionate to the problem of opiate dependence. Less than one in every thousand Canadians uses opiates regularly and yet author Peter Appleton has calculated that we spend approximately $5 billion annually on enforcement: conservatively, about $200,000 for each opiate addict.

Opiates also represent a loss to taxpayers, some $2 to $4 billion annually in untaxed distribution revenue. Some of this amount is seized by the government through its "anti-drug profiteering program." This program allows the currency of convicted drug distributors to be seized and their property sold. In the case of heroin and other opiates, the amounts seized appear to be in the range of $5 million per year, or less than 0.5 per cent of all untaxed income.

There is also an international agenda here; the United Nations continues to co-ordinate global policy, urging that all nations adhere to the 1961 Convention on Narcotic Drugs, and its dictates of criminal sanctions for the possession and distribution of certain drugs. The opiates are the drugs of the third world. The UN's current power brokers — the United States, the Soviet Union, China, France, and Britain — do not have territorial control over production and distribution and are not culturally tolerant of opiates. The developing countries may give diplomatic assurances to their economic masters that the trade is being eradicated, but worldwide increases in opium production during the 1980s suggest that political realities are quite different.

There are alternatives to the model of criminalization for controlling opiate use and abuse. Methadone was first synthesized as an alternative to heroin during the 1940s in wartime Germany, when it was feared that the country's supply lines of opium poppy might be destroyed. In the early 1960s, in the United States, medical researcher Vincent Dole and psychiatrist Marie Nyswander developed a new way of using methadone: as a method of treatment for heroin addiction. The couple had remarkable international political success in convincing various governments of the value of their program and, indeed, methadone maintenance has emerged in the last twenty years as Canada's treatment of choice for heroin dependence.

In reality, we are simply replacing dependence on heroin with dependence on an equally addictive drug, methadone. But Dole and Nyswander were also altering the existing approach towards opiate dependents: control by medicine was to replace control by police. The user would be able to get methadone by prescription, regularly, thus eliminating the need for a less predictable cat-and-mouse manoeuvring with the criminal law.

Methadone was said to have the advantage of a long-lasting effect — the drug needs to be taken just once a day. It was also argued that methadone tends to block the effects of heroin and other opiates, thus making the purchase of heroin less likely.

It is rarely the opiate of choice, however, for most opiate dependents. Although it fulfils a physical and mental need, most men and women who have used both heroin and methadone report that methadone is less enjoyable and more difficult to withdraw from.

The non-euphoric qualities of methadone apparently make it a better candidate for legitimacy than drugs like heroin or smoking opium. Lawmakers view a medically prescribed dependence as preferable, the similar pharmacological consequences of the two drugs notwithstanding. Methadone maintenance programs provide for a cultural redefinition of the opiate user, from criminal to addict. They offer a way out of a desperate and criminal lifestyle, but they also require a compromise.

Eddie Burns has been on the methadone program in Vancouver for many years. As he became older he realized that he was still opiate dependent, but he didn't want to risk further imprisonment or police surveillance. He agreed to the bargain of maintenance, but not without reservations. "I think it was De Quincey, he was talking about opium. It's like owning a magic carpet, and you ride the magic carpet every day, and then one day someone takes your magic carpet and locks it in the closet, and says you can't ride the magic carpet anymore.

"I went there last month to pay my bill," he continued. "I'm not on welfare, I've gotta pay them. There's about twelve people waiting to get in there. Not one of them knew me. They were all young people, street people. And I'm goddam sure none of them were heroin addicts. Not a one of them. . . . I know a good part of them sell their methadone . . . they got on that program for one purpose, to get methadone to sell it, to augment their welfare."

Many of those in charge of methadone maintenance programs worry about the diversion of the drug into the underground economy. Methadone and a host of other pharmaceutical opiates have street prices far above the minimal costs of legitimately prescribed use. A day's supply of methadone or a single tablet of Dilaudid will sell on the street for over $50.

Canada's guidelines for methadone maintenance make medical doctors the agents of control. The "pharmacological management" of the opiate dependent is currently said by the federal government to involve four phases: a three- to six- month "stabilization" period; "maintenance," to be reassessed at least every six months; "withdrawal, to be individually determined and time frame flexible"; and "follow-up," a form of "post-withdrawal aftercare." Random urine testing during all four steps of the program must occur at least twice a week. In the event of a positive urine test for other opiates, or illegal drugs, a patient may have his or her methadone withdrawn.

Canada's methadone programs require oral use of the drug, and so they have limited appeal for those involved in the black market. Methadone is typically mixed with an orange drink before distribution; if injected, this combination will tend to make the user quite ill for about twenty-four hours. The programs' other conditions are similarly restrictive: those dependent on opiates will be permitted to use this drug only if they do not use any other illegal substances, and if they subject themselves to an ongoing program of treatment, with the ultimate goal of abstinence.

In a 1990 information letter, Canada's Bureau of Dangerous Drugs, a division of the Health Protection Branch of Health and Welfare, added that "carrying privileges" — the right to take methadone at home — "should be limited" and that for the first 90 to 180 days of the program, a urine test should be taken from the "patient" every day.

In its final report in 1973, the Le Dain Commission suggested that the federal government consider implementing heroin maintenance programs, on an experimental basis. "For the present, our recommendation is not that heroin maintenance be made as generally available as methadone maintenance, but that it be something which approved treatment units should be able to resort to as a transitional measure to attract from the illicit market opiate dependents who will not respond to methadone."

This suggestion, though it seems to have been a very restrained first step, with a very restrained objective, has never been acted upon. If there has been any policy change over the past decade, it has been to increase controls over opiate dependents: limitations on methadone use, more frequent requests for random urine testing.

This "get tough" approach has had the consequence of increasing drug-related crime. "Now, the police take all kinds of credit for stamping out heroin, but they don't tell you what they've got in its place," Eddie Burns said. "You see the users resorting to all that drug store stuff, all that garbage." Crime statistics support this interpretation. Armed robberies of Canadian pharmacies have increased dramatically during the 1980s, from an average of about 60 per year in the late 1970s to about 150 per year today.

E.V. Wilson, the assistant director of Canada's Bureau of Dangerous Drugs, has suggested we might follow the lead of some American states and train pharmacists in the use of handguns. In a recent year in New York state, more pharmacists were killed in the course of their work than were police officers. "One objective is to help some pharmacists over the psychological hurdle of actually using firearms," Wilson told an Ottawa conference in the 1980s. "Another is to prepare them to deal with the psychology of actually killing a human, should this happen in the event of a robbery."

The message of this logic is that we are to risk our lives to ensure that opiate dependents are not able to gain access to their drugs of choice. And, if they become too confrontational, we'll have to kill them. What we do to opiate dependents in our culture is already brutal and thoughtless; we hardly need to increase the social risks for this usually marginal and indigent population. Support and assistance are needed, and the mutual trust of an opiate maintenance program is a good place to start.

It is commonly argued that heroin maintenance will never work, that it was a failure in Britain and will be a failure in Canada. Robert DuPont, an American psychiatrist who has held a number of government positions related to drug treatment, told the U.S. National Drug Abuse Conference in the late 1970s that making heroin available would not help to eliminate the profit in the illegal market. "Such clinics in Britain have not taken the profit out of the illegal heroin traffic," he said, "and they would not do so here. In order to make heroin unattractive to criminal suppliers, we would have to make heroin as available as we now make Aspirin or antihistamines."

DuPont's conclusion that clinics in Britain have not eliminated the illegal trade was accurate enough, but his other claim was an exaggeration. The potency and risks of heroin will always separate it from a mild analgesic or a decongestant. The choice is not between DuPont's corner-store free-market trade in heroin and the status quo. There are and have been other models of heroin maintenance.

The British currently have fewer than 10,000 heroin addicts. This is less than 10 per cent of the U.S. rate, and about 20 per cent of the rate in Canada. The British approach to heroin began to assume a public form with the appointment by the minister of health of distinguished physician Sir Humphrey Rolleston and a panel of medical doctors. They were to report to government on the problems of morphine and heroin addiction.

The Rolleston Committee report of 1926 set out two categories of addicts for whom doctors might appropriately prescribe: "those in whom a complete withdrawal of morphine or heroin produces serious symptoms which cannot be treated satisfactorily under the ordinary conditions of private practice" and "those who are capable of leading a fairly normal and useful life so long as they take a certain quantity, usually small, of their drug of addiction." (In America, at about the same time, heroin was being touted as a public enemy, not recognized as a valid part of medical treatment.)

For about thirty years, the recommendations of the Rolleston Committee were put into practice in England, without incident. But in the mid-1950s the United States pressured the United Nations to demand an international ban on the use of heroin. In 1955, Britain complied. The government's announcement of prohibition provoked a wave of opposition from the British medical profession, and in early 1956, less than one year later, the Home Secretary informed the House of Commons that the doctors had emerged as the victors. "The Government has been advised that it is not possible under the present law of the country to prohibit the manufacture of heroin."

The number of known heroin addicts in England climbed from about 100 in 1960 to about 500 in 1965. This prompted two reports from a group of seven physicians and one pharmacist, led by Sir Russell Brain. The second Brain report of 1965 heralded dramatic limitations on the right of British doctors to prescribe heroin to opiate dependents. Brain II recommended that only certain doctors be licensed to dispense to these addicts, and that "treatment centres" be established in London and other major cities.

The Brain II recommendations became law in 1968, and the number of opiate dependents in Britain continued to grow, to about 3,000 by 1969. With the clinics in operation, the numbers initially stabilized at about this figure. Between 1969 and 1972, injectable heroin, methadone, and occasionally other opiates were supplied, by the clinics, to the addict population.

But in the mid-1970s, the clinics became increasingly restrictive: new patients were not given injectable heroin, but, more typically, oral doses of methadone. There were now two classes of patients: the long-term injectors and the drinkers of methadone. According to policy researcher Arnold Trebach, doctors had become uncomfortable with providing drugs for non-medical reasons to a group of young and deviant individuals who were mostly unproductive. If they were to *treat* these men and women, they would insist on placing greater controls on their behaviour: to engage in a more intrusive policing of their health.

These changes have been followed by a strengthening of the illicit heroin trade within Britain. Seizures of heroin have increased significantly during the past twenty years. If Britain's system of heroin maintenance has not worked, it is because it has not always attracted addicts from an often desperate and criminal lifestyle. For at least half of all users, drinkable methadone is an inadequate substitute for injectable heroin.

Opiate maintenance programs have rarely been content with maintenance. The agenda has typically become more ambitious, for reasons that are not really clear. The physician and his prescription pad have replaced the police officer and his choke hold, but the game of social control continues. We've simply mixed our gatekeepers. Opiate dependents remain criminals deserving of punishment, but they now have an additional or alternate identity — that of addicts, in need of treatment.

There is probably little enthusiasm for heroin treatment centres in Canada today, however. The use and occasional abuse of cocaine has eclipsed heroin, both in quantity and in the popular imagination. But heroin and other opiates are still bought and sold on Canadian streets, particularly those of Montreal and Vancouver. The last twenty years of enforcement and criminal activity have also brought a new range of synthetic opiates from pharmaceutical firms, and an increasingly restrictive regulation of access to methadone.

The criminalization of heroin and other opiates has been

a failure, based on the unlikely premise that only prohibition will prevent Canadians from becoming a nation of narcotic addicts. The policy is extremely costly, inefficient, and hypocritical, and inconsistent with a mandate of public health.

If public health is the cornerstone of our policies of drug control, and infringing civil liberties is seen as a tolerable cost, why are we focused on methadone or other opiates at all? It would seem more appropriate to turn our attention to tobacco and alcohol and their more pronounced risk of premature death. A recent research study from Ontario's Addiction Research Foundation revealed that 20,000 deaths in that province in 1985 could be linked to drug use. Tobacco was identified as the culprit in more than 13,000 of these cases, alcohol in more than 6,000. Opiates were responsible for 15 deaths.

For men like Ken and Eddie Burns, Les Podolski, and Hugh Ford, opiates have been a source of great pleasure, and a source of great pain — imprisonment, dependence, and violence. Government could have lessened this pain, if there had been the political will to move towards a safer existence for those who ingest powerful painkillers.

Instead we seem focused on the alienation of these users, expressing revulsion for their habit in the language of the criminal law. As Eddie Burns put it, "If someone could just convince me that what I'm doing is wrong when I take a needle to my body and I shoot some heroin into me — never mind all the things it takes to get the money and all that — if they can convince me, logically, that I'm doing something morally wrong in that simple act, taking a drug, I'd have quit right away."

NOTES

There are many good sources of information about the health and social consequences of opiate use. See, for example, T.C. Cox et al., *Drugs and Drug Abuse: A Reference Text* (Toronto: Addiction

Research Foundation, 1983), pp. 105–28; E.M. Brecher et al., *Licit and Illicit Drugs* (Boston: Little, Brown, 1972), pp. 1–183; A. Weil and W. Rosen, *Chocolate to Morphine: Understanding Mind-Active Drugs* (Boston: Houghton Mifflin, 1983), pp. 80–92; and B.K. Alexander, *Peaceful Measures: Canada's Way Out of the War on Drugs* (Toronto: University of Toronto Press, 1990), pp. 129–66.

For a very thorough discussion of the problems that surround heroin and methadone in North America and Britain, see A. Trebach, *The Heroin Solution* (New Haven: Yale University Press, 1982). For a good indication of police concerns about heroin, and a reasonably comprehensive picture of the heroin problem nationally and internationally, see Royal Canadian Mounted Police, *National Drug Intelligence Estimate, 1988 / 1989* (Ottawa: Supply and Services, 1990), pp. 16–37. And for a discussion of the role of opiates in the emergence of Canadian narcotics legislation, see N. Boyd, "The Origins of Canadian Narcotics Legislation: The Process of Criminalization in Historical Context," 8 *Dalhousie Law Journal* (1984): 102–36. For an indication of the extent of opiate involvement in premature death see Addiction Research Foundation, *Drugs in Ontario* (Toronto: Addiction Research Foundation, 1990).

This chapter was also informed by a series of interviews, by newspaper and magazine articles, by archival retrieval from the National Archives of Canada, and by a number of specific requests for government correspondence, pursuant to the Access to Information Act.

In addition to those works cited above, scientific evidence substantiating the medical and social consequences of opiate use can also be found in S. Siegel et al., "Heroin Overdose Death: Contribution of Drug Associated Environmental Cues," 216 *Science* (1982): 436–37; J. Westermeyer, *Poppies, Pipes and People: Opium and its Use in Laos* (Berkeley: University of California Press, 1982); H.K. Beecher, *The Measurement of Subjective Responses: Quantitative Effects of Drugs* (New York: Oxford University Press, 1959); L.N. Robins, J.E. Helzer, and D.H. Davis, "Narcotic Use in Southeast Asia and Afterwards," 32 *Archives of General Psychiatry* (1975): 955–61; and T. Arnold, *American Diplomacy and the Narcotics Traffic 1900–1939* (Durham: Duke University Press, 1969). The figure of $200,000 in enforcement costs per opiate addict is obtained by assuming that one third of drug enforcement efforts are directed towards heroin; given that heroin is said by the RCMP drug-policy manual to be its drug of highest priority, this one third estimate would appear to be conservative. See P. Appleton and A. Sweeny, "Canada's Monstrous Drug Problem," *Globe and Mail*, February 24, 1987.

LIFE IN THE FAST LANE

Behind all the greed and the violence, the need to
make laws and the itch to break them, there is
just this handful of leaves, medicine for the
journey.

— CHARLES NICHOLL

Allan Andrew has spent most of his adult life in the drug
trade. He has been a heroin user, a marijuana user and
distributor, and a cocaine distributor.

"If I'd stuck with the pot, I would've been all right," he
said. "I would have got less time and the heat wouldn't have
focused. At the time I wasn't aware of how bad cocaine is. I
didn't think there was a big deal about it. But now, let me tell
ya, it's the most deadly drug there is."

Allan Andrew started using drugs when he was about
twelve, beginning with alcohol and tobacco, and then moving on to marijuana and heroin; he'd tried cocaine, but
never liked it. He is close to forty now, and he has been in jail
for the past five years, sentenced in 1986 to sixteen years'
imprisonment for conspiracy to import twenty-five kilos of
cocaine. Allan is a small, energetic, and friendly man, described by one prison worker as "a decent, normal kind of
guy, a little crazy, but a decent, normal kind of guy."

Allan Andrew's view of cocaine needs a little qualification; this may well be the most dangerous of illegal
drugs, but it appears to be much less destructive than tobacco or alcohol. Cocaine and its more refined derivative,
crack, begin with the coca plant. In the hills of Peru, Bolivia,
and Colombia, Indians have cultivated this shrub for thousands of years. In these cultures, people chew the dried

leaves of the coca plant, gradually applying powdered lime, ashes, or some other alkali to the surface of the leaf. In most instances a stick is dipped into a pot of lime or ashes and then rubbed on the leaves in the mouth. This wad of leaves is slowly sucked for about thirty minutes, the interaction of acid and alkali numbing the mouth and tongue, the coca producing a mildly stimulating effect. Coca is valued, in cultural terms, both as a recreation and a medicine. Some coca leaves taste like wintergreen, other varieties like green tea.

In *The Fruit Palace*, an account of his travels through Colombia and the cocaine trade, British journalist Charles Nicholl described the effects of a *mascada*, a mouthful of coca leaves, mixed with lime, "The effects come on gently, scarcely noticeable until you learn to recognize them. Your mouth is numbed where the quid sits. You salivate a lot. You are not hungry, nor thirsty, nor tired. You are cool and buoyant. Chewing coca is not a 'high' as such, not a 'drug experience.' It is more of a load lightener. . . . One might quantify the effect by comparing it to a strong cup of black coffee, except that the mode of ingestion makes it smoother, longer and more elastic than a caffeine hit."

This form of coca use is vastly different from the present use of cocaine in Canadian and American culture. The impoverished hill people in the mountains of South America have learned to integrate the coca plant into their culture; yet we, among the globe's best-educated citizens, have not.

The response of most Western states to this phenomenon has been to encourage eradication of the coca plant. We have a problem with the more refined derivatives of this shrub, derivatives that we have encouraged; so we demand that these hill people of the third world, who have been using coca safely for thousands of years, burn their crops.

Cocaine is a white crystalline powder that has become increasingly popular in Canada during the 1980s. While convictions for marijuana, heroin, and other illegal drugs have remained constant or declined, convictions for cocaine have increased 500 per cent between 1980 and 1990.

In urban Canada, cocaine sells for about $100 a gram, typically folded into a square of glossy paper. The cocaine user usually places a little of the drug on a mirror, chopping it into very fine particles with a razor blade, then using the blade to draw a line of cocaine across the glass. A mirror withstands the razor a little better than most surfaces and ensures that none of the drug will be left undetected. The less patient consumer simply places some amount of the drug on the tip of his finger and sniffs it directly into his nostril, in crystalline chunks.

Popular culture dictates that some denomination of paper currency be rolled into a cylinder, and the line of powder drawn through the cylinder into the nostril, the first half of the line for one nostril and the second half of the line for the other. A plastic or paper straw is equally functional, provided that it is cut open after use, and its residue consumed.

There are others who inject the drug, and still others who smoke cocaine, the more potent "freebase" cocaine, or crack. In Colombia today, *basuko*, a dried cocaine paste, halfway between the extract of the coca plant and cocaine, is emerging as the coca product of choice among urban Colombians. Charles Nicholl describes the effects of smoking the peach brown powder: "it is a rougher, milder, and — above all — far cheaper version of coke. . . . You might feel giddy, benevolent, chattery, even vigilant after a *sucito* — a joint of basuko. But you are soothed rather than fired up."

But the more refined products, cocaine and crack are the chosen drugs for the current political culture in North America, their stimulant properties enhancing one's sense of personal power. Cocaine is an entrepreneurial high, giving energy, endurance, and appetite suppression. In an era of "lean and mean" individualism, the drug seems a logical choice.

It may be that the resurgence of cocaine in North America symbolizes a resurgence of the politics of self-interest. Cocaine is the right stuff for the corporate culture, a drug that allows you to "take charge," "kick ass," and "compete in the international marketplace." A little powder up the nose stimulates both physical and mental performance.

And yet, ironically, cocaine is anathema to those who profess this ideology. When George Bush declared war on drugs in 1989, it was cocaine that he spoke about, shaking a plastic bag full of the product at the camera, and talking about the need for action at home and in South America.

For Allan Andrew, cocaine was an opportunity that fell into his lap. In 1978, he had been introduced to a man in California who had taken twenty-five kilos of cocaine from Miami. "I didn't like it, but it seemed to be the jet-set drug."

He took four ounces of the drug up to Canada to see if there was a market. "I pass it all around and . . . Holy Smokes. These guys want it and I can sell this for $3,500 an ounce . . . I'm making about $130,000 on a kilo, so this is a hell of a good deal."

The twenty-five kilos travelled from southern California to Bellingham, Washington, in the armrests of a Cadillac, and were collected by Allan Andrew and stuffed into a gym bag. He had paid a pilot to fly him from Bellingham to Chilliwack, a short hop over the Canadian border, where he had been assured there was no airport Customs. A woman would be waiting there in a van.

"We land and we taxi up to the end of the runway, the very first sign I see says Customs. I says, 'There's a Customs here, you idiot.' He goes, 'Oh no, I must have looked at the wrong city. I'm gonna get out of here.' I says, 'Fuck you. We're here now. I'm getting out.' "

Andrew left the plane with the gym bag of cocaine and walked towards the Customs building. He told a Customs officer coming towards him that he had to go to the washroom first and would meet him inside in a minute.

"Meanwhile, the pilot, he turns the plane around and just guns her. The guy's standing there, he's going, What?"

In the confusion Andrew and his twenty-five kilos of cocaine hopped into the waiting van. "The guy can't see me, he doesn't pick up that we're leaving in the van. He's just standing out there, baffled. So, now I'm in the cocaine business. The twenty-five kilos, it took me about three months to get rid of all of it."

The project produced over $700,000 in profit for Andrew and his two partners, Dave Rich and Stacey Harris; the downside was the product itself. "I started realizing what coke does to people. During this six months, Stacey, this 250-pound maniac, started consuming a vast amount of cocaine. He started getting really psychotic, right?"

According to Allan Andrew this tension reached a peak when the three men sat down to split up the proceeds of their enterprise. There was an argument over how much cocaine Stacey Harris had consumed, and hence the size of his share of the $700,000, "Stacey picks up this big chair. I duck, but one leg catches Dave on the head. So now, Dave stands up. He's kinda dazed. He goes, 'I don't have to take this shit from anybody.' He starts walking away. I'm up already. Stacey grabs a leg that broke off and smacks him on the head again.

"Now I jump on Stacey and wrestle, and he's big and I'm small. But I get him away and I get him in the bathroom. Dave's got a big gash. I can see grey matter. I poured baby powder in there. We're on the second towel — it's just full of blood — when Stacey comes rushing in the bathroom with this fish gaff on a broom stick."

While his two partners wrestled in the bathroom, Allan Andrew went to the kitchen to find a large butcher knife, "The biggest one I can find. I go in there. Now they're in the bathtub. Stacey's got his back to me. Dave's scared. I can see he's bleeding. I have this butcher knife and I just can't stick it in him. I can't do it. All I can see in my mind is a picture of him going 'Aaaagh,' pulling the knife out, and chopping me into little pieces."

Andrew returned to the kitchen with the butcher knife

and then took the whole drawer of knives outside, and threw them off the balcony. By opening the sliding door, however, he created something of a suction effect. About one third of the $700,000 cash was swept out the door. Thousands of twenty-, fifty-, and hundred-dollar bills were sent swirling over a five-acre farmyard.

This stopped the conflict. Over the next couple of hours the three men tracked their money down, ultimately losing only about $4,000 to the sliding door and the wind. For Allan Andrew it was a sobering lesson about cocaine. "I didn't really know at first, and I was in a tight spot. That's why I went for the first twenty-five kilos. Then I saw how easy it was, and the money that was there and I got greedy."

But it's not clear that the cocaine was the architect of madness or absurdity in this scenario; Stacey Harris was apparently aggressive, with or without cocaine, and was said by fellow prisoners to be "difficult." Allan Andrew was eventually arrested and convicted on the basis of Harris's testimony, and the testimony of the pilot who flew him over the border with the twenty-five kilos of cocaine. Both Harris and the pilot bargained their way out of later trouble with police by agreeing to participate as prosecution witnesses at the trial of Allan Andrew.

The cultural image of cocaine as a dangerous drug is pervasive, but users demonstrate a diversity of reactions. One man in jail for murder said of his pattern of abuse: "I'd take seven grams, pour it on the table, and using a credit card, just spread the whole line across the top. It got to the point I'd wake up in the morning, blood dripping out of my nose. I'd have my sink full of cold water, stick my face in the sink, and suck water up my nose to get the crust, blood, congeals, and stuff out. Once that was cleared up, I'd start again."

The homicide — he shot a friend in the head with a hunting rifle — occurred when he was very drunk. Though alcohol was the trigger, he believes that cocaine also has some responsibility for his crime. "I always had a loaded gun in my apartment. I refer this back to the paranoia of the cocaine. You're always scared that somebody's after you." A seven-gram-a-day cocaine habit had also taken its toll on his finances, septum, and nasal passages.

For one young woman, however, the availability of large amounts of cocaine has not posed similar problems. In her mid-thirties now, she is generally regarded by those in her community as a sensible and pleasant person, her time occupied with two children and a small business that she created. During the 1980s, she and her husband were given several ounces of cocaine. They used it steadily for about two months, until it ran out.

"I liked it. You could get too speedy, and that wasn't good, but we just continued to do it until it was gone. Sometimes it would make me nervous in bed at night when I could hear my husband's heart pounding; I'd be paranoid that he was going to have a heart attack. But mostly I didn't really think about it. We just kept doing lines. I wish I'd kept some."

Research literature suggests that cocaine, in itself, does not create aggression. In low doses, cocaine improves reflexes, creates a sense of well-being, inhibits appetite, and increases blood pressure and respiration rate. In high doses, cocaine, like other central-nervous-system stimulants, can produce nausea, vomiting, cold sweats, tremors, muscle twitches, paranoia, convulsions, and death.

For most people who have experienced its effects, cocaine is not a source of stubborn dependence, nor a substantial physical risk. In *The Steel Drug*, a research team at Ontario's Addiction Research Foundation identifies occasional use with few adverse consequences as the most probable outcome of experience with cocaine. In their study of 111 users, the authors describe a range of consumption, from about once a year to daily, with more than 95 per cent of those sampled falling somewhere between these extremes.

Cocaine began life in 1860 when German scientist Albert Niemann isolated the drug from the leaves of the coca plant, producing a fine white powder. And for the remainder of the nineteenth century, the reputation of cocaine flourished, extolled and recommended, and used by American physicians as a treatment for opiate dependence. Sigmund Freud described his article "Uber Coca" as "a song of praise to this magical substance." This summation was probably more an expression of personal taste than a description of empirical reality, but it convinced a generation of physicians of the therapeutic values of the drug.

Cocaine became the first local anaesthetic in medical use and, as a consequence, revolutionized surgery. It is still used today for some operations in the eye, nose, throat, and mouth. Cocaine was also the original "pick-me-up" in Coca-Cola and a number of other tonics and wines, hailed by North American doctors in the late 1880s as a panacea for a wide range of illnesses: hay fever, head colds, stomach irritability, and depression. It was also used as a stimulant to athletic performance, and as a preventive for female masturbation, the drug applied topically to numb the clitoris and vagina.

A mix of concerns about cocaine was, however, developing. The damaging consequences of stimulant abuse — dependence, paranoia, and extreme agitation — were becoming apparent. And the patent-medicine industry, the principal distributors of cocaine, were an economic threat to doctors and pharmacists. When the patent-medicine makers suggested self-medication in advertising that urged the avoidance of physicians, they ran afoul of the emerging state-sanctioned professions of medicine and pharmacy. An article in *The Canadian Pharmaceutical Journal* in 1908 described the drug's use as "a danger spot of threatening proportions." Moral crusaders were uniting with church leaders, physicians, pharmacists, politicians, and police to denounce the new drug.

In 1911 the various concerns about this method of consciousness alteration reached the floor of the House of Commons. Mackenzie King, then minister of labour, introduced legislation to prohibit the possession or sale of the drug. He noted that, "according to the medical men, the cocaine produces worse effects than opium." He quoted the Vancouver chief of police on the need for more intensive surveillance of the waterfront, and the Montreal chief on the destruction of young people caused by cocaine. So cocaine was criminalized, with possible jail terms for use and distribution.

The "social gospel" movement that permeated Canadian society between 1900 and 1930 was a necessary backdrop for the passage of this legislation. Personal morality became the object of social control. With Christianity as a guide, the criminal law could be used to eliminate undesirable forms of moral conduct. Salvation was not to be achieved through the chemical alteration of consciousness, particularly when that chemical emanated from the pagan hill tribes of South America.

Penalties for cocaine use and distribution, like penalties for marijuana and opium, increased significantly during the 1920s, in response to the perceived moral threat of the drug. Emily Murphy contributed a chapter on cocaine to her influential book, *The Black Candle*, tying the drug to interracial sexuality, sexual promiscuity, and violence.

From the 1930s to the late 1960s, cocaine use was relatively sporadic, apparently concentrated in the entertainment industry. There was a minimal increase in use during the late 1960s and early 1970s, as Canadians became more conscious of drugs generally; but the most significant changes in consumption began in the late 1970s. Increased interest in cocaine during this period reflects a renewed interest in all stimulants, and follows the increased consumption of amphetamines in Canada and the United States during the early 1970s. Cocaine is a much more seductive stimulant than amphetamines, however, providing a thirty-minute burst of energy that is often accompanied by an almost overwhelming sense of pleasure.

Canada's best-known reference text on drugs and drug abuse says of cocaine abuse: "Although the effects of chronic cocaine use have not been fully researched, some reliable observations have been reported. Nervousness, excitability, agitation and paranoid thinking commonly occur, as do hypersensitivity, mood swings, memory disturbance, insomnia, and impotence. . . . If the drug is sniffed, constriction of the blood vessels in the lining of the nose eventually may lead to local destruction of tissue, and may result in perforation of the nasal septum."

The reference text goes on to note the strong similarities between cocaine and amphetamines, in terms of their pharmacological properties, and adds, "Death by overdose from either cocaine or amphetamines is indeed rare when compared to death by overdose from opiates or barbiturates. However, the death rate from accidents, suicides, and homicides is higher among heavy users of amphetamines than among the general population. Whether the same is true among heavy users of cocaine has not been documented."

There is probably little doubt on this last point; heavy users of cocaine are, like heavy users of amphetamines, stimulant abusers. In most instances of daily intravenous injection, and in many instances of daily sniffing, the drug of choice is irrelevant to the consequences of agitation and paranoia. Amphetamines have the political and economic veneer of pharmaceutical acceptability, however, whereas cocaine resonates with images of pagan hill people, alien rituals, and violent South American drug lords. We classify amphetamines (commonly known as speed) as controlled drugs. There is no penalty for possession, and a maximum penalty of ten years' imprisonment for distribution. Cocaine is legally classified as a "narcotic." There is as much as a seven-year penalty for possession, and life imprisonment for distribution.

The difference between cocaine and amphetamines is the cultural context in which they are used. Cocaine was popularized in the 1970s by the entertainment industry, tying the drug to socially desirable professions: music, televison, film, and sports. Cocaine had the cachet of glamour and prohibitive expense; it was the caviar of illegal drugs. Amphetamines have little mass appeal, particularly in the wake of the 1970s and the claim, emanating from the drug culture itself, that "speed kills."

The production of cocaine in South America increased between 1980 and 1990, in order to meet the growing demand from North America and Europe. From 1980 to 1990, the price of cocaine has declined and its availability has increased. The drug remains expensive relative to most other illicit substances, but its use is no longer confined to the affluent. By the late 1980s, about 10 per cent of Canadians and about 20 per cent of Americans between the ages of eighteen and twenty-nine had used cocaine. The RCMP's most recent annual Drug Intelligence report notes: "The majority of cocaine abusers across Canada are now males in the 20 to 40 age group, followed by females in the same age group. There is no identifiable socio-economic stratification of these cocaine abusers. Intelligence indicates, however, that in larger centres, younger and less affluent abusers may be associated with the nightclub culture, and may support their habits by selling cocaine to peers."

According to RCMP Intelligence reports, the price of a gram of cocaine is now less than half its 1980 price of over $200 and the price of a kilo of cocaine is about one-quarter of the $100,000 that was required for its purchase in 1980. The prices have been cut by distributors supplying the drug to North America and, in turn, by distributors in North America.

The reason for the drop in price is not clear. A price cut can attract uncertain buyers to the market and increase the consumption of those already in the market. But it can also reflect a glut of the product, relative to consumer demand. Cocaine may be losing its cachet as the inaccessible caviar of our culture at the very time it is becoming a global agribusiness.

In our culture, it is generally a "party" drug, consumed by a range of young people in social situations. There is some associated violence, but this flows mainly from particular social settings in which the drug is used and distributed, and from the kinds of people who are inclined to become involved in the business. In the United States, the abuse of cocaine is a more serious problem, but the difficulty is again more closely associated with social arrangements than the pharmacology of the drug. In New York City, about one-third of the annual toll of almost 2,000 homicides can be tied to cocaine and crack. In over 80 per cent of these cases, the murder suspects and the murder victims are either black or Hispanic, and under the age of thirty.

Public-policy researcher Paul Goldstein and his colleagues examined the role of cocaine and crack in homicide incidents in New York City. They found that while 3 of 414 homicides could be said to be "caused" by the consumption of cocaine or crack, 152 of the 414 were associated with disputes over the territory for cocaine or crack, disagreements over debt collection or quality of product. Of the three homicides motivated by the consumption of crack or cocaine, two also involved the consumption of a significant amount of alcohol.

Goldstein offers an example of the the most common type of cocaine homicides. "The victim was a twenty-four year-old black male, standing with a female at a telephone booth in a drug-sales location. He was approached by a thirty-year-old black male, who shot him in the head three times, using a nine-millimetre automatic. The victim was a low-level crack dealer, working for a higher-level dealer, but trying to freelance by taking over a portion of the big dealer's territory."

There has been some of this traffic-related violence in Canada, but comparatively little, and certainly the portrait of homicide in New York City is very different from the portrait of homicide in Canada. But cocaine's seductive dangers can be found in both locations. The drug is like alcohol in its tendency to promote or at least be associated with social disruption. Police forces across the country have found that an angry man on cocaine is more difficult to contain than an angry man who is very drunk. The cocaine abuser is not falling down or sedated; there is a focused intensity to his hostility.

This does not mean, however, that alcohol is a less dangerous drug than cocaine, merely that we in the West have no cultural blueprint for wise or responsible use of cocaine. While a few hundred Americans may die annually from the direct effects of cocaine, thousands are killed each year in the battles that flow from this unregulated, illicit market. In Canada there are fewer battles, and fewer deaths related to distribution and to consumption. The cocaine-related homicide rate is about ten times as great in the United States as in Canada. (This is part of a profound difference between the two cultures: there are about 20,000 homicides annually in the United States and about 600 in Canada.)

For many if not most cocaine distributors, however, violence and cocaine distribution are entirely separate worlds. For a man I'll call Rob Grant, cocaine connotes not street violence but wealth, lawyers and developers, and parties fuelled by fine wines, high-quality marijuana, and Colombian cocaine. The Canadian justice system has spent a lot of money on Grant, a chubby middle-aged American, and it is not clear that we have accomplished a great deal. Crown prosecutor Ian McKinnon recalled Grant's 1986 trial. "I never took this case personally," he said, but added, "I wish he'd stop writing Ottawa, though; he's creating a lot of paper work for me."

Rob Grant is not like most people in Canada's penitentiary system. With his short grey hair and softly pleasant features, he looks more like an accountant or a lawyer than popular culture's image of a trafficker. The traces of social and economic privilege are easily discernible. He is not violent; he has never carried a gun or employed strong-arm tactics.

During the late 1960s and early 1970s, Rob Grant had marijuana flown from Mexico to the United States on a weekly basis, unloading around Tucson and delivering to the Chicago and San Francisco markets. His twelve-ton-a-year delivery business fell apart when an informant infiltrated their delivery scheme, and Grant was charged in California with conspiracy to import marijuana. Knowing that he was facing something like five to seven years' imprisonment, Grant jumped bail, leaving California for Canada, settling first in Toronto in 1971, and then in Vancouver in 1973.

In 1975, Grant went to Medellín for about four months, at the time that the cocaine cartel was being formed. He'd never liked marijuana, tobacco, or any other drugs, but unlike Allan Andrew, Rob Grant found that he enjoyed cocaine, mixed on occasion with a little champagne or cognac. It was the mid-1970s, and life on a rented estate in Medellín was very pleasant. "One guy brought his stuff from Bolivia, the other guy brought some stuff from Ecuador, we brought our stuff up from Peru. And everyone sat around for the night, sampling different products. And I'm looking over this house we'd rented. There was a fifty-acre estate there, with three servants, with the waterfall on the back part of our property, falling about a hundred feet. Everything was done in marble."

He started to move cocaine to the United States, about a pound at a time, but his brother was arrested in Costa Rica and sent back to the United States to face outstanding marijuana charges in California. When his brother was released from jail, the two returned to the business in a much larger way.

"From '81 to '83," he began, "we were doing coke, really in large quantities in the States, dropping a hundred keys at a time, wholesaling the L.A. market. And I don't think we were even a tenth or a hundredth of it." He laughed.

By Canadian standards, Rob Grant was a fairly major cocaine dealer. But by American standards, moving a hundred kilos a month was and is unspectacular. The Los Angeles cocaine market is a multibillion-dollar business, serving hundreds of thousands of users. Grant's connections in California were just one step away from the Medellín cartel, and while he may have had a role moving more than $50 million of cocaine annually in Los Angeles, he was a tiny part of that city's distribution network.

Rob Grant started using a lot of cocaine in 1981, following the death of his wife at the age of thirty. They had been together since the early 1970s. During their time together in Colombia, they had to move to Medellín because her rare heart condition could not accommodate the oxygen-depleted elevation of Bogotá. When her heart gave out in Vancouver, Rob Grant found that he cared less about taking risks.

"That's when they got on to me," he said. "And it was all because I wasn't paying attention to what I was doing. I was on a self-destruct mode."

Just before the death of his wife, Rob Grant was charged in Calgary with possession of 150 pounds of marijuana for the purpose of trafficking. The case went on for more than two years, involving scores of weekly court appearances in Calgary and Vancouver. In 1982 he pleaded guilty to the charge and received a fine of $10,000. (From an economic point of view, it was not a good bargain for the state. The police and court costs totalled more than $100,000.)

Meanwhile, Grant continued to distribute cocaine in the United States and marijuana in Canada. He rarely left his home in Vancouver, organizing distribution with his brother in the United States, and with others in Canada. He was also becoming a multi-millionaire — the owner of a restaurant in an affluent residential area of Vancouver and an office building in Nanaimo, and a major investor in a gold-mining operation in Nevada — if only temporarily.

The gold-mining operation concluded in 1983 in disaster, for reasons unrelated to the cocaine business or the project itself. Grant's brother was killed, along with five others, in the crash of a small plane near the mine site. For Rob Grant, it was the end. He was contacted about taking over his brother's connections in California, but he wasn't interested.

He remained in Canada, using cocaine, "mostly with either developers or lawyers, partying." He was arrested in 1985 and charged with conspiracy to import cocaine. "I had been at this lawyer's house all day under surveillance, with all these lawyers, partying. And I went down to the office and they came in and arrested me."

In the summer of 1986, Rob Grant pled guilty in the Supreme Court of British Columbia to conspiracy to import cocaine. The evidence against him came from authorized wiretaps and from one of his partners, a former Los Angeles police officer, who was stopped at the Canadian border and charged with importing about a pound of cocaine. He pled guilty to the charge of importing, received a sentence of seven years' imprisonment, and agreed to testify against Grant.

Justice Trainor of the B.C. Supreme Court sentenced Grant to eighteen years' imprisonment for importing a pound of cocaine. Crown prosecutor Ian McKinnon had asked the judge to impose a life sentence. The judge justified the eighteen-year term with the comment, "You inflicted, I'm sure, pain and suffering and heartache on many individuals without any concern for their welfare or their future and the cost to them in terms of health and happiness and the cost to our society in terms of those ruined lives . . . are directly attributable to you and to your own selfishness. . . . There must be the force of deterrence to other people who are tempted to engage in this same kind of business that brings so much tragedy."

This rhetoric is typical in the sentencing of convicted cocaine distributors, particularly those thought to be in the upper echelons of the industry. The sentence imposed on Rob Grant is longer than that imposed on 99.5 per cent of all of Canada's cocaine traffickers.

The rhetoric serves certain social and political purposes, rejecting coca and its derivatives as recreational drugs of choice. The portrait constructed in aid of the policy of criminalization paints the distributor as a selfish predator, and the user as a tragic pawn. Free will or choice is said to be an illusion, and "ruined lives" are a natural consequence of the distributor's actions.

The reality is much less simple. Most users are not tragic pawns, but willing consumers; they report no serious adverse consequences from the consumption of cocaine. There is also no evidence that cocaine distributors are more selfish or less concerned with their clients' welfare than are other entrepreneurs. Like the distributors of alcohol, the distributors of cocaine market a product that has acknowledged physical risks. Some users may consume the drug in an irresponsible manner, and do harm to themselves or others. Most kinds of drug distribution — alcohol, opiates, tobacco, marijuana, cocaine — could be described in the terms employed by Justice Trainor: "the kinds of businesses that bring so much tragedy."

In empirical terms, the industries that bring the greatest human tragedy are alcohol and tobacco. The federal Ministry of Health and Welfare and Ontario's Addiction Research Foundation estimate that 35,000 Canadians will die prematurely from tobacco this year, about 15,000 from alcohol consumption, 100 from cocaine, 50 from opiates, and 15 from marijuana. (In the United States the surgeon general has estimated 346,000 deaths from tobacco, 125,000 from alcohol, 2,000 from cocaine, 2,000 from opiates, and 75 from marijuana.)

The construction of these figures and their absolute accuracy might be imprecise, but there is no doubting the general trend. Cultural beliefs notwithstanding, the "ruined lives" Justice Trainor lamented seem more likely to result from tobacco or alcohol use than from cocaine use, even when differences in per-capita consumption are taken into account.

Rob Grant's "ruined life" had little to do with cocaine. In 1985, his father died. The death of his wife in 1981 and his brother in 1983 had already pushed him to the margins of the cocaine industry. "I haven't really been interested in dealing since my brother's death. Y'know, I've done a few little things, but the one I'm busted on is a complete phony deal."

What really bothers Rob Grant about his trial, however, is the conduct of members of the legal profession. "My agreement for putting all this free coke out was that when I needed a lawyer, they were going to be there to help me out. Now, two and a half years later, I haven't seen hide nor hair of them."

Grant has made several allegations about lawyers and cocaine use, in relation to his trial. The Law Society of British Columbia has investigated the individuals concerned and found no evidence to substantiate these allegations. I asked Crown prosecutor Ian McKinnon if this means that the legal profession is generally clean in the matter of cocaine, suggesting to him that it would be reasonable to suppose that cocaine is used by lawyers in Vancouver, and in most other Canadian cities, regardless of the merits of Rob

Grant's specific allegations. "I'm told that it is," he said, "and I believe that it is."

"It's really strange," Rob Grant began. "The major criminal lawyers who do a lot of drugs . . . they'll sit around with you and do it in their office, while they're interviewing you."

Rob Grant's sentence of eighteen years' imprisonment was upheld by the British Columbia Court of Appeal, one of Canada's most substantial terms of imprisonment for this offence. Justice Taggart said of the punishment, "While I think it may be a sentence higher than the sentence that I would have imposed had I been in Mr. Justice Trainor's place, I do not think that it is so high that it warrants interference by this court."

Rob Grant will be eligible for release in the early 1990s, and as an American citizen, may be deported to the United States at that time. The lesson that he believes he has learned is that business and pleasure do not easily mix. "My criteria for lawyers now is that they do not hang around with this drug crowd, they have nothing to do with drugs, and they're super ethical. I would never go again for this fallacy. They're your buddies, you do drugs with them, and everything else."

Grant is less critical of the police. "I never felt any hatred between us," he said. "Sometimes they even helped me. One time in Arizona I told a cop I knew that it looked like a good day for flying. He said, no, I don't think it's a good day to go flying. And I'm glad we didn't. There were police all over the airstrip. . . . It was always a game between us and them.

"The desire for the drug is always going to be there," Grant concluded. "They made me a precedent — with my sentence, people weren't going to follow me. But that didn't work. The price has fallen by a third since I came in and the volume has increased."

Rob Grant's claim is understatement. In the five years that he has been in jail, the price of a kilo of cocaine has dropped by more than half. In the face of increasing convictions for cocaine distribution and use, the amount entering the country has increased, the price of the drug has been cut, and its purity improved. To counter Rob Grant's distribution of $45,000 of cocaine, we have spent about $1 million of public funds on police enforcement, trial, and imprisonment. This expenditure continues to grow, during his imprisonment, at about $50,000 annually.

What are we going to do with Rob Grant and those who have since followed him and thousands of other Canadians into the cocaine trade? Should we opt for longer sentences, build more jails, and increase the share of public funds that we target for drug enforcement?

The most recent RCMP Drug Intelligence estimate says of cocaine use in Canada, "Canadian cocaine statistics took some rather startling leaps in 1988 . . . lower prices, higher purity and wider availability at both the wholesale and retail levels continued to make cocaine more accessible to all socio-economic groups. Supplies remained more than ample, and availability was noted in all parts of the country." In the United States, imprisonment for cocaine distribution typically brings between two and four times the length of sentence imposed in Canada. Nevertheless, use of cocaine in America is between two and four times more common than the use of cocaine in Canada, and the price is about 30 per cent lower than the Canadian price.

A similar dysfunction exists on the international level. Since George Bush declared war on drugs, the total area of coca cultivation in South America has increased. The RCMP's 1989 Drug Intelligence report notes, "Estimates for Colombia stand at over 27,000 hectares, while estimates of between 70,000 and 100,000 hectares for Bolivia compare with 1987's range of 40,000 to 60,000 hectares. The total area currently under cultivation in Peru is conservatively estimated at 200,000 hectares, of which some 140,000 to 180,000 hectares are believed to be located in the primary growing area of the Upper Huallaga Valley."

The coca leaf is cultivated in Peru, Bolivia, and Colombia, the largest harvest coming from Peru, followed by Bolivia and Colombia. Colombia is the centre of the cocaine trade, the principal centre for processing a rudimentary coca paste into cocaine hydrochloride. The white powder is then shipped from Colombia to the world's markets; the RCMP estimates that 80 per cent of the world's cocaine comes from Colombia, and more specifically, from cartels in Medellín and Cali.

The effect of intensified efforts to dismantle the cartels and to eradicate the coca plant has been to change the way in which the industry is structured. The laboratories that manufacture cocaine have moved from central locations in Colombia to a range of bases in Bolivia and Peru. The RCMP's Drug Intelligence report indicates that success in this war is very unlikely: "All available evidence indicates that coca production in the source countries is set to expand in the future, unless existing pressing economic problems are resolved speedily, which seems unlikely. . . . The lack of resources to combat drug trafficking, the dependence of so many peasants on the alternative cocaine-generated economy, the lack of a cohesive crop spraying program, the lower remuneration achieved from substitute crops and the promise of rich rewards from the new and expanding European markets can only lead to continued production of coca and cocaine, in the absence of any viable alternative means of employment."

For Rod Stamler, the politico-economic situation of cocaine in South America is markedly similar to that of heroin in Asia. What he culled from ten years at the helm of the RCMP's Drug Branch has led him to believe that the American strategy of intervention in South America is flawed. "Every time you disrupt an organized crime group, when

you know where it is and you know how it operates . . . you
end up with something different."

Stamler recognizes the political limitations of supply reduction as a social strategy. He argues that experiences with
heroin in Asia should be considered more carefully, "If you
look at the last twenty years in the Golden Triangle area, the
efforts on crop substitution and so on have really been
tokenism to begin with, and have really done nothing to
change the drug production or limit the drug production
from that area. It has intensified, if you will, the involvement of insurgent army groups, and politically motivated
individuals who also get involved in the drug trade. If you
look at Southeast Asia, and look at what's happened over the
years, you see exactly what's going to happen in South
America . . . if you increase enforcement to the extent
where you're going to have some impact on the drug production in that area, you're going to alienate the people of
that particular area, with respect to central government.
You're going to have the involvement of organized crime in
between, and perhaps an insurgent-type army group that
has political and territorial interests that also will control the
drug trade.

"In Bolivia," Stamler continued, "when the United
States army went in and started blasting the cocaine labs, the
natives there resented that very much because it disrupted
their income flow, and what happened in the long run was
that the natives aligned themselves with the Colombian
organized crime groups . . . and the central government in
La Paz really lost control over territory."

For Rod Stamler, the ultimate answer to the problem of
cocaine is to be found in strategies that aim to reduce consumer demand in North America. "You have to keep an eye
on the supply line," he began, "but my feeling is that the
most you can do is to control organized crime, with that kind
of effort. You'd have to have crop substitution and then
you'd have to give preference to that particular crop in the

world marketplace, and countries are not willing to do that."

Stamler suggests that the political economy of Colombia itself is at the heart of the system of cocaine distribution: "Their organized crime is deeply entrenched in their society . . . the criminal organization is meshed into Colombian society, where maybe every tenth politician is a member of an organized-crime group, and every second or third police officer . . . and there are lawyers and accountants, and so on, all the way through the system."

Charles Nicholl's analysis, from firsthand experience, is similar: "the whole Colombian power-base is so deeply implicated, through bribes and kick-backs and drug-related political funds, that any concerted action against the drug racket has a built in softness, one hand waving a cudgel while the other pockets a share of the proceeds. The big busts are good propaganda, but it is always the small fry who get caught, while *los peces gordos*, the 'fat fish,' swim on happily in their fortified haciendas and Miami-baroque mansions."

In Canada and the United States as well, *los peces gordos* are rarely arrested. Cocaine distribution in Canada is centred in Toronto, Montreal, and Vancouver. RCMP Intelligence indicates that agents and associates of Colombian drug cartels are living in Montreal and Toronto, and that they are involved both in the shipping of cocaine from the United States and source countries and in the distribution of the drug across Canada. These individuals are said to be in constant communication with their associates in the United States, the Caribbean, and South America. The report argues that, although Canadians or Americans may be employed at various stages in the operations, control over shipping and distribution remains securely in the hands of Colombians.

What should be added, however, is that most of the capital generated by the cocaine trade remains in Canada and the United States. It takes about 500 kilograms of coca leaves to make 1 kilogram of cocaine. The farmer in Bolivia, Peru, or Colombia will receive about $500 for supplying this half-ton of coca leaves; the refined product will find its way to thousands of Canadian nostrils, costing the attached consumers about $100,000.

Cocaine arrives in Canada by sea, by land, and by air. Mexico is used as an important point of transshipment for the organizations involved in the distribution of illegal drugs, the so-called *narcotraficantes*. In October 1988, about five tons of cocaine (street value $450 million) was seized in Northern Mexico. The market price of cocaine in North America was unaffected by this loss. A seizure of five million grams could not produce a jiggle in the cost charged to consumers.

The cocaine that ultimately reaches Canada may be brought across by land from the United States. The drug typically travels from one of the source countries to Florida, on to New York City, and then on to Toronto and Montreal. On the West Coast, the cocaine travels from Colombia to Mexico, to California, and then up Interstate 5, into Vancouver.

Some cocaine arrives on container ships in the ports of Toronto, Montreal, and Vancouver. And a little more arrives by commercial aircraft, either concealed in air cargo or carried by the passengers. But the private aircraft provides the preferred means of importing cocaine into Canada. The RCMP report notes: "Canada's vast unpopulated areas make it a natural target for cocaine smuggling by air. Canada's landscape, proximity to the largest cocaine consuming nation in the world and rapidly developing domestic market increase the likelihood of such flights in future."

It is virtually impossible for enforcement efforts to be effective against private aircraft, unless there is a tip-off. (This apparently occurred with the largest seizure of cocaine in Canadian history. In April 1989, a small plane landed at a small airstrip near Fredericton, New Brunswick, with a cargo of 500 kilos of cocaine. Three men were arrested, two Colombian nationals, and one Canadian.) There are too many private landing strips, and too many remote areas in which private landing strips can be hastily constructed. And there are too many small private planes, easily able to fly out of the range of radar.

The portrait of cocaine distribution within Canada is no more encouraging. There is occasional violence and violent death associated with the trade: a few dozen homicides annually and hundreds of assaults. The report of two recent arrests in Montreal speaks for itself: "In early 1988 authorities in Montreal seized 18 kilograms of 93 per cent pure cocaine, as well as $54,000, three handguns and two rifles. . . . An undercover operation in February 1988 resulted in the seizure of eight kilograms of cocaine, as well as quantities of other drugs, $154,000 in cash, one Uzi submachine gun, two 12 gauge shotguns, one .38 calibre and two .45 calibre handguns, 12 sticks of dynamite, and four detonators."

The distribution of cocaine is generally more organized in Montreal and Toronto than in Vancouver, and more likely to have firearms attached. Over the last five years, the number of cocaine traffickers in Canada investigated by the RCMP has almost doubled, from just over 1,500 in 1985 to a little under 3,000 in 1990. This increased enforcement activity reflects, at least to some extent, the increased use of this drug.

About 80 per cent of convicted cocaine distributors are jailed; the rest are usually fined. Of those jailed, about half receive a sentence of one month to two years in prison; 49 per cent get a sentence between one and seven years; 1 per cent receive a term of more than seven years. Most of those convicted are user/distributors, selling grams and occasionally ounces. They work with hundreds of dollars, not hundreds of thousands. The public balance sheet with most of these 2,500 individuals is also disproportionate: we spend tens of thousands of dollars on enforcement, trial, and imprisonment, responding to mere hundreds of dollars of drug distribution.

In 1988, the RCMP investigated a total of 893 individuals who they believed were distributing amounts of one kilogram or more — by the force's own admission, a mere fraction of their real number. The greatest growth in enforcement efforts over the past five years has occurred in investigations of individuals who are distributing less than twenty-eight grams of cocaine, the street-level dealers of single grams. The RCMP investigated 165 of these low-level dealers in 1984, and 960 in 1988.

The RCMP suspects that motorcycle clubs are deeply involved in the distribution of cocaine. The report notes: "Many of these gangs derive the bulk of their drug related income from cocaine trafficking and importation. The proceeds are then frequently diverted into legitimate business ventures such as bars, real estate, and motorcycle repair shops. Outlaw motorcycle gangs, especially Hells Angels, are increasing their involvement in cocaine trafficking, and numerous kilogram and multi-kilogram amounts were seized from these gangs in 1988."

The portraits of cocaine distributors are as diverse as the Hell's Angels, Rob Grant, and Allan Andrew. None is an anomaly, none atypical. There is, rather, a mix of men and a few women who work in the cocaine trade, some violent, and some non-violent, some wearing suits, some wearing jeans or leather. There is not even a common denominator of greed; the street-level dealer of cocaine is often less interested in the money than in the drug itself.

Most of those who are caught and processed through criminal courts are socially and economically disadvantaged consumers and distributors who sell or use their drugs in public settings, on the street, or inside bars or nightclubs. Yet even this apparently brazen disrespect for the law is rarely stopped; the police cannot be everywhere at once. In the most careless and thoughtless of circumstances, the distribution of cocaine, and other drugs, usually proceeds unhindered.

The picture of cocaine in Canada is one of disproportionate spending, inefficient enforcement, a relatively small user population, and little violence. Can we afford to integrate these drugs into our culture? In the United States about 60 per cent of those who have used cocaine have used it fewer than 10 times in their lives, about 30 per cent have used it between 10 and 99 times, about 6 per cent between 100 and 999 times, and less than 3 per cent on more than 1,000 occasions. Moreover, of those who have used cocaine daily, less than 25 per cent appear to continue with this pattern of consumption over the long term. In another survey of American high-school seniors defined as recent users of cocaine, less than 4 per cent reported that they had tried unsuccessfully to stop taking cocaine; 20 per cent reported that they had tried but were unable to stop smoking tobacco.

Research in Canada tends to confirm the findings of American survey research. In a recent study of cocaine use in British Columbia, the Co-ordinated Law Enforcement Unit found that about 55 per cent of those who had used the drug had used it fewer than 10 times, about 35 per cent between 10 and 99 times, and again, as in America, less than 10 per cent more than 100 times. Compulsive use of this drug is the exception to the more general rule of moderation or ultimate lack of interest. There are tragedies but, as with alcohol, they are not the usual course of events.

Much of the claim that cocaine is highly addictive comes from animal research. Findings of self-reported human behaviour do not support this hypothesis, but some researchers hold, however surprisingly, that animal research provides a better barometer for understanding human beings.

In one such study, two rhesus monkeys in small cages were

given the opportunity to press a lever for cocaine, with the possibility of continuous reward. One monkey died of convulsions after three days, the other after five days. In another study, three monkeys in cages, when given a choice between cocaine and food, chose cocaine almost exclusively. In a third scientific experiment, twelve rats were given an opportunity to continuously inject cocaine. The ten rats that opted for continuous injections experienced a 30 per cent loss in body weight, and a number of convulsions over the course of a month.

This research is often trotted out to demonstrate what might happen to human beings if cocaine were to be made more available, but psychologist Bruce Alexander questions their conclusions. "Generalizing these animal findings is dubious, for many reasons ... monkeys are gregarious, active, curious animals, with a great resistance to being handled or restrained. The same is true of wild rats, and to a lesser extent, of their laboratory-bred descendants. Cocaine self-administration studies isolate such creatures in small cages, where they are surgically implanted with a cannula and tethered twenty-four hours a day to the injection apparatus.

"There is virtually nothing for these creatures to do in their solitary confinement," Alexander concludes, "but to press a lever on the wall that produces a temporary euphoric stimulation. There is little basis for concluding that these animals would consume as much cocaine in a more natural habitat. In fact recent data indicate that rats housed in isolation self-inject much more cocaine in daily self-administration tests than rats housed more naturally."

Much of this animal research is spurious science. Researchers cut open and occasionally kill animals in order to make the political rather than scientific claim that cocaine is a very dangerous drug. When we scrape away the moral residue that popular culture imposes and look at coca and its derivatives as a problem of public health, some different conclusions emerge.

Stimulant abuse is a real problem in our culture, and cocaine is the most seductive of stimulants. The most popular methods of ingestion — sniffing and smoking — are more likely to produce dependence than is oral consumption. And for those who inject cocaine intravenously, the risks are greater, attributable to injection itself and its increased risk of overdose. For most users, however, cocaine is not a source of dependence or a serious health problem.

In South America, coca is both a medicine and a recreation. To the hill people in the mountains of Colombia, Bolivia, and Peru, it has always been something of a blessing. To young black men in American ghettos, the more refined cocaine and crack are avenues to wealth, their pharmacology also delivering the illusion of being on top and in control, if only fleetingly.

As the industry is more dangerous than the drug itself, a solution to the problem of cocaine may be found in a regulation of the product and a system of taxation that gives preference to consumption of the drug in its least potent and least refined forms. Specifically, in an era of decriminalization or legalization, government policy should encourage, at least in fiscal terms, the chewing of coca leaf over the injection, smoking, or sniffing of the refined drug.

This drug is not going to go away. We can choose to live with it or we can fight it. And the solution will be global, in political, economic, and social terms. There can be no real progress until the consuming countries begin to negotiate with the producing nations and their cocaine industries. In the 1880s we said that coca and its derivatives were miraculous medicines. Fifty years later we regarded consumption of the drug as morally offensive. Another fifty years on, some of us are claiming that it is a recreational intoxicant, a party drug.

Cocaine has been pursued for a mix of reasons, at different times, and in different places. For the foreseeable future it will be business as usual, as tons of cocaine leave South America annually for Canadian and American markets, with most of the profits remaining in North America.

There seems little reason to believe that much will change. Yet when used in a typical pattern of moderation, cocaine seems no more a threat to Canada than alcohol or tobacco, and probably much less. When cocaine is abused or when it works as a catalyst for aggression, it is not the drug itself that is responsible for the problems that develop as much as the predisposition of the user.

In the Sierra Madre mountains of South America, the Indians chew the equivalent of about $1/4$ gram of pure cocaine every day in their *mascadas*. There are no indications that this gradual intake of the drug over the course of the day is inconsistent with good health or social productivity. With Canadians who sniff similarly small amounts of the drug, there is no indication of a substantial risk to health.

But the game goes on. There is an official script about cocaine, calling for callous distributors, weak, corruptible users, and "ruined lives." The everyday reality, however, is far less exciting: that melodramatically ruined life is an exception, most users are mere pleasure seekers, and most distributors are simply small-time entrepreneurs trying to sell enough product to finance their own consumption.

NOTES

There are many good sources of information about the health and social consequences of cocaine use, covering the range from coca leaf to crack. See T.C. Cox et al., *Drugs and Drug Abuse: A Reference Text* (Toronto: Addiction Research Foundation, 1983), pp. 225–31; B.K. Alexander, *Peaceful Measures: Canada's Way Out of the War on Drugs* (Toronto: University of Toronto Press, 1990), pp. 167–215. For more particular information regarding cocaine, see two more comprehensive books on cocaine itself: P.G. Erickson et al., *The Steel Drug: Cocaine in Perspective* (Toronto: Lexington Books, 1987), and L. Grinspoon and J. Bakalar, *Cocaine: A Drug and Its Social Evolution* (New York: Basic Books, 1976).

For a compelling and engaging description of Colombia and its cocaine trade, see Charles Nicholl, *The Fruit Palace* (London: Pan Books, 1986). For a good description of the cocaine trade and its consequences in New York City, see P.J. Goldstein et al., "Crack and Homicide in New York City, 1988: A Conceptually Based Event Analysis," in *Contemporary Drug Problems*, Winter 1989: pp. 651–87. For a good indication of police concerns about cocaine, and a reasonably comprehensive picture of the cocaine trade nationally and internationally, see Royal Canadian Mounted Police, *National Drug Intelligence Estimate, 1988/89* (Ottawa: Supply and Services, 1990), pp. 40–56.

This chapter was also informed by a series of interviews, by newspaper and magazine articles, by Hansard, by archival retrieval from the National Archives of Canada, and by a number of specific requests for government correspondence, pursuant to the Access to Information Act.

For estimates of cocaine use in Canada and the United States see B.K. Alexander, "Drug Use, Dependence and Addiction at a British Columbia University: Good News and Bad News," 15 *Canadian Journal of Higher Education* (1975): 13–29; P.M. O'Malley et al., "Cocaine Use Among American Adolescents and Young Adults," in N.J. Kozel and E.H. Adams, eds., *Cocaine Use in America: Epidemiologic and Clinical Perspectives*, NIDA Research Monograph No. 61 (Rockville, MD: National Institute on Drug Abuse, 1985); P.G Erickson et al., *The Steel Drug: Cocaine in Perspective* (Toronto: Lexington Books, 1987), pp. 33–59; and M. Eliany, ed., *Licit and Illicit Drugs in Canada* (Ottawa: Ministry of Supply and Services, 1989).

THE ILLEGAL SMILE

*The dose that would actually kill man is very
high indeed, really well beyond what would be
achieved by almost any amount of smoking. . . .
The drug is really quite a remarkably safe one
for humans, although it is really quite a
dangerous one for mice and they should not
use it.*

— J.W.D. HENDERSON,
Director of the Bureau of Human Drugs,
Health and Welfare Canada.

In the summer of 1990, David Bayley was convicted of possession of marijuana for the purpose of trafficking, and sentenced to five months' imprisonment. He had been under police surveillance and was stopped while driving his old grey Acadian on a city street. RCMP Constable Derrick Hobson explained to the judge that he could smell marijuana and found a joint in the ashtray; when he and his colleagues searched Bayley's car they found twelve ounces of marijuana in the trunk, along with a set of scales positioned at one gram. The drugs were valued at close to $2,000. They also found more than $800 in cash, an application for social assistance, and a social services slip giving Bayley a night's accommodation at a skid-row hotel.

Although David Bayley was later successful in an appeal against his conviction, he was like most of those who go to jail in Canada, a young man with little education, no stable family life, and inconsistent involvement in the labour force. His arrest is also typical of marijuana control in Canada: it is the most obvious users and distributors who are apprehended. The state sentences about 5,000 Canadians to jail every year for distribution of the drug, and hundreds annually for possession. More than 90 per cent of those jailed for cannabis receive sentences of less than six months in prison.

Yet, the seriousness with which police take marijuana is inconsistent. At rock concerts, for example, police typically ignore cannabis consumption. And not every police officer charges in every instance of marijuana use. Some police officers will charge on all occasions, some will confiscate the drugs but not charge, and still others will ignore the violation.

This inconsistency goes hand in hand with twenty years of ongoing disrespect for marijuana law among the Canadian and American publics. The most recent national Health and Welfare data indicate that more than half of all Canadians between the ages of twenty and forty-four have used marijuana; U.S. figures are similar. And these are very conservative estimates; many users are unwilling to admit consumption, notwithstanding the telephone interviewer's promise of anonymity.

Marijuana is the product of the hemp plant, and its intoxicating properties are found in the flowering tops of the female plant. These tops create a sticky resin, responsible for the potency of the final product. To attain greater strength, growers harvest the aromatic buds before seeds form; these tops are dried, and stored away from light and air, in order to increase their shelf life.

Over the past twenty-five years, the growers have developed a variety of potent strains of marijuana. In the late 1960s and early 1970s, the product was usually "shake," the dried leaves of the plant, with the occasional beginnings of flowers. In the 1990s, shake is a small part of the market; various strains of the resinous female flowers now dominate.

Since the late 1960s there has always been hashish, the caked resin from the hemp plant, and hash oil, a dark liquid drug, extracted from this resin with solvents. In the Netherlands, there are currently as many as seven varieties of hashish for sale, from different regions of the world and, correspondingly, about a dozen strains of marijuana. As in the alcohol market, consumers exercise different preferences, within a similar price range. Some prefer hashish or oil, and others marijuana. Within each form of cannabis there are also preferences, for "Afghani Black" or "Blond Lebanese," for "Thai Stick" or "California Red Hair." Not unlike those in search of ale or lager, Bordeaux or Chardonnay, cannabis consumers have constructed an elaborate market for the exercise of their psychoactive preferences.

Marijuana control began in Canada in 1923 with a single sentence in Hansard: "There is a new drug in the schedule." One year earlier in *The Black Candle*, Emily Murphy had written a chapter entitled "Marihuana — A New Menace." She concluded this chapter: "It has been pointed out that there are three ways out from the regency of this addiction: 1st — Insanity. 2nd — Death. 3rd — Abandonment. This is assuredly a direful trinity and one with which the public should be cognizant in order that they may be warned of the sharp danger that lies in even curiously tasting poisons which have been inhibited, or which are habit forming."

For the next forty years there was little use of marijuana in Canada and little knowledge of its effects, consumption generally confined to those in the entertainment industry. Despite this lack of public interest in the drug, the Narcotic Control Act, drafted in 1961, raised maximum penalties for distribution of marijuana from fourteen years to life imprisonment. Just a few years later, marijuana became popular in Canada and the United States, tied to the anti-war movement and to a developing culture of sexual experimentation among young people. In the House of Commons it was not the health effects of marijuana that came under debate, but its social and cultural connections. Members spoke of "demoralization," of "eroding the moral fibre of young people," and of a threatening "new morality." Marijuana was perceived to be synonymous with undermining parental authority and challenging the societal ethic of productive labour.

When the Trudeau government appointed the Le Dain Commission in 1969 to inquire into the "non-medical use of drugs," marijuana was at the top of the political agenda. There were two major reports from the commission, *Cannabis* in 1972 and *Final Report* in 1973. The commissioners recommended that marijuana possession no longer be a criminal offence, convinced that the health and social risks posed by consumption did not merit criminalization. Somewhat paradoxically, the commission recommended that distribution of marijuana remain a criminal offence, as part of a policy of discouraging use. Under the Le Dain guidelines the Canadian government was to tolerate consumption but to forbid any mechanism of distribution that would enable that consumption.

When marijuana offenders first began to appear in Canadian courts, the judiciary adopted what sociologist Pat Erickson has called "a get tough policy." In the late 1960s about half of convicted marijuana users were jailed for their offence of possession, some for as long as two years. Despite this significant threat, marijuana consumption continued to grow. In 1967 there were about 1,000 possession convictions in Canada; in 1975 there were more than 40,000.

In the face of increasing defiance of the law, and with limited jail space, the Canadian judiciary began to move away from imprisonment as the punishment for possession. By the mid-1970s, most users were fined, a smaller number placed on probation or given conditional or absolute discharges, and about 5 per cent imprisoned. During the past fifteen years, this pattern of sentencing has persisted, though the number of people facing marijuana charges has decreased significantly.

The RCMP charged more than 25,000 Canadians with

cannabis offences in 1977; they are now charging about 10,000 Canadians annually. "These figures are reflective of the RCMP's drug enforcement policy of targeting at the higher levels of drug trafficking organizations," they explain. "Prevailing economic conditions . . . may have encouraged more individuals to participate in drug trafficking activities for quick financial gain, while advanced technology such as computers and hydroponic cultivation were increasingly utilized in the drug trade." However, this image of police moving away from street-level enforcement and targeting more sophisticated entrepreneurs is still far from the realities. Most arrests and convictions are based on distribution schemes that involve a few hundred dollars and the degree of sophisticated delivery allegedly employed by David Bayley.

Successive federal governments have almost ignored the Le Dain Commission's recommendations regarding marijuana. In 1980 the Trudeau government announced in its throne speech that it was "time to move cannabis offences to the Food and Drugs Act and remove the possibility of imprisonment for simple possession." No legislation was introduced, and the promise was abandoned. Then Solicitor General Robert Kaplan has indicated that when the matter came to Cabinet after the throne speech, there was no consensus on the legislation, and no commitment to proceed.

So the game goes on. The RCMP's most recent Drug Intelligence estimate notes that the domestic cultivation of marijuana has been increasing through the late 1980s, but that "even at its top-end price, domestic marijuana is less costly than any of its imported competitors. . . . The preference for hashish in both its solid and liquid forms may be attributed to the fact that it is generally more potent than marijuana."

This needs some qualification. The top end of the marijuana market in Canada is often domestically produced

material, an ounce selling for as much as $450. And prefer-
ence for hashish is more one of a cultural or individual taste
than a matter of potency. In Ontario and Quebec, hashish
from Lebanon and Asia dominate the cannabis market; in
British Columbia, locally produced, Mexican, and Asian
marijuana dominate the market. Potency — resin content
— can be comparable in marijuana and hashish, and is
critically affected by such variables as seed stock, the gender
of the plant, sunshine, temperature, soil content, and exposure to air and light after harvest.

As the RCMP have noted, the domestic production of
marijuana has continued to increase in Canada into the
1990s. With more sophistication in the technology of growing and the options of indoor, greenhouse, and outdoor
harvests, domestic production is often seen as preferable to
smuggling the product from Asia, Mexico, Jamaica, or the
Middle East. An eight-by-eight room given to indoor growing might yield over $100,000 in profit annually.

The advantage of importation, from the distributor's
perspective, is quick profit. Marijuana can be purchased for
less than $100 per pound in countries like Mexico or
Thailand, and sold for $2,000 to $3,000 per pound in
Canada. As the Canadian market is estimated to be about
five hundred tons per year, the potential income amounts to
about $2 billion dollars annually, in the wholesale trade
alone. The profitability of hashish is much the same. Smuggling by air or sea through foreign contacts has the advantage of a cheaper, more plentiful product and, hence,
higher profit, but it also requires substantial co-ordination
and more risks.

Robert "Rosie" Rowbotham knows all about those risks.
He is a major importer of hashish and has staged Canada's
most prominent show trials on marijuana, using the court as
a forum for the cause of legal change. He is currently
imprisoned in Ontario's Collins Bay Institution, a medium-
security penitentiary known to the local residents and pris-

oners as "Disneyland North" because of its red tin spires sitting atop a castle-like stone building. Rowbotham challenged the moral legitimacy of the law, and lost. With his fourteen-, seventeen-, and twenty-year sentences, he is something of a martyr for marijuana, locked up for his political beliefs about the legitimacy of marijuana distribution.

On this morning he was dressed in a Hawaiian motif, white shirt and floral trunks. "I'm on Maui at Lahaina, I don't know about you guys." Never mind that it's November, that he's serving a seventeen-year sentence for importing some uncertain number of tons of marijuana into Canada. And never mind that the judge at one of his more recent trials handed out a sentence of twenty years and described him as a "social bloodsucker."

The guards are laughing. "Yeah, sure, Rosie. Looking good."

Rosie was born in Belleville, Ontario, a little over forty years ago. In the summer of 1968 he had his first contact with the criminal law. He arrived at a friend's home to pick up an ounce of hashish and found it cut and wrapped in forty pieces — done as a favour, he was told. Arrested shortly after leaving the house, he was charged with possession of hashish for the purpose of trafficking. "I understand now what he and the Mounties were doing. I didn't understand then, but if we had taken off we would have made it."

Rowbotham was convicted of possession and sentenced to thirty days in jail. He later drifted to Toronto's Yorkville, and then to the site of his rise to prominence, Rochdale College. Rochdale was the name given to a concrete building just to the west of the fashionable section of Toronto's Bloor Street north of the University of Toronto campus. An experiment in student co-op housing, Rochdale became an important part of Toronto's illegal drug trade, and the subject of much public concern. It is now a residence for senior citizens.

Robert William Rowbotham was, if not a student, at least a keen practitioner of business and commerce. In his early days in Rochdale, there was often a line-up of forty to fifty people outside his door, waiting to buy marijuana, hashish, and LSD. "On a weekend I could probably pick up $2,500 to $3,500. That was a lot to me."

Rosie shifts in his chair and smiles. The curly brown hair is getting pretty grey. He's spent almost eleven of the past thirteen years in jail. His marriage has dissolved, and he's only two years into a seventeen-year sentence. It's the longest sentence ever handed down in Canada for the distribution of cannabis, except for the twenty years that he previously received for the same crime.

Through the early 1970s Rochdale became the nemesis of the RCMP drug squad, and Rosie became one of their major suspects. He was stopped and searched on about fifty occasions, without being arrested or charged. Then, in December 1973, sixteen crates of Lebanese hashish arrived at Toronto's International Airport. There were phony invoices for a phony company that had a post-office box for an address. The police uncovered the drugs only through a routine check but, once alerted, followed the men who picked them up. Robert Rowbotham was charged with conspiracy to import approximately one ton of hashish.

The strategy of the Rowbotham defence was to proselytize, and, at times, to shock. At his preliminary hearing, he distributed T-shirts with a stencilled picture of a large penis devouring Ottawa's Peace Tower, and the words "Rowbotham versus Regina." He admitted dealing in marijuana, but argued — and still argues — that he was not guilty of conspiring to import this particular shipment of hashish. He urged — and continues to urge — the legalization of marijuana. In May 1977, he told county court judge Stephen Borins prior to sentencing that there was nothing morally wrong with using or distributing marijuana.

Judge Borins must have seemed, at least initially, to offer

some hope for the defence. He had just written an important decision in a case against a cocaine distributor, a man by the name of Shand. In that instance, he considered the physical and social harm of cocaine, and the circumstances of the offender, and came to the conclusion that a seven-year minimum term amounted to "cruel and unusual punishment."

The appearance of author Norman Mailer in defence of Rowbotham elevated the public visibility of the case. Barbara Amiel managed to both bitch and coo about Mailer's testimony in a feature article in *Maclean's*. "For close to four and a half hours, the gravelly, sexy voice of Norman Mailer carefully instructed a respectful court on the meaning of karma and the balance of justice in the cosmos. When it was all over the court had effectively been asked — in somewhat mystic and literary phrases — just why they were bothering to try this case at all. And then Norman Mailer got on a plane and went home."

Toronto rock promoter John Brower testified that he, John Lennon, and Yoko Ono had spent an enjoyable evening in December 1969 smoking marijuana with two of the five Le Dain commissioners. And a survey of graduating students at Osgoode Hall Law School revealed that over 85 per cent had used marijuana, and that 70 per cent intended to continue use after graduation. The *Globe and Mail* printed the news across the top of its front page.

None of this had much impact on the case, however. Patrick Duffy prosecuted Rowbotham in 1977; he then defended him in 1985 and 1988. Duffy is a friendly family man in his fifties, "a decent human being," according to most.

As Duffy recalls, Rosie was unreasonably optimistic about his chances of convincing the court of the moral legitimacy of his argument. "One day Rosie comes to me," Duffy said with a chuckle, "could I drive him back to the subway? I said,

I suppose so, but not without your lawyer's agreement and consent. I mean, I'm the Crown attorney, you know."

On the drive to the subway, Rosie told Duffy that, when it was all over, there would be no hard feelings. He would not sue for false arrest or false imprisonment. He also told him that marijuana was going to be legalized.

"And I told him, not in my lifetime. I didn't have any personal dislike for the guy. He's intelligent, engaging. But he was a high-profile drug dealer. We caught him with a ton of hash, which even in those days was an enormous amount, and my job was to prosecute him, convict him, and get him a big sentence."

In May 1977, Judge Stephen Borins sentenced Robert Rowbotham, the man *Maclean's* dubbed "Johnny Reeferseed," to fourteen years in prison. On Christmas Eve, in 1980, he was released on parole. A little over a year later, in April 1982, after an eleven-month undercover operation, Robert Rowbotham was arrested and imprisoned, charged with conspiracy to import over $50 million of hashish, allegedly from Lebanon.

The first of two trials ran from February 1984 to June 1985, and cost taxpayers a little more than $6 million. The prosecution relied on telephone interceptions and bugging devices to build their case. It was said to be an elaborate conspiracy, with Rosie as chairman of the board, and other accused cast as corporate president, junior partner, courier, and so on. The prosecutor, Chris Amerasinghe, was seeking a life sentence for the "Chairman of the Board" of "the Mr. Bigs."

Prosecution witness Dr. John William Dalrymple Henderson was the director of the Bureau of Human Drugs in Canada's Department of Health and Welfare. Dr. Henderson trained as a medical doctor and worked as a surgeon and pharmacologist before joining the federal government's health bureaucracy in 1977.

After explaining that much research about the effects of cannabis takes place on mice, Dr. Henderson was asked by Crown prosecutor Amerasinghe to extrapolate to humans. "The dose that would actually kill man is actually very high indeed," Henderson responded, "really well beyond what would be achieved by almost any amount of smoking . . . the drug is really quite a remarkably safe one for humans, although it is really quite a dangerous one for mice and they should not use it."

Patrick Duffy began his cross-examination of Dr. Henderson: "If my notes are correct, you told us basically these things about the use of cannabis . . . there is little evidence of heart damage that we know about?"

"Yes."

"As far as we know, it does not damage the liver?"

"That is right."

"Except . . ."

"With alcohol, yes."

". . . that it is unconvincing that it does any chromosome damage?"

"Yes. . . ."

". . . Are you telling me that there is any connection . . . between the use of marijuana or hash . . . and lung cancer or any kind of cancer that is scientifically established?"

"No, I am not. I am not able to tell you that."

This was a fairly accurate summary of existing scientific evidence. Marijuana's major risk is associated with the ingestion of smoke. There are no filters provided on marijuana cigarettes, and the smoke is usually held in the lungs longer than tobacco smoke. Some scientists have suggested that one marijuana cigarette might be as harmful to the lungs as five or more tobacco cigarettes. However, such precise comparisons are ultimately confounded by variations in individual rates of use over time, the extent of inhalation, and the chemical composition of the product.

Research indicates that the average marijuana smoker

will smoke three to five cigarettes per week, in contrast to the tobacco smoker's two hundred cigarettes. Neither tobacco nor marijuana is benign, but the cardio-pulmonary risks of marijuana are slight in comparison, the physiological addictiveness of tobacco being the key to the distinction.

The other significant cost of marijuana consumption is the sedative effect of the drug, potentially decreasing productivity, and imposing a risk to others, if the user decides to drive a vehicle or operate heavy machinery. Marijuana is, however, a much less potent sedative and has many fewer physical consequences than does alcohol. Unlike other popularly used drugs such as alcohol, tobacco, and caffeine, marijuana has not been scientifically linked to cancer or heart disease, although there are likely connections in cases of extremely heavy use.

As for the other claims about marijuana — that it impairs the immune system, that it leads to chromosome damage, brain damage, and an "amotivational syndrome" — there is no sound empirical support, though "amotivational syndrome" probably relates to the drug's sedative effect. Unlike alcohol, which is quickly eliminated from the body, marijuana is stored in the fat cells and eliminated slowly, over days or weeks; however, the health consequences of this difference, though not well understood, have not been shown to be significant.

The Rowbotham defence's most dramatic evidence about the effects of marijuana came in testimony from the rock musician Neil Young, whose brother Robert had been charged as a co-conspirator in the Rowbotham case.

"I have smoked grass for twenty years myself," Neil Young told the court. "I have held down a good job. I have continued to be very productive. . . . I would say that these people [the accused] knew that cannabis is not seen to have a detrimental effect, especially compared to alcohol, cigarettes, heroin, cocaine, barbiturates, amphetamines, et cetera, et cetera. Cannabis is in a different ball park. These people know that. I know that."

Asked by prosecutor Chris Amerasinghe if he really saw nothing wrong with cannabis use or distribution, Young responded, "Yes. . . . The only thing that's wrong with the use of cannabis is the government doesn't make any money from it, like it does from alcohol and tobacco."

In June 1985 Judge Eugene Ewaschuk (known to his colleagues as "Tex") passed sentence on the accused. "I should add that I strongly disagree with Neil Young's comment that cannabis is harmless," he wrote. "One has only to look at the rock stars themselves to see how graphically the abuse and even death that drug use can lead to. Cannabis use is particularly harmful to young Canadians. As I stated earlier, it leads to drug experimentation. Additionally, the pernicious properties of cannabis are, amongst other effects, mind altering, and hence harmful as well to adults."

Justice Ewaschuk sentenced Rowbotham and his associates to a total of ninety-five years' imprisonment. Rowbotham received the most severe penalty, twenty years. "Drug traffickers are amongst the worst kinds of criminals in society," Ewaschuk wrote. "Young people steal to buy their drugs. Addicts break and enter to get drugs. Addicts become prostitutes to get money to satisfy physical and psychological drug cravings. Drug traffickers profit from the misery and crime of the drug users. Drug traffickers live off the avails of other people's crimes and are thus social bloodsuckers."

The rhetoric has little to do with the reality of marijuana use and distribution. Marijuana "addiction" is purely psychological, the physical consequences of withdrawal virtually non-existent. The drug is not as potent a psychoactive as alcohol or tobacco, and not empirically connected to "misery and crime," as alcohol is. And the description of the marijuana distributor as a "social bloodsucker" seems, again, empirically difficult to support.

In March 1988, the Ontario Court of Appeal overturned the convictions of Robert Rowbotham and his ten associates, eight men and two women allegedly involved in various marijuana distribution schemes. The $6 million trial would have to be replayed. The court did not take issue with the philosophical direction taken by Justice Ewaschuk — with his talk of "social bloodsuckers" and the like — but with his technical mastery of the Rowbotham case.

The Court of Appeal indicated that Justice Ewaschuk had made a number of substantive and procedural errors. The jury-selection process had given an unfair advantage to the prosecution, two of the eleven accused had gone through the entire trial without a lawyer, their requests for representation consistently denied. Justice Ewaschuk had also ordered one of the accused out of the courtroom during legal argument, and continued the trial in her absence. And he had refused to give the federal government's legal advice on wiretap evidence to defence lawyers.

The government decided that plea bargaining was preferable to another trial, but Rosie did not like the terms: ten years. He had already spent six years in jail and this would guarantee at least another four before release.

Patrick Duffy was expressing exasperation. "I told him — Bob, this isn't a legal case anymore, it's a political case. You've taken on the Canadian government. "But," Duffy continued, "he threw down the gauntlet."

In May 1989 Robert Rowbotham was sentenced to seventeen years' imprisonment for conspiracy to import hashish. On the day prior to sentencing, new charges were laid, relating to his alleged distribution activities during his seven months on bail. There will be another trial, and the prosecution will be relying on a videotaped conversation between Rosie and a police informant in order to make its case. The allegation is that Robert William Rowbotham has once again been involved in the distribution of cannabis and its derivatives.

Rosie Rowbotham has already spent more time in jail than the overwhelming majority of those convicted of manslaughter, multiple sexual assaults, or a series of armed robberies. (The typical sentence for manslaughter is six years' imprisonment, for violent sexual assault three years, and repeated armed robbery six years.)

"I'm costing the taxpayers $50,000 a year, but they don't give a fuck. Why should I give a fuck?" said Rosie. "It's their money."

"Simon Morgan" cost the Canadian taxpayers much less. Simon Morgan isn't his real name. Unlike Rosie, Morgan makes pragmatic choices. Like Rosie he is, or was, the kind of boy your mother warned you about.

Sex and drugs and a genial machismo are a strong part of both R.W. Rowbotham and Simon Morgan. For Rosie, however, it was much more than a business; ultimately it was a political struggle against the federal government. For Simon Morgan, marijuana distribution was an exciting game.

"I like to think of it," he began, "as one of the last real *laissez-faire* types of capitalism."

Simon Morgan spent a decade in the marijuana business, in Britain in the late 1960s and in Canada in the 1970s. He was a university student with access to a large number of willing consumers. "I was never really involved in anything else . . . cocaine, once or twice, LSD, once or twice . . . but I decided I wanted to stay away from things like that because of the kinds of people that you ran into. The farther you move away from marijuana and hash, the heavier the scene is likely to be.

"There's a kick in it," he continued. "There's nothing like walking through Customs loaded with dope and making it. The buzz you get when you're walking away with your back to them is unbelievable." He laughed. "I'll tell you another thing — and that's about the buzz when you're not walking away from them." He groaned.

On the night that he was arrested, Morgan was lying in bed, listening to someone walking on the roof of his top-floor apartment. He saw the police car from his window and heard the knocking on the downstairs door a few minutes later. His landlady let the two policemen into the building, and just moments later they knocked on his door.

In a moment of carelessness Morgan had violated one of the cardinal rules of dealing: "Don't pollute your own doorstep." Keeping large amounts of any illegal drug in your house dramatically increases the likelihood of apprehension. And given that cannabis is more bulky than other drugs, this rule is particularly important. (Other rules also make police intervention more difficult: never talk on the phone, sell only to people you know well, and never tell people any more than they need to know. Those who appear in criminal court have almost always violated one or more of these rules.)

The two officers were from the city police force. Although they didn't have search warrants, Morgan suspected that they had writs of assistance, documents that could justify a search. He invited them in, and they began to look through his apartment. They found a small amount of marijuana, but this was not of interest to them.

Morgan recalls, "I said, 'Of course I smoke dope. I'm not going to deny that to you.' And they said, 'Well, if that's all we've come here for, we're not going to embarrass ourselves.' "

After half an hour the police tired of the search, sat down beside Morgan on the bed, and told him that it looked like they wouldn't get him this time.

Morgan winced. "I couldn't believe it. They told me who the informer was . . . her husband or boyfriend had recently been busted and in order to get him off she was selling people out."

The police officers were on their way out when one decided to use the toilet before leaving. "I can hear the brown paper wrapper, as he's undoing the dope. He finishes his piss and he comes back in and he sits down on the bed and says, 'Simon, I'm disappointed in you.' " Within three hours, Morgan had been taken before a justice of the peace, charged with possession for the purposes of trafficking, and released upon a personal recognizance. He was back in his apartment by four o'clock in the morning. He had declined to make any statement to police.

"I felt violated. They had no right to come in my apartment and take my shit. . . . MY shit." Morgan laughed. "It's not THEIR shit, it's MY shit. . . . They'd just deprived me of a couple of thousand dollars and I was not well disposed towards that. I still had a stash . . . I had money in the fridge. It wasn't like I was wiped out, but I was pissed off.

"That taught me something — this is a game. And the issue is, which of the players has power and what is the story?" Morgan returned to the business of marijuana distribution with something of a vengeance. "My main reaction to getting busted was to say, 'Okay, you fuckers' . . . the first thing I did was to go back to Europe, organize a load of dope and import it. . . . It was all done in the Christmas mail. It was a nice little scam — not a big thing — but it gave us enough working capital to go to Jamaica."

Morgan flew down to Jamaica with three friends for a working holiday. Three of the four men were business partners — they had $20,000 in cash, and were looking forward to a substantial return on this investment and three weeks' relaxation.

Naive young Morgan and his partners fit every police composite of the "drug fiend/dope dealer." They all wore their hair to their shoulders and were incessantly displaying a rather boisterous approach to social life. A night with four Jamaican prostitutes had cost them $5,000, apart from the women's fee: two of the women discovered some of their cash and left with it.

On a day that began with a mickey of rum and a side order

of eggs and bacon, one of the four fell in the street outside the bar. "I got out into the street just in time to see Fred crash, he cut himself pretty bad. . . . I'm saying, 'You all right, man?' He's saying, 'Yeah, yeah, I'm all right.' We put him in the back of the car and we took him home."

Fred was dead. "Pretty bizarre," Morgan continued. "Here we are, the attitude between the legality of alcohol and marijuana . . . there's a statement right there. This guy would have literally had to stuff a pound down his mouth so he couldn't breathe to die from marijuana. But here he was, dead."

Morgan and his two partners had been in Jamaica for under ten days; they had already been robbed of $5,000 and now there were only two of them. Morgan and his friend Jeff decided, however, that they would not lose sight of their objective — that "Fred would have wanted us to continue."

During the next two weeks the men organized the importation of ten pounds of hashish oil. Morgan and his partner carefully unwrapped cigarette cartons, took out the cigarettes, and replaced them with their weight in hash oil, poured into condoms, which were then tied closed and surrounded in the cartons by crumpled newspaper. Another nine pounds of oil were poured into the cavities of wooden carvings. The men drilled holes, poured in the oil, and then plugged the holes with wooden stoppers. They concealed their carpentry by sanding and then staining the carvings. As they boarded their flight to Canada, their mood was optimistic.

"We get on the plane . . . and we walk through Immigration, and they were waiting for us." Morgan and his partner Jeff were stopped by Customs officers and charged with importing narcotics. They would face a minimum term of seven years in prison if convicted.

Morgan figures that an informer was responsible for his arrest, "It turns out that one of the women who was around the villa a lot was the sister of the woman who sold me out on

the first charge. She flew back to Canada a few weeks before
we did. . . . I think I was sold out by the same person on both
charges."

Morgan and his partner were turned over to the RCMP. At
this point he reminded himself of his earlier dealings with
Canada's criminal-justice system, "This is a game — and the
question is, who has the power and what is the story?" On
the way from the airport Morgan and his partner rode
together in the back seat of the RCMP car. They were not
allowed to speak to each other, but were able to write
messages on their hands with their fingers. They silently
agreed that they would confess to importing the one pound
of hash oil in the cigarette packages, but deny any knowledge of the nine pounds found in the wooden carvings. This
would be, by implication, the work of their late partner,
Fred.

"Nobody really believed that for a minute," Morgan
recalled. The prosecutor placed the value of the hash oil at
approximately $100,000, and the judge noted that Morgan
had been charged while awaiting trial on an earlier charge of
possession of two pounds of hashish for the purpose of
trafficking. Morgan's application for bail was not granted.

But he did receive one very good piece of news after the
ten pounds of hash oil had been analysed. The certificate of
analysis described the substance not as *cannabis indica*, but as
cannabis sativa. In other words, Morgan had been sold marijuana oil, not hash oil. The black sticky tar was worth less
than $10,000. The gravity of his crime had been lessened by
the unethical conduct of his suppliers.

When Morgan came to trial on his first charge of possession for the purpose of trafficking, he argued that the two
pounds of hashish was his; he told the jury that he was guilty
of possession, but not guilty of possession for the purpose of
trafficking. This was a difficult argument — the police had
valued the hashish at $10,000 and had found scales in Mor-
gan's apartment.

But Morgan told the jury that, whatever its value on the street, he had paid only $1,600 for the hash. As a student with little income and a committed cannabis smoker, he needed to buy in bulk.

"I was on the stand for seven hours . . . and here are all these people. . . . And, you know, the truth, the absolute truth, and nothing but the truth. . . . They, however, are stuck with conjecture. They're in the realm of pure theory."

After more than ten hours' deliberation, the jury brought in a verdict of not guilty. "My friends in the court stood up and they cheered. . . . This judge gets up and he's steaming, he's thinking there are twelve idiots here."

What the judge knew about, and the jury did not, was the more serious charge of importing that Morgan still had to face. The judge found Morgan guilty of possession, fined him $500, and sentenced him to seven days in jail. Within a few weeks he had served his sentence, won a second bail hearing, and been released on a bond of $50,000. He was now waiting for the second trial on the charge of importing.

Morgan remained out on bail for over two years. His lawyer believed that sentences for marijuana distribution were gradually being reduced, and that Morgan could be the beneficiary of this leniency. A friend from the university had posted the $50,000 bond in order to secure Morgan's release on bail. Morgan returned to dealing marijuana and hashish, thinking that, if he could make enough money to cover his friend's loss, he would leave the country. He didn't want to face the possibility of seven years in jail.

But he didn't manage to make enough money to cover the value of his friend's home, and so ultimately went to trial, his beard shaved off and his hair cut. He was wearing a suit and tie. His lawyer told him of the bargain he had made with the prosecutor: two years' imprisonment for a plea of guilty to the reduced charge of possession for the purpose of trafficking the single pound of marijuana in the cigarette cartons.

But in the courtroom the Crown reneged on the bargain

and led evidence with respect to all ten pounds of the drug. Morgan was convicted, and held in custody, to be sentenced five weeks later.

On the day of sentencing Morgan's lawyer retaliated by reneging on his bargain with the prosecutor, arguing for no more than three months in prison.

"The Crown attorney just about dropped in the courtroom. My lawyer said he was not going to go along with two years, given the circumstances of my life, and the chance to leave the city for the university in the fall . . . two years would take me to a different place in the world, it would take me away from all that."

Simon Morgan was sentenced to ninety days' imprisonment, and was released in time to resume his university studies in the fall. He explains the court's leniency by pointing to his support from the university, his lawyer's skills, and his own attitudes towards the police. "I didn't give them a lot of tongue. I was polite to them. And they treated me all right . . . these guys treated me like a human being.

"We played class differences to the hilt," he continues, "the tie, the jacket, the university support. We were arguing that we didn't really belong in the criminal court.

"I spent six months in prison. It taught me about the futility of imprisonment. It didn't deter to the extent that I was involved after that. Ultimately when another kind of life came along, it deterred me completely, because it just wouldn't be worth losing.

"Clearly I made a lot of mistakes. I was far from perfect in the judgments that I made, but, by and large, my impression is that it's a very honourable business. . . . There are a few assholes around but basically because the business is repetitive, there are very few. . . . It's not in anybody's interest in the long run to do a rip-off. It's a short-term gain, for a sacrifice of the long term. It's the long term that you want to think about. The object is capital accumulation."

The RCMP places the current value of the industry at $5

billion annually, about $200 for each of Canada's 25 million residents. That $200 will purchase an ounce of high-potency marijuana. It can be rolled into about fifty cigarettes, each of which will get the user high at least twice: the net cost of a single cannabis high, about $2.

Marijuana is typically the least expensive of legal and illegal drugs. An alcohol high usually costs more than $2 and a tobacco habit between $4 and $8 dollars per day. A gram of cocaine will, with some restraint, provide the user with about five separate highs: the net cost, $20 per high. And with heroin, the price of a high is even more prohibitive, a day's consumption typically starting at $100.

In 1991, there are about 2.5 million Canadians using marijuana and hashish. About one in every thousand is brought before the criminal courts each year. Those we convict are typically poor young men who use and sell marijuana in public; they are occasionally sent to jail for short terms. Those at the top of the distribution pyramid — Rosie, or men like Bob Pascoe, Pat Roberts, and Gary Sexton — are one in a thousand, sentenced to five years or more for their marijuana crimes.

If the Marlboro man had shoulder-length brown hair, he would look something like Bob Pascoe. There is the same middle-class sense of self assurance, the slightly rugged features, and a western drawl. The seizure of Bob Pascoe's six-ton cargo in the late 1980s was the end of a game that, at one point, was earning over a million dollars annually. Pascoe was convicted of conspiracy to import marijuana in 1988 and plea-bargained a term of seven years. He is now out of prison, on parole, living with his wife and five children, involved in legal business ventures.

Pascoe never carried a gun, and never associated with people who carried guns. (In western Canada guns are very rare in the cannabis business, although this has been less true of the industry in Ontario and Quebec.) He argues that there is a lot of trust in the marijuana business — he once

had his truck loaded in California with 600 pounds of marijuana on the basis that he was Bob from Canada, soon to
return with the proceeds from his sales. "Can't imagine
doing that in straight business deals," he said.

Pat Roberts is a short, somewhat stout and balding man in
his early forties. In 1987 he was convicted of flying about
half a ton of marijuana into Atlantic Canada in a small plane.
He was released from jail in 1989, after serving about two
years of a five-year sentence for importing.

Pat Roberts is currently enrolled in the School of Business
Administration at Simon Fraser University. In the spring of
1990 controversy arose when the Department of National
Defence revealed that the death of a pilot and the loss of a
$35 million CF-18 had occurred during a test mission for the
war against drugs. Roberts pointed out that the CF-18 could
never follow the smaller plane of the smuggler into remote
airstrips; a CF-18 would be of no assistance to the enforcement effort, unless it was able to shoot a smuggler out of the
sky. A spokesman for the drugs section of the RCMP agreed.
Roberts also suggested that $35 million could have bought a
lot of education and support for those with drug-abuse
problems.

Roberts is unapologetic about his former occupation.
"People say that I abused the privilege of being a pilot by
putting my skills and airplanes to such use. I don't accept
that. At the risk of my freedom and my life, I brought a
relatively harmless product to people who chose to use it, of
their own free will. Contrast that with what we've seen
recently in the Persian Gulf: highly sophisticated aircraft
flown by young heroes, killing and maiming innocent
women and children in the thousands. I don't have any
difficulty justifying my use of aircraft. But they're heroes,
and I'm on parole."

The seizure of Gary Sexton's cargo in the late 1970s was a
record for Canadian police forces — thirteen tons of Colombian marijuana. Sexton and his partners began to distribute

marijuana in Newfoundland and in parts of Ontario in the early 1970s, making expeditions to Jamaica and Colombia. In early 1974 Sexton was arrested at Toronto Airport with a Tia Maria bottle full of hash oil. He had the receipts for the alcohol and so could hope to establish that he had been deceived by somebody who wanted him to act as a courier. But when a lawyer told him that it would cost almost $10,000 and two years of court appearances, he decided to leave. Police issued a warrant for his arrest.

He travelled to Newfoundland, and then south to the island of Antigua to begin a deal that would bring two tons of Colombian marijuana into port in Newfoundland. The two tons eventually found their way to port just outside of St. John's but were soon confiscated by police and traced to Gary Sexton. Another warrant was issued for his arrest.

He remained at large for almost two years, until arrested on Saltspring Island in British Columbia. He was flown back to Newfoundland and given ten years for importing the two tons of Colombian marijuana. Sent to Springhill Penitentiary in Nova Scotia, he obviously impressed prison authorities with his sense of humour and his initiative. A little over a year into his sentence he was given a three-day pass to attend a Jaycee convention. He was an enthusiastic participant on Friday and Saturday, but on Sunday he was absent, en route to Montreal. He remained at large again for almost two years, surfacing when his thirteen-ton cargo was confiscated on the west coast of Vancouver Island.

"At this point bail was becoming difficult." He laughed. Gary Sexton is turning forty, his shoulder-length hair flecked with grey. There is a Newfoundland lilt in his voice and a little mischief in his laugh. In 1979 he was sentenced to ten years' imprisonment for conspiracy to import approximately thirteen tons of marijuana. He served a little over four years before release on parole. When he looks back to his days as a smuggler, the picture resembles a dream, a script from another lifetime. Sitting in a sailboat off the coast of Colombia at midnight, bathed in the warm scents of the tropics, listening to the sound of the Colombian cutter disappearing, its cargo of hundred-pound bales of marijuana now covering his deck.

There are some commonalities among Canada's more sophisticated marijuana distributors. Rosie, Simon Morgan, Bob Pascoe, Pat Roberts, and Gary Sexton, all endorse the political values of the 1960s generation: make love, not war; question authority; and have a good time. And this remains the challenge and the threat of marijuana, feared not for its ultimate physical or social consequences, but for its challenge to dominant cultural scripts.

Vancouver's Granville Mall is a gathering site for socially and economically disadvantaged youth. Marijuana and hashish are sold at $10 to $15 per gram. The police use the area for what is called a buy-and-bust transaction.

In one recent case an undercover policewoman approached two young men and asked if they could sell her a gram of hash. She indicated in court that she had chosen the two because they were wearing blue jeans and looked a little scruffy. One of the two men was interested in pursuing the woman romantically, or at least sexually, and so they complied with her request, finding her a gram of hashish. They were then charged with trafficking and taken into custody to await trial and, ultimately, a typical jail sentence of less than six months in prison.

This is the essence of the buy-and-bust technique — use decoys to approach potential drug distributors, and then arrest upon delivery of the product. It is a technique that is most likely to succeed with people who have few social skills and little in the way of economic resources.

For almost ten years Rod Stamler was director of the drug-enforcement program for the RCMP. His appointment in 1980 was unexpected. Stamler had little experience in drug control, having spent his career with the complexities of corporate and commercial crime.

"In hindsight I see why," he said. "They selected me because, at that time, the RCMP wanted to move street-level marijuana enforcement to looking at organized crime, looking at the money-flow situation and moving upwards and getting the people that really counted, rather than picking up all of these cases out there. And that was the directive I got."

At the time of his retirement Stamler was also assistant commissioner of the Force. He is a friendly and energetic man, highly regarded by his former colleagues. He now works for Peat Marwick, his area of specialization, drug-control policy. He does not believe that marijuana consumption is morally different from alcohol consumption, but worries about public safety. "How do you test impairment with marijuana? That's my only question. You can smell alcohol, you can see it, and you can test it." Like alcohol, marijuana can be detected in blood and urine, but unlike alcohol, it cannot be subject to a breath test. Given human-rights concerns and difficulties in data interpretation, blood and urine tests are unlikely to be widely used.

Rod Stamler's interest in controlling impaired driving is understandable, but takes us away from the more important issue. Should marijuana consumption be criminally prohibited? Do users who are not driving need to be subject to penalties of up to seven years in prison, and distributors subject to life imprisonment? Is there a kinder, gentler way to control this drug?

The Leidesplein branch of Amsterdam's Bulldog Coffee Shop looks across the Leidesplein square to the curved windows, balustrades, and turret of the Municipal Theatre, a nineteenth-century elegance in brick. On the side of the Bulldog's building there is a McDonald's sign, and two buildings down, a Heineken sign. On the front of the building that faces The Bulldog there are two more signs, the symbols of Burger King and Coca-Cola.

The tubular neon of "The Bulldog Palace" is a little more

difficult to spot in this mix, its red and blue scrawl under-written with a more formal blue neon, "Cafe," "Cocktails." The rules of the establishment are displayed in the window in a simpler print: no hard drugs, no aggression, no one under eighteen will be served, no stolen wares, and no alcohol.

The Bulldog is one of about 300 "coffee shops" in Amsterdam, offering a menu of fresh squeezed orange juice, coffee, and marijuana. At the Easy Times coffee shop a few blocks and a canal away, beer is added to the list of choices, but the other rules remain — no hard drugs, no aggression, no one under eighteen, and no stolen property. Bob Marley overlooks the bar, his face emblazoned on the Jamaican flag that hangs above the beer dispensers.

In most of the Netherlands' coffee shops price lists are tacked discreetly to the wall. Two grams of "sinsemilla — skunk," grown locally in Amsterdam, is a top-of-the-line product, costing about $17 Cdn. Hashish from Nepal and Kashmir is similarly priced; Colombian marijuana and Afghani hash are about half the cost. Buying in bulk merits a discount, nine grams of "sinsemilla — skunk" for the price of eight, and so on.

The patrons of the Bulldog, like the patrons of other coffee shops, range from late teens to mid-forties, and tend to be cheerful, if somewhat disaffected and slightly dis-solute. There are also the "double parkers," those who stop their cars or bicycles only long enough to make a purchase.

The Netherlands is the only Western state that permits the sale and possession of the drug, and its European neigh-bours, most particularly, Germany, fear leakage into their countries, despite more widespread consumption within their own borders. The Dutch policy seems to be working. While 10 per cent of Canadian youth use marijuana reg-ularly, only 2 per cent of Holland's youth do. The rate of casual use of the drug is also lower in the Netherlands. The price of marijuana is about two-thirds of the price on Canadian streets. Since the introduction of decriminalization in 1975, the country's rate of consumption has declined.

The Netherlands has not fully legalized cannabis: there is no tax collected on Dutch marijuana revenues; as a consequence of consistent pressure from the international community, the Netherlands cannot acknowledge the business of marijuana distribution as a source of legitimate income. It is legal to consume and to distribute in the country, but not to earn income from the drug.

Yet the Netherlands seems to have about the best solution for this problem, aside from this anomaly of tax avoidance: fewer committed users, no public social or economic costs for courts, imprisonment, or the production of criminal records.

Meanwhile, thousands have gone to jail, losers in this late-twentieth-century twist on cops and robbers. The policing tools are now a telephone receiver, a bugging device, and, as always, the cultivation of informers.

There seems to be a good case for decriminalizing marijuana use, and for permitting distribution, with government regulation and taxation. But it seems unlikely that this will happen quickly. No government wants to be labelled "soft on pot," and the current regime is determined not to be soft about anything: drugs, criminals, the unemployed, or Iraq.

But greater tolerance is required, at least in the case of marijuana. The drug has apparently found its way into the homes of our role models. It has been used by provincial premiers, federal cabinet ministers, Supreme and county court judges, National Hockey League players, and thousands of doctors and lawyers. Few of these people are likely to see their marijuana consumption, present or former, as morally offensive.

The obstacle to marijuana reform is inertia. The government is reluctant to change the law, wary of appearing to promote the drug. Cannabis distributors and consumers, fearful of detection and apprehension, have not organized effectively to legitimize their industry. After almost seventy years of cannabis prohibition, we have a stalemate. As Pogo would have it, we have seen the enemy and they is us.

NOTES

There has been a lot written about marijuana, particularly since 1967. Unfortunately, there is not a lot of valuable reading; the tenets of scientific study have not always been observed and the value of research has often been compromised by bias — both for and against marijuana.

The issue of the drug's health effects has been widely canvassed. The best sources of information are G. Le Dain, *Cannabis: A Report of the Commission of Inquiry into the Non-Medical Use of Drugs* (Ottawa: Information Canada, 1972); E.M. Brecher and the Editors of Consumer Reports, *Licit and Illicit Drugs* (Boston: Little, Brown, 1972), Part VIII; A. Weil and W. Rosen, *Chocolate to Morphine: Understanding Mind-Active Drugs* (Boston: Houghton Mifflin, 1985), chapter 9. For a slightly more alarmist but essentially consistent account of the drug's effects, see Cox et al., *Drugs and Drug Abuse* (Toronto: Addiction Research Foundation, 1983), pp. 212–25. For a comical example of work with an anti-marijuana bias, see M. Miller and M. Gold, "The Diagnosis of Marijuana Dependence," 6 *Journal of Substance Abuse Treatment* (1989): 183–92. For a comical example of work with a pro-marijuana bias, see J. Margolis and R. Clorfene, *A Child's Garden of Grass* (New York: Ballantine, 1978).

The best history of marijuana is probably E.L. Abel, *Marihuana: The First Twelve Thousand Years* (New York: Plenum, 1980). The best description of marijuana use in contemporary culture is probably W. Novak, *High Culture: Marijuana in the Lives of Americans* (New York: Knopf, 1980). The plant and its cultivation are most exhaustively considered in R.C. Clarke, *Marijuana Botany* (Berkeley: And/Or Press, 1981). For a general understanding of the phenomenon of marijuana use, see A. Weil, *The Natural Mind* (Boston: Hougton Mifflin, 1972), pp. 73–97.

The history of marijuana control can be found in M. Green, "A History of Canadian Narcotics Control: The Formative Years," *University of Toronto Faculty of Law Review* (1979): 42–79. For a contemporary history of control, see N. Boyd, "The Question of Marihuana Control: Is De Minimis Appropriate, Your Honour?" 24 *Criminal Law Quarterly* (1982): 242.

The most comprehensive information with respect to current enforcement strategy can be found in RCMP, *National Drug Intelligence Estimate 1987/88* (Ottawa: Supply and Services, 1988): see, particularly, "Cannabis," pp. 76–96. These annual RCMP publications give a good sense of the way in which cannabis is distributed in Canada, and of current prices and availability. Information about what happens to cannabis users and distributors in court can be found in *Narcotic, Controlled and Restricted Drug Statistics* (Ottawa: Bureau of Dangerous Drugs, Health and Welfare Canada, 1968–86). (For sentencing patterns relating to marijuana offences, see Tables V, VII, and XII.) Unfortunately, in 1983 information about cannabis was dropped from these annual reports. Though it is possible for researchers to gain access to cannabis sentencing data, the information is no longer made public as a matter of course.

The most comprehensive understanding of the current application of criminal law to cannabis is to be found in B. MacFarlane, *Drug Offences in Canada*, 2nd ed. (Toronto: Canada Law Book, 1986). The statute that applies specifically to cannabis is the Narcotic Control Act, Revised Statutes of Canada, 1985, Chapter N-1.

POTIONS FROM THE MEDICINE MEN

When you actually spell it out to them, look this is what you've got to do, cut back on your pills, cut back on your booze, and change your diet, they say, hell, what are the trade-offs? They'd rather enjoy a nice meal, have a glass of wine, and take their pills.

— BRIAN BIRD

The pharmacy is a hybrid, offering the consumer the options of both pursuing pleasure and relieving pain. It is also a halfway house for legal and illegal drugs. Illegal drugs can be transformed into legal drugs if they are prescribed for relief from pain or the treatment of illness. And legal drugs can be transformed into illegal drugs if they are used without a physician's approval.

LSD, amphetamines, and tranquillizers began life in this century as pharmaceuticals. They were developed in laboratories, and valued for their potentially therapeutic mind-active effects. Today, only the tranquillizers remain in medical use, not generally tied to youthful consumption in pursuit of pleasure. LSD and "speed" were not particularly successful as therapies, LSD culturally defined as the drug of the hippies, amphetamines as the drug of choice for motor-cycle gangs.

LSD was discovered by a Swiss chemist in 1938 when he was trying to develop medical drugs from ergot, the fungus that attacks cereal grains. He became aware of the psychoactive powers of the drug when he accidentally consumed a few micrograms in 1943. The Swiss pharmaceutical company Sandoz marketed the drug worldwide for the next twenty years, predominantly to psychiatrists. In Canada it was imposed on research subjects at McGill University. In the late 1960s it became valued by Canadian and American youth for its ability to change perceptions and enhance sensations.

Amphetamines were developed in Germany during the 1930s, and first marketed in North America under the trade name Benzedrine. These long-lasting and powerful stimulants of the central nervous system were widely prescribed by doctors during the 1950s as a treatment for depression or the suppression of appetite. Soviet factory workers were given amphetamines in an effort to increase productivity, and allied troops during the Second World War were also provided with the drugs, to enable them to continue fighting, despite physical exhaustion. In the late 1960s young users injected amphetamines intravenously.

Tranquillizers are a relatively recent invention, first developed and marketed in North America as anti-anxiety drugs during the 1950s. For millions of Canadians taking tranquillizers and sedatives with legitimate prescriptions, the pursuit of pleasure is a part of the agenda of use, along with the reduction of stress and anxiety. The elderly, and particularly elderly women, typically face declining health at the same time that they are being socially and economically disempowered. In these circumstances a mind-altering sedative may provide both enjoyment and relief.

If drug taking is to be defined as legitimate, it must be seen either as a culturally acceptable recreation like alcohol or tobacco or as a therapeutic treatment. Tranquillizers and other sedatives are medically legitimated as chemical strategies for relieving tension and anxiety; they are said to be useful medicines. Like many other mind-active drugs, however, tranquillizers sedate and alter mood; they carry risks of dependence and risks of difficulty in withdrawal.

When Brian Bird began to practice pharmacy in 1965, there was virtually no use of the drugs that most of us know as tranquillizers. Librium was introduced in 1960 by the international firm of Hoffman LaRoche, and was followed quickly by Valium and Mogadon. Hoffman LaRoche claimed that these new drugs were non-addictive, and preferable to barbiturates for the relief of insomnia and anxiety. These new sedatives — the benzodiazepines — were also safer than barbiturates in overdose.

"We didn't dispense as much daytime sedation as we do now," he said. "We didn't do very much of that at all. Really, the classification didn't exist. If you're under stress now, it's tension, anxiety, you phone your physician and say, 'Look, I'm going through a bad time.'

"I had a physician phone me the other day," Brian Bird continued, "and he said, 'Well, Brian, I've just got a fellow, his business is going down the tubes and he's in a lot of trouble.' And the first thing he gets him is daytime sedation, and the second thing was sleeping medication.

"It isn't a matter now of seeking counselling, or a matter of saying, 'Well, look, there's tough times. Can you tough it out?' It's let's treat it right away. Treat the infection."

Discomfort and distress are no longer considered natural or necessary, and a chemical "solution" is less expensive and socially demanding than treating the social and political problems that underlie the discomfort and distress. Physicians, pharmacists, and pharmaceutical corporations, benefit economically from the simplicity of chemistry. After a paid consultation, the doctor's prescription pad sanctifies a drug experience as a medical treatment. The pharmacist is then paid to deliver the product to the consumer, receiving a dispensing fee each time the prescription is filled. And after every transaction, the drug company receives its share of the proceeds.

The Narcotic Control Act, the Food and Drugs Act, and Regulations to the Food and Drugs Act create various offences, punishable by imprisonment, for selling drugs without a doctor's oral or written prescription. The only exceptions to this policy are alcohol, tobacco, and caffeine.

We have not always distributed drugs in this way. Before the turn of the century the patent-medicine industry followed their initial success in the marketplace by advertising their products more widely and intensively, in newspapers, magazines, and medical journals. They pointed out that their form of treatment was inexpensive, compared to the alternative of the physician, and less intrusive. (They also went on to make more suspect claims. In one instance a patent medicine was said to be a "microbe killer," and in another, a restorative of "female weaknesses." Dr. A. L. Taylor's "Pain Annihilating Liniment" was said to provide "the oil of life for man or beast." One advertisement began with the headline "The Doctors Did No Good" and asked, "Do you want a strange man to hear all about your particular diseases?")

Though various associations of physicians and pharmacists sought restrictive regulation of the patent-medicine trade, governments in Canada and the United States were initially reluctant to intervene. In 1904, an amendment to the Post Office Act was introduced in the House of Commons by then postmaster general Sir William Mulock. The section read, "It shall not be lawful to transmit by mail any books, magazines, periodicals, circulars, newspapers or other publications which contain advertisements representing marvellous, extravagant, or grossly improbable cures, or curative or healing powers, by means of medicines, appliances or devices referred to in such advertisements."

The Commons was not receptive to Mulock's initiative, the opposition claiming that the medical profession was simply being territorial. Two days after its introduction, the amendment was withdrawn. The power of the patent-medicine industry to set out "grossly improbable cures" remained intact, protected by freedom of speech. In the early years of the twentieth century the conflict continued, the journals and newsletters of Canadian physicians and pharmacists increasingly denouncing the sale of patent medicines, citing the often fraudulent claims of the manufacturers and their non-professional status as dispensers of drugs.

Two critical changes in Canada and the United States brought an end to a free market in mind-active drugs. First, the therapeutic and diagnostic competence of the medical profession was improving. Vaccines for diphtheria and tetanus were developed, and surgical intervention was becoming increasingly effective. And most significantly, a better understanding of the role of hygiene in the transmission of disease had greatly improved life expectancy. Public confidence in the emerging science of medicine began to grow.

Second, deceptive advertising was bringing the makers of patent medicine into disrepute. Samuel Hopkins Adams, a "muckraking" journalist in the United States, began to crusade against patent-medicine companies and the shady business practices they employed in marketing potentially addictive drugs. He published his work in a two-part series, "The Great American Fraud," in *Collier's Weekly* in 1905; the American Medical Association distributed 150,000 copies of the publication.

Adams gave detailed evidence of the fraudulent claims of these entrepreneurs, citing men and women who had died from diseases that the medicines were designed to cure, and revealing laboratory reports of the presence of worthless or potentially addictive drugs. "Don't Dose Yourself with Secret Patent Medicines," Adams warned, "Almost all of which are frauds and humbugs. When sick consult a Doctor and take his Prescription: it is the only Sensible Way and you'll find it Cheaper in the End."

As sociologist Paul Starr has noted, the message from Adams and other critics of patent medicines was that, in the absence of regulation, entrepreneurial interests were dan-

gerous to health. Physicians who could combine entrepreneurial skills with professional qualifications were to
be given social and moral legitimacy.

In Canada, as in the United States, the federal government committed itself to legislation that would better regu-
late patent medicines. In September 1907 representatives
from provincial pharmacy organizations met in Toronto to
organize the Canadian Pharmaceutical Association; the
Parke-Davis drug company was a major sponsor of the initiative. The focus of the agenda, apart from the drafting of a
constitution and by-laws, was Bill 99, a controversial piece of
legislation that was being designed to control the patent-
medicine trade.

This trade, the greatest threat to the economic well-being
of Canadian pharmacists and physicians, gave the Canadian
Medical Association and the Canadian Pharmaceutical Association their initial organizational impetus. Parke-Davis
and other drug companies tied their economic interests to
the associations' agendas. By forming a national and united
voice and making representations to the Canadian government, this coalition of interests influenced the shape of the
legislation.

Under this new approach, access to drugs would be controlled by the profession of medicine. The drug company,
the physician, and the pharmacist would each receive a
share of the income from drug distribution for producing,
prescribing, and dispensing the drugs of therapeutic choice.
Though consumers would pay more for their drugs, there
was to be a benefit in public safety from this application of
professional knowledge. In the early years of the twentieth
century, Canadian health professionals and certain drug
companies made significant strides, gradually taking
political, economic, social, and cultural authority over
medication.

The Proprietary or Patent Medicine Act, passed by the
House of Commons in 1908, came into force in 1909. It

permitted patent medicines containing opium or small amounts of alcohol as "a solvent or preservative" to be sold. Cocaine was to be prohibited as an ingredient. But the most important limitation on the patent-medicine industry was a legal stipulation that the ingredients be displayed on a label attached to the product. The consumer's interests were to be better protected; there was no longer a philosophy of *caveat emptor* in the business of drug distribution in Canada.

Between 1850 and 1920 Canadian society became more industrialized and urbanized; professional associations arose to service and to structure these emerging communities. The unintended consequence of this move to a more centralized and economically productive form of community was the development of an urban underclass. For a solution to their attendant social problems Canadians of this era turned, in large measure, to God; they were almost uniformly committed to a religious interpretation of social life: salvation, redemption, and charity were the means of social change.

The combination of these features — a visible and disaffected underclass, and an emerging professional class, linked by a religious world view — gave rise to what has been called the social gospel movement. Consciousness alteration, in so far as it deflected one's attention from spiritual matters, was to be resisted. Sociologist Glenn Murray has written of these years, "The notion that God was involved in the process of personal transformation could very easily be developed into the idea that God was involved in the social processes of change. . . . In time no aspect of the community's life, from the home to Parliament, was unaffected by this tide of moral reform."

Appropriate medicines and appropriate recreations were determined in a political context in which science could be structured by Christian precepts. Physicians could prescribe and pharmacists could dispense the opiates of "Christian" pharmaceutical companies, but the smoking opium of Chinese merchants was criminally prohibited. Drug taking as recreation was morally repugnant, but the professional team of the drug company, physician, and pharmacist could provide a morally acceptable reason for indulgence: their drugs were to be taken in pursuit of medical treatment.

There has been little change in these moral scripts during the past eighty years. Tranquillizers, rather than opiates or alcohol, are the current mind-altering sedatives of choice for the medical profession. Pharmacist Brian Bird questions the anomalies in the way in which we categorize drugs. He doesn't believe there are differences among a middle-aged woman taking prescribed Valium regularly, a daily consumer of alcohol, and a young man smoking marijuana regularly.

"Our society has created a situation," says Bird, "where there's got to be a resolution for whatever problem I've got, and if part of my resolution is that I need to have a medication, I'll use it. . . . You know, there's still a lot of mystique in pharmacy. People used to come to me and I would say, well you can take Tylenol No. 1 or you can use a 222, or one of these drugs that are over-the-counter pain relievers. But now, Tylenol No. 3 is so accessible. If I've got a headache, why take a Tylenol No. 1 when I can get a prescription for 100 Tylenol No. 3?" The irony here is that Tylenol No. 3 contains codeine, a derivative of opium, a drug that in different circumstances is the subject of criminal prohibition.

"There was a time when we didn't even label what the drug was," recalls Brian Bird. "We couldn't counsel patients on what the drug was. We couldn't tell them what they were taking. The directions were on there: Take one capsule four times a day . . . but physicians would not encourage us talking to their patients about their medication. That was only twenty-five years ago." For the first half of this century Canadian physicians did not encourage Canadian pharmacists to question or evaluate the chemistry that they dispensed.

The need for mood-altering drugs is responsible for most

of the prescriptions written by Canadian physicians and dispensed by Canadian pharmacists. About 40 per cent of the prescriptions that Brian Bird fills each day at his pharmacy are for tranquillizers and other sedatives, and a further 30 per cent for painkillers, mostly Tylenol No. 3.

In the 1990s pharmacists are very involved in the dissemination of information about drugs; their economic and political power has expanded over the past two decades. The pharmacists now share responsibility for the prescription and communicate information about a given drug, its effects and its contra-indications. Physicians have generally been very accommodating of this development, at least in part because the increasing role of the pharmacy has not required any lessening of the social and political power of the physician.

For pharmacists like Brian Bird, this has meant an increased sense of social responsibility. "These people have a great faith in the fact that when I fill out that prescription for them, and I give it to them, and I tell them what it will do, and talk about the medication, and what the end result will be, and the side-effects may be, they walk away feeling good about it."

Tranquillizers, the most popular of medications, are about twice as likely to be prescribed for Canadian women as men. This gender difference can also be seen in the prescribing practices of American, British, and Irish physicians. Recent surveys of use suggest that about 10 per cent of Canadian women and about 4 per cent of Canadian men have used tranquillizers at least once in the past year. There is some evidence of slight declines in the extent of use over the past decade, but mostly there have simply been shifts away from long-acting tranquillizers such as diazepam (Valium) to short-acting tranquillizers like triazolam and lorazepam.

Tranquillizers are most commonly used by women and men over the age of thirty; the heaviest concentration of users is found in the population fifty years of age and over. About 10 per cent of all men and women who use these drugs use them daily throughout the year; three of four daily tranquillizer users report that their lives are stressful.

All tranquillizers share anti-anxiety, sedative/hypnotic, muscle relaxant, anti-convulsant, and amnesic properties. The differences between the drugs are explained in terms of half-life variations. Some of these drugs have a longer half-life, producing more of a hangover effect. Tranquillizers with a shorter half-life may, however, produce other potentially more unpleasant consequences. Triazolam, for example, while usually taken as a sleeping pill and eliminated within four hours of ingestion, has been linked with unusually high levels of daytime anxiety.

Tranquillizers are usually referred to by physicians as "minor tranquillizers," in part to distinguish them from "anti-psychotic" tranquillizers such as chlorpromazine, and in part because it is more comforting and socially acceptable to be using "minor" tranquillizers. Physician Andrew Weil has noted of this distinction, "Minor tranquillizers are not, as their name implies, mild drugs. There is nothing minor about their effects, the problems they can cause, or their potential for abuse."

Brian Bird notes that the Canadian statistical profile of tranquillizer users fits his pharmacy well. "Well, you would start, definitely, with a woman . . . the senior . . . the woman who's under the stress, the strain, the anxiety, women who've got a problem with their kids. . . . The stress is there. You just read it in their face, the stress is there.

"And then of course they need their sedative at night . . . if the marriage is falling apart they keep it together because of the kids. I do get a lot of stories. I know so many people so well; people have great faith in their pharmacists."

Brian Bird, like other pharmacists working in communities, has assumed, in part, the physician's role of counselling patients about drug use. "People give you their trust, and I'll sit them in my office and talk to them privately. And they have a real problem. They don't have a sense of their own self worth.

"In most cases," he continued, "you're probably going to find that person who might be abusing Valium or Xanax, or whatever benzodiazepine we're talking about, will also probably be indulging in more alcohol than he or she probably should. It's almost a given. They go real well together. And people like taking them together. And of course you get very comatose very quickly."

But friendly advice does not necessarily change behaviour. "When you actually spell it out to them, look this is what you've got to do, you've got to start to monitor your health, cut back on your pills, cut back on your booze, and change your diet. They say, hell, what are the trade-offs? They'd rather enjoy a nice meal, have a glass of wine, and take their pills."

There has been a considerable amount of research on the effects of tranquillizer use. In one experiment, healthy volunteers who received daily doses of the drugs for two weeks showed some level of psychomotor impairment and reported a lowering of alertness. The effects disappeared after use was discontinued. This is generally a consistent research finding: the effects of tranquillizers disappear when use ceases. However, one British researcher, comparing brain scans of groups of normal subjects, daily tranquillizer users, and alcoholics, has found more enlargement in the ventricular spaces of the brain in alcoholics and tranquillizer dependents than in the normal population. These enlargements are thought to indicate a greater brain atrophy. And though the enlargements for tranquillizer users were not as marked as those for alcoholics, they were, nonetheless, significant.

Another American study compared tranquillizer users and opiate users on a range of psychometric indices: tests of intelligence, tests of memory, and visual-spatial skills. The tranquillizer users showed considerably more impairment than those who were using either opiates alone or no medication.

But the public threat posed by tranquillizer abuse is more significant than its private consequences. In one study of motor-vehicle accidents, a team of British researchers linked general-practitioner prescriptions to records of hospital admissions and deaths in more than 40,000 cases. The researchers found that the prescription of minor tranquillizers is highly correlated with an increased risk of serious motor-vehicle accidents and fatalities. Other research has established that this increased risk is particularly evident in the morning; after taking a tranquillizer at night, the user may still have up to 85 per cent of the dose in his or her body the following morning.

Chronic long-term users of tranquillizers will typically experience some difficulties in withdrawal: perceptual disturbances, and hypersensitivity to auditory and olfactory stimuli. Also common are sleep disturbances, muscle pain, and nausea, the antitheses of sedation and muscle relaxation. A gradual withdrawal is generally recommended by physicians, though there is no guarantee that the regimen will always be followed or continued.

"There still is a degree of agitation on withdrawal," Brian Bird observed, "but you're able to taper people down, you know, in good faith, in good practice you'll taper people down. But they want . . . it's the same as having booze, it's the same as having a cigarette. What are you going to do? The patient's got to want to have to stop it."

Chronic long-term users of tranquillizers are likely to have previous histories of alcoholism, or other forms of drug abuse, although such daily long-term use is relatively rare, primarily linked to emotional instability. For many women, tranquillizers have become the mind-altering sedative of choice. Alcohol dependence is less socially acceptable and more visible, and most other opportunities are to be found in the uncertainty of the illicit market.

Ruth Cooperstock has argued that because women in

Western societies are more likely than men to express their feelings, they are more likely to perceive emotional problems, and to report these to their physicians. Indeed, women are more likely than men to receive a prescription for tranquillizers. Shirley Small of Toronto's Support Services for Assaulted Women has suggested that tranquillizers can work to compound the problems that women face, "When a woman has been beaten and goes to a doctor she's more often than not given a tranquillizer, which tends to make her problem worse. She tends to become more passive and she's more likely to be endangered. This way of treating the problem, as a sort of neurotic problem that these women have, is really disgraceful."

The disproportionate use of these drugs by Canadian women is not representative of any physiological or structural difference between men and women. If this is a disease, it appears to be social, economic, and political in its origins. A recent survey by Health and Welfare Canada found that widows, and separated and divorced men and women also make a disproportionate use of tranquillizers. And certain occupational categories have been associated with particularly high levels of consumption: housewives, the retired, students, and the unemployed. Income and educational level have not correlated with accelerated rates of use or abuse.

Psychiatrists H. Petursson and M. Lader have described the men and women who appear for treatment of tranquillizer dependence in a number of vignettes in their 1984 Oxford University Press publication, *Dependence on Tranquillizers*. In one, a forty-two-year-old housewife sought a doctor's assistance with withdrawal from tranquillizer dependence. She had always been highly strung, worried about constriction in her chest, headaches, and a lack of energy. She was first prescribed the tranquillizers lorazepam and nitrepam at the time of her mother's death. For the next two years, she was extremely worried about her father's continuing ill health, and she gradually increased her dose of lorazepam from one milligram per day to about eight milligrams per day.

Also typical of daily tranquillizer users was a twenty-nine-year-old male who presented himself for treatment after using tranquillizers for about six years. He described himself as inadequate, introverted, anxious, and tense. He had a very irregular employment record, which apparently contributed to a pattern of excessive drinking.

These portraits share similarities: stressful lives and compromised relationships. But daily users of tranquillizers are single and married, male and female, rich and poor, university graduates and public-school dropouts. Although the motivations underlying this pattern of consumption are similar, there is a social and economic diversity in the population that uses.

Some users ultimately recognize tranquillizers as more of a problem than a solution. "Beth Walters" was afraid of the drugs when they were first prescribed, believing that they could become addictive. She had been to a gastro-enterologist about a nagging stomach problem. After finding no detectable pathology, he prescribed a tranquillizer and an anti-depressant, to be taken daily. When Beth expressed concern about dependence, she was told that it was only a psychological phenomenon, and that the drugs were quite safe.

After a couple of months of taking pills as prescribed, she stopped, afraid that she was becoming addicted. She had little difficulty withdrawing. Her family later told her, that while she was taking the drugs, she seemed to be travelling in slow motion. "Now I don't go to a doctor if he's a pill doctor," she said.

Her mother-in-law was an alcoholic who was first prescribed tranquillizers during hospitalization in the 1970s. She had been committed to the hospital in an effort to "dry her out" and was given the drugs to help her with her adjustment to sobriety. After release from hospital, Walters's mother-in-law went back to drinking, and continued taking tranquillizers. She remained dependent on both drugs until her death some years later.

For Joel Lexchin, the prescription of tranquillizers all too often means that social and family problems are being converted into a form of medical disease. Lexchin has been an emergency-room physician in Toronto for more than ten years, responding to the crises that come daily from the city's streets. He is also the author of a 1984 book, *The Real Pushers: A Critical Analysis of the Canadian Drug Industry.* He argues that doctors are inclined to prescribe tranquillizers because of their own time constraints, the advertising of pharmaceutical companies, general social pressure, and a lack of alternatives.

Lexchin identifies the reliance of physicians on drug companies as a significant obstacle to the delivery of medical services, "There's no requirement for you to keep up your knowledge about prescribing, go to so many courses a year, or anything like that. As a result, doctors tend to rely on the drug companies because the way that the information is presented is very accessible. The ads are much easier to read than the journal articles." The literature of drug advertising supports Lexchin's conclusion. Tranquillizers have been urged by drug companies in circumstances "when anxiety and tension create major discord in parent-child relationships" and have been advocated for women with young children, "when reassurance is not enough."

Lexchin notes that the drug-company representatives who travel to doctors' offices are essentially trained salespeople, "It's even easier than looking at the ads, because you don't have to read. All you have to do is listen to what they're saying. Some of the courses that are run by the drug companies are also quite pleasant, and a lot of the time they run an evening thing where you get dinner and some wine, and you hear a lecture." A survey of Ontario physicians during the 1980s revealed that the province's physicians attend physician-sponsored seminars about half as often as seminars sponsored by drug companies. The survey also revealed that pharmaceutical company representatives visit doctors in accordance with how often they prescribe drugs; the most substantial prescribers receive the greatest number of visits, in some instances at least weekly. And a few doctors report the receipt of benefits from drug companies: meals, stationery, travel expenses, office services, and computer hardware and software.

The problem that Lexchin identifies is not limited to the prescription of tranquillizers. For university researchers, faced with diminishing public-sector contributions, the monies provided by drug companies are typically a welcome source of funding. "The information that they present about using drugs may be perfectly valid," says Joel Lexchin, "but as Sherlock Holmes remarked to Watson when Watson said, 'But the dog didn't bark,' 'That's the point, Watson, what didn't happen?'

"The questions that get answered and the research that gets done and communicated is obviously biased by 'where the bucks are,' " Lexchin suggests. "If there aren't any bucks, then you don't even pose those questions, because you won't be able to get the money to find the answers." Alternatives to drug solutions, though theoretically sound and possible to implement, are difficult to finance.

Pharmaceutical companies are, understandably, not interested in pursuing non-drug solutions to the problems of anxiety and stress, or non-drug solutions to any medical problem. And Western culture itself, dominated by white males, actively resists the professionalization of alternative vehicles for delivering medical services: acupuncture, homeopathy, chiropractic, and midwifery. In *The Real Pushers*, Joel Lexchin wrote, "The dominant medical paradigm, reflecting the society in general, identifies illness as residing in the individual. In the case of organic diseases, there is an

organism that has invaded the body or a biochemical mechanism that is malfunctioning. In the case of social problems, there is an inherent personality flaw in individuals
which evokes socially unacceptable conduct. Chronic unem-
ployment is known to lead to depression and eventually to
an increase in the suicide rate, but because the disease has
been isolated from its social roots, depressed unemployed
workers are deemed to have an individual medical problem,
and are treated with a tricyclic antidepressant."

When he looks to the pharmacy and the practices of
physicians in prescribing mind-active drugs, Joel Lexchin
fears that little has changed over the past hundred years.
"Whether it's tranquillizers now, or opium and alcohol fifty
to a hundred years ago isn't too important . . . in both cases
the prescription reflects a certain naivety among doctors in
believing that these things are going to help, without really
trying to look at the evidence to see whether or not they
do."

Jim Elliott would probably agree with this assessment.
During the past two decades he has been in more than one
hundred hospitals and long-term-care facilities, an advocate
for both labour and management, negotiating contracts for
health-care workers. Jim Elliott isn't his real name; he wants
to continue working in the health-care field.

"There is massive tranquillization in long-term-care facilities," he begins. "A lot of overprescribing, a lot of sedating.
Doctors are less able to spend time with elderly patients.
And the men and women in long-term-care facilities are
more and more aged, less able to care for themselves.

"The elderly revert to their childhood behaviours without tranquillization. I've seen a man eating soap, another
eating Comet. They can carry out physical and sexual attacks, and even stab each other. In one instance, some
elderly men urinated on their clothes to protest a requirement that they walk down the hallway. They're institu-
tionalized, and they don't like it."

For Jim Elliott, tranquillization of the elderly is more a political than a medical strategy. Without the option to sedate "residents," the labour costs of Canada's nursing homes and other long-term-care facilities would increase significantly. Elliott urges that the elderly deserve more, socially and economically, than the quick fix of a sedative or tranquillizer.

Tranquillizers are different from most other mind-active drugs in that their goal is not to intensify sensations but to shield the user from the effects of daily life. While alcohol, tobacco, marijuana, and cocaine are typically taken as a life-affirming pursuit of pleasure, tranquillizers and other sedatives are the drugs of the timid or the disappointed, taken to insulate the consumer from life's social burdens.

LSD and amphetamines are the other side of the pharmaceutical coin, taken to heighten and embellish the senses, if only temporarily. They are the best-known of the mind-active formulations that have been rejected as medically useful drugs, despite much early promise and support.

They are not the only pharmaceuticals, however, that may be put to subversive use. There are the opiates in pharmaceutical form, from Tylenol No. 3 to Percodan, to Dilaudid. There are other hallucinogens, such as MDA. And there is PCP, a drug first developed as a surgical anaesthetic. All these drugs are referred to by the RCMP as "chemical drugs." All originated in a laboratory and were designed for therapeutic purposes. And although the opiates may have medical approval in certain circumstances, the hallucinogens, amphetamines, and PCP are thought to have no valid medical purposes. These are typically manufactured by "contrepreneurs" for the illicit market.

LSD or "acid," is one of the most potent drugs in existence; its effect will be experienced with a dose of little more than one millionth of a gram. When the drug is purchased on the street, it may be in either tablet form, inside a tiny transparent chip of gelatin, or soaked into a piece of paper.

The gelatin chip is known as "windowpane acid," the impregnated paper as "blotter acid." A single dose typically sells from $4 in Toronto, Montreal, and Vancouver, to $15 in the Yukon.

Physician Andrew Weil notes that, "for the most part, people who took LSD in the early days had pleasant trips. They talked about experiencing powerful feelings of love, mystical oneness with all things, union with God, and a deeper understanding of themselves. . . . From the very first, however, it was apparent that not everyone who takes LSD has a good time. Some people had bad trips: they became anxious and panicky, afraid they were losing their minds and would be unable to return to ordinary reality. They almost always did return, when the drug wore off twelve hours later, but some of them remained depressed and anxious for days afterward, and a few had lasting psychological problems."

MDA is a similarly priced hybrid of an hallucinogen and a stimulant. A variation on the amphetamine molecule, MDA produces, like other stimulants, feelings of physical and mental well-being. But it also produces what might be termed psychedelic or hallucinogenic effects. Unlike LSD, however, it rarely changes visual perceptions. Though many users claim to have lasting psychological benefits from experiences with hallucinogens, there is no substantiating scientific evidence.

Hallucinogens are the most consistently policed of pharmaceutical drugs. There are about 1,000 criminal charges in Canada each year for possession or distribution of these drugs. In contrast, there are a few hundred charges annually for "trafficking in amphetamines."

Hallucinogens are not likely to be abused over time, though they may well produce severe difficulties in particular instances. "The substances in this class probably have the lowest potential for abuse of any psychoactive drugs," Andrew Weil suggests. "In purely medical terms, they may be the safest of all known drugs. Even in huge overdose, psychedelics do not kill, and some people take them frequently all their lives without suffering physical damage or dependence.''

Amphetamines, or "speed," are often described as the poor man's cocaine. As these synthetic stimulants are longer lasting and typically produce less euphoria than cocaine, they are less likely to be a source of dependence. The problems of the popularly prescribed amphetamines first began to surface in Canada and the United States in the late 1960s and early 1970s, with a developing culture of intravenous injection appearing in most major cities. "Young 'speed freaks' who fell into this pattern of use experienced very bad effects on their bodies and mind," Andrew Weil writes. "After only a few weeks they became emaciated and generally unhealthy. . . . They became jumpy, paranoid, and even psychotic. The drug subculture itself, realizing the dangers of shooting amphetamines, warned people about it with the phrase 'speed kills.' ''

At the same time there was increasing criticism of the promotional practices of pharmaceutical companies, and the prescribing practices of physicians. Within a decade, the legal and moral descriptions of these drugs were no longer considered useful for depression or suppression of appetite; they were culturally connected with rebellious and disaffected youth.

However, amphetamines may provide some benefit in some circumstances. Andrew Weil notes, "Some college students use them to study. Truckers and other drivers sometimes take them for long-distance travel. . . . Athletes sometimes use them to play big games. Actors and dancers take them occasionally to perform. Used in this way — that is, taken by mouth on occasion for specific purposes or projects — amphetamines do not usually cause problems, especially if people rest afterward. Problems arise when people take amphetamines all the time, just because they like the feeling of stimulation.''

Amphetamines are available in Canada only on the illicit

market, manufactured at clandestine laboratories in Quebec and Ontario. They are sold on Canadian streets in the form of tablets or powder; the product can be injected, sniffed, or taken orally. The current market price of one gram of methamphetamine — the most potent form of amphetamines — ranges from $80 to $150. Police intervention in the amphetamine trade often involves surveillance of what are called "precursor chemicals," the ingredients necessary to produce amphetamines in the laboratory. While police cannot look over the shoulders of the multinational chemical companies that sell these wares, the companies have agreed to report suspected illicit activity. Most police arrests arise from information about the sale or distribution of the chemical P2P, phenyl-2-propanone.

The RCMP suggest that motorcyle clubs control most of the distribution of amphetamines in Canada, and a significant amount of the drug's production; they also implicate the clubs in the LSD and the MDA markets. The latest RCMP Drug Intelligence estimate notes: "Although their involvement in the more lucrative cocaine trade is growing steadily, outlaw motorcycle gangs continue to be implicated in the manufacture and distribution of chemical drugs."

Ontario and Quebec motorcycle groups are also thought to be involved in the production and distribution of PCP. Phencyclidine was first developed as a surgical anaesthetic for human beings, but did not, like ether, render a person unconscious. Patients reported strange mental states, visual disturbances, and out-of-body experiences after being given the drug. It was abandoned for human beings, but put to use in veterinary medicine. Animals were unable to tell their doctors that they disliked PCP's side-effects.

The drug is typically smoked, but can be ingested as a pill or sniffed as a powder. It impairs co-ordination and may produce nausea and dizziness. Its mental effects are quite unpredictable, but are likely to include a sense of mental and physical distance from external reality, a feeling of uncontrolled drunkenness, and distortions of time and space.

PCP is known on the street as "angel dust," or more dismissively and accurately, as a horse tranquillizer. It is used mainly by unemployed men between the ages of eighteen and thirty. In any given year it is consumed by less than 0.05 per cent of the adult population. Its effects are so disabling and so unpredictable that repeated or daily consumption is very unlikely. For most people, any form of consumption would probably be unattractive, regardless of the drug's legal status.

There are three ways in which pharmaceuticals are converted to illegal use: diversion from legitimate medical supplies, illicit manufacture, and illicit importation, usually from the United States. Opiates are typically diverted from pharmacies. The opiate dependent may seek prescriptions from more than one doctor; forge prescriptions; commit break, entry, and theft; or resort to armed robbery of the pharmacy. (For most tranquillizer dependents, such actions are not necessary: physicians will typically prescribe their drug of choice.)

During each of the past five years Canada has experienced slightly more than two hundred incidents of pharmacy break, entry, and theft, mainly in Ontario, Quebec, and British Columbia. In each of these years there were between fifty and one hundred armed robberies of pharmacies. There is no effective way of calculating the extent of "double doctoring" (seeking more than one prescription) or prescription forgery.

LSD, MDA, and amphetamines are controlled by the Food and Drugs Act. LSD and MDA are "restricted" drugs; there is a penalty of up to six months' imprisonment for possession and up to ten years for trafficking. Amphetamines are "controlled" drugs; there is no penalty for possession and up to ten years' imprisonment for trafficking. PCP and pharmaceutical opiates are controlled by the Narcotic Control Act; they can elicit up to seven years' imprisonment for possession, and up to life imprisonment for trafficking.

Like the line between legal and illegal drug use, social

attitudes towards "narcotics," "controlled," and "restricted" drugs are confounded by our cultural beliefs about medicine and pharmacy and by the arbitrariness inherent in our legal designations of acceptable and unacceptable drugs.

"Bob Howard" has distributed LSD, amphetamines, and marijuana, cocaine, and heroin. He graduated from marijuana to LSD because "the profit margin was greater. It was easier to conceal. To go downtown with four ounces of marijuana was a risk, but I could take a thousand hits of acid with me, easily concealed."

He could buy an ounce of the drug for $80 and divide it into 140 hits, to be sold for $2 each. But Howard only "dabbled" in LSD. Amphetamines became his personal drug of choice, and intravenous injection his preferred method of ingestion. "A speed rush is kind of hard to describe. I've heard it described as an orgasm, but I don't think that quite fits. I've heard it described as better than one. Your blood's going from your toes to your head and back, it's like a wave, the first wave, and there'd be little ones ever after."

He became involved in distribution of speed, and increased his own use of the drug, "I dealt a lot of speed . . . but the effects weren't the same. . . . At one point, as well as affecting my body, speeding up my heart rate, and giving me rushes, I was right off the deep end, hallucinating and paranoid." At the time of his arrest several years later on charges of armed robbery, Howard was no longer using amphetamines. He was robbing convenience stores to pay for daily injections of cocaine and heroin.

Hallucinogens and amphetamines are drugs that most people have little interest in, given their capacity to significantly alter reality for twelve hours at a time. But they seem mundane beside the surgical anaesthetic, PCP, a drug that can remove consciousness for days. The first time that Robbie Robidoux used PCP, he and five co-accused sniffed a gram in a holding cell, while awaiting a court appearance on a charge of assault.

Robbie was told by the others that taking PCP was like smoking two pounds of marijuana, so he dug in with some fervour, sniffing large quantities. When the six prisoners were led up a set of stairs into the Toronto courtroom, they began to lose their ability to walk. They fell all over each other in front of the judge, and when they tried to speak, they could only make incoherent and slurred noises. The judge decided to adjourn the case.

The men were taken to hospital for observation. Robbie didn't recover his speech completely for several days. He later learned to take smaller doses of PCP. "I'd smoke it, just one or two tokes. If you took five, you couldn't walk."

Robbie Robidoux first came into contact with drugs in training school, when the Province of Ontario provided him with free tobacco. He had been abandoned at the age of seven by his mother and father and sent to a training school for both delinquent and neglected boys. Released at age sixteen, he was full of anger and resentment, a young man with no family, no education, and no future. He began to drink a lot of alcohol, "Drinking was making me a lot tougher than I really was. . . . I found out where my dad lived and I took a case of beer over. I really hated the guy. We drank the case of beer and I ended up punching him out. I didn't mean to do that. . . . I hit him and I cut his face. But for me it was all that anger, so the alcohol sort of really helped give me the opportunity."

Within a year of his release from training school, Robbie Robidoux had been convicted of robbery for stealing a car at knifepoint. At age seventeen, he was sentenced to three years' imprisonment in Kingston Penitentiary. He had been drinking heavily at the time of his offence. By this time he had also experimented with LSD.

In jail Robbie Robidoux gained a reputation as a young man prone to violent outbursts. He would fight and smash windows in a berserk rage. He wasn't an intimidating size, and he had a strong fear of being used or abused by other prisoners or by prison authorities. He learned that if he lost control easily, people would leave him alone. "When I'd go, I'd just go. I didn't give a fuck what happened. And then they would have to deal with it. They'd come in, six of them, and one of them's got a needle. And their only goal is to get you on the ground so they can stick you with it. You're fighting all the way, but you can't fight six people."

Robidoux was given a virtually permanent prescription for tranquillizers; when he became violent, he was treated with more powerful depressants. "There was certain drugs you didn't want to get," he said. "Chlorpromazine — you don't get high, all you do is get zonked and you don't want to do anything. All you want to do is eat. Eat and sleep. Eat and sleep."

There was a purpose in spending so much time and effort to obtain mind-active drugs. "Every day that you're high in prison is a day you're not doing time," Robbie explained. Drug taking is a triumph over the regime of control and has been a common pastime in Canada's jails for at least twenty-five years. Correctional Services Canada may have a prisoner's body, but it will not always have his mind, and it will almost never have his soul.

They are all available, at least from time to time: alcohol, marijuana, cocaine, amphetamines, LSD, heroin, and even tranquillizers. Valium was widely prescribed for prisoners during the 1970s, but when violence was determined to be one of the withdrawal effects, Correctional Services Canada restricted consumption and replaced Valium with other tranquillizers. For Robbie and many other prisoners, tranquillizers produce an enjoyable high, particularly when more desirable alternatives are unavailable. Four or five of the pills are taken at once, and the user falls asleep, waking up a few hours later ravenously hungry and somewhat euphoric. The downside of the experience is the irritability that often follows eating and euphoria.

Robbie Robidoux's early years of confinement are not all that different from those depicted in Ken Kesey's *One Flew*

Over the Cuckoo's Nest. He would stand in a line to receive his medication in a little cup, trying to fool his keepers into giving him a double dose. And like the Randal McMurphy of Kesey's imagination, he was given electric-shock treatments, apparently to control his aggressiveness. In the early 1970s this "therapy" was commonly employed with unmanageable prisoners at Kingston Penitentiary.

"I had it done seven times," he began. "They'd tie you down to this bed with leather straps around your arms and legs, and a metal band around your head. They'd give you sodium pentathol. That part was pretty good because you got a bit of a blast and the room would go around . . . they'd give you shocks to your brain, hoping that they could knock you out of your box and you'd be a real calm guy."

Robbie Robidoux believes that he is lucky to have survived his shock treatments without obvious disability. During the time that he was in the psychiatric centre, the men in the cells to his left and right both committed suicide.

Robbie was learning that, if he behaved outrageously, he would be given tranquillizers, or, if he slashed himself, opiates to kill the pain of his injury. These were desirable drugs. If he went too far, however, he could be subjected to chlorpromazine and other, even more potent anti-psychotic tranquillizers, or to electric shocks.

During his time in jail, his drug intake shifted from alcohol to tranquillizers, and then to amphetamines. "The very first time I did speed was in Millhaven Penitentiary," Robbie began. "It was, like, wow, what a blast. I went out and played floor hockey and I scored about twelve goals. I was just all over the place and I wasn't tired, and I thought, does this stuff ever give you a boost."

During the mid-1970s amphetamines, his drug of choice, were supplemented by prescriptions of Valium and occasional prison home brew. He was released to a halfway house in 1975 but broke the nose of another resident, and was sent back to penitentiary. He was released and then taken back to penitentiary nine times between 1975 and 1980. He was rarely on the street for more than a few weeks.

It was during this period that he shifted back to alcohol as his drug of choice. He had been awake for twenty-one days, injecting speed. "I was really fucked up. I had to go to a hospital and get them to give me Novahistex cough syrup. It actually put me to sleep for three days. After that I thought, you know, people on speed are mean; it brought out the worst in people. The same, I think, today, as what cocaine is doing."

During the time that he spent on the street Robbie drank heavily, after taking a number of tranquillizers. "I'd gone through fifteen riots and smashups. I really didn't care about things. I was really angry. . . . I would pop all these pills and then go to the bar and start drinking . . . guaranteed to be in a fight."

On all of the occasions that led to his return to penitentiary he was very drunk and very belligerent. At one point he was taken, for evaluation, to Penetang, a maximum-security institution that houses the criminally insane. He and four or five other prisoners with alcohol problems were placed in a small room, naked, and asked to drink alcohol. They were then observed and tested for their responses to stress while under the influence. Robbie does not believe that this initiative was of any assistance. "I always found the bug house a lot more scary than the joint," he said.

In 1979 Robbie Robidoux moved to Edmonton, apparently to distribute cocaine. He was drinking a lot of alcohol and taking tranquillizers, "At that point in my life it just seemed to me, the higher the better." He was involved in an incident with his partner in the cocaine trade, a karate expert. Robbie slashed the man's arm with a knife, and was charged with attempted murder. In 1980 he was sentenced to three years in jail for assault causing bodily harm.

He was released from a psychiatric facility in 1983 and moved to a suburb of Vancouver. On the day that he finally found a job, Robbie decided to celebrate by drinking. He came back to the house very drunk, and when the couple that he was staying with complained about his behaviour, he picked up a knife and held them in the room for about two hours. The screaming and shouting alarmed the neighbours and they called police. Robbie was arrested, and charged with unlawful confinement and unlawful assault with a weapon.

When Robbie sobered up in a psychiatric facility, he attempted suicide by overdosing on pharmaceuticals, and slashing his wrists. "If this was how I treated my friends, well I didn't want to live with myself," he said.

When he next woke up he asked where he was. "You're in Coquitlam," a doctor responded. Robbie was terrified. He didn't know Coquitlam was a suburb of Vancouver; he thought it was part of the afterlife.

While awaiting trial he experimented with heroin, injecting the drug daily. "I got sick at first, but sick is just part of it. You didn't want to eat much. You like chocolates, candy and stuff like that, but real food, ugh. You end up sleeping a lot, you're really happy and your body feels really good. I thought I'd have a problem coming off it. But I didn't, though I've seen a lot of people going through withdrawal."

Robbie was convicted of assault with a weapon, and sentenced to seven years' imprisonment. He was also declared to be a dangerous offender, convicted of "a serious personal injury offence" and having displayed "a pattern of persistent aggressive behaviour . . . showing a substantial degree of indifference."

This marked a turning-point for Robbie Robidoux. His loss of control had horrified him. He didn't believe that he was a dangerous offender, and he realized that he didn't want to spend the rest of his life in jail. At the age of thirty-one he stopped taking tranquillizers and other medication, and vowed that he would never drink again. The only drugs that he used after his sentence were tobacco and marijuana.

In 1985 Robbie started to take correspondence courses at the university, enrolled in the violent-offenders program, and made a promise to himself to run the Vancouver marathon. "I realized that if I want to keep in control of what I'm doing, I have to really monitor myself. I have to be really sure about what's going on."

Prior to 1987 Robbie Robidoux had spent no more than a few months on the street at a time. Between the ages of seven and thirty-four he spent over 90 per cent of his life institutions, mostly penitentiaries. He has been out on the street for almost four years now, and though this time has not been without difficulty, there has been a remarkable change in his lifestyle.

"There was a lot of irresponsibility. And also being very violent, very angry, being hateful, and being very negative. But when you don't have anything to look forward to, you don't care. There's no light at the end of the tunnel. There's no light to get through there."

After taking virtually every mind-active drug, legal and illegal, Robbie has concluded that there are some important differences. He hasn't taken any pharmaceutical other than aspirin since 1984, and feels that his use of tranquillizers contributed to his behavioural problems.

"If I have children," he said, "and I know they're going to get into something, because we live in that kind of society. If they are going to do any drugs, cigarettes, alcohol, pot, cocaine, whatever, the only one that I would probably recommend is pot, or hash. Leave the cigarettes alone. Leave the heavy drugs alone. Certainly people can get lazy, and there are people who are lazy because of pot. But it's people letting pot take control of them. It's like any drug — if you allow it to get a hold of you, it allows you to be irresponsible."

There are no guarantees for Robbie Robidoux. He has still to make the transition from the educational institution to the community, and drugs will continue to be a part of his life. He has been smoking over two packs a day for more than twenty years. Alcohol will continue to be a temptation. He's no longer interested in drugs like heroin, cocaine, or PCP, though he has come to believe that marijuana can be helpful to him occasionally. Robbie Robidoux is a reminder that the line that we draw between legal and illegal drugs distorts and obscures the realities of mind-active drugs. And the line that we draw between drug taking as medicine and drug taking as recreation is similarly suspect.

Leslie Dan is a soft-spoken man in his fifties who has made a success of Novopharm, Canada's largest drug company. The most recent corporate report notes that the financial success of the company will now allow it "to make an evolutionary step into original research and development of innovative pharmaceuticals." Asked if the line between legal and illegal drugs can be seen as a matter of pharmacology, he responded cautiously.

"I think it's up to the government to decide what medications are considered restricted or not restricted. What you may find is that some medications in Canada may not be restricted, and in other countries they are restricted. Well, some so-called hard medications, yes, they're all illegal, but there are some medicines which may be controlled, so there is some grey area here. I think this is a term coined by the public as opposed to the regulatory agencies or the law. The law says that certain medication can be sold only against prescriptions. Now, once the prescription is obtained by a patient, and the patient gets the medicine, it's not considered illegal. Yet, if for some reason the patient doesn't use it for his betterment, or her betterment, and sells it on the street, then it becomes illegal."

Leslie Dan agreed, albeit cautiously, with Joel Lexchin's claim that doctors may have a preference for a drug solution, even when other non-drug treatments might be more viable. "Whether a doctor writes a prescription or not, this is not up to us to comment. That is the medical doctor's decision. . . . I think Dr. Lexchin is right, that many of the brand-name companies [Novopharm is a generic-drug producer] are constantly interested in coming up with a new form of medication, sometimes without any significant therapeutic advantages. Just like car dealers come up with new features every year to attract the buyer. He's right that there are many other ways of solving health problems besides taking medication."

The delivery of pharmaceuticals into Canadian communities requires a number of interlocking networks: drug companies, physicians, pharmacists, police, government regulators, and patients. Ontario's Lowy Committee was asked in 1988 by the provincial Liberal government "to examine all matters pertaining to the acquisition, distribution, prescribing, dispensing and use of prescription drugs in Ontario."

Their recommendations were presented to then health minister Elinor Caplan in July 1990. "Physicians are not well prepared educationally for prescribing the thousands of drug products available," they began. The committee went on to recommend more support for continuing medical education about prescription drugs, and wrote of "the need to communicate to the patient the importance of proper drug use."

Recommendation 8.9 suggested that pharmacists be compelled to keep patient-medication profiles; recommendation 11.5 suggested that physicians develop guidelines prior to 1992, "in order that prescriptions for hypnotics, sedatives, and tranquillizers be issued for the shortest possible time and clearly marked 'no repeats,' unless there is a clinical indication to the contrary." The Canadian Medical Association and the various provincial medical associations have been reluctant to impose such a policy on their membership, saying that prescription is a decision to be made by the individual physician.

Recommendation 7.16 recognized the problem of doctors learning about drugs from pharmaceutical salespersons and requested that manufacturers and physicians "develop and publicize ethical guidelines for physician/industry interaction, which also deal with the industry's involvement in continuing medical education." Recommendation 7.17 requested "the establishment of a department of clinical pharmacology in each Ontario medical school."

The drift of the Lowy report is clear: doctors don't know enough about drugs and need more than the messages of the drug companies if they are to do their job properly. Physicians have also assisted tranquillizer dependence by allowing prescriptions to be refilled indefinitely. And yet medical associations are reluctant to interfere.

On the subject of public education, the Lowy report notes, "This Inquiry agrees that the objective must be a change in public attitudes toward drug use. . . . It is important to persuade the public not to take powerful medications needlessly, as it is to persuade people not to smoke."

At the turn of the century Canadian physicians were prescribing opiates and alcoholic tonics for their distressed patients. At the same time, drug companies were beginning to develop amphetamines and tranquillizers with possible therapeutic benefits. Pharmacists, at the request of physicians, began to dispense these products to willing patients. But whether the prescription was for opium, cocaine, or alcohol, as in the early days; for amphetamines in the 1950s; or for today's minor tranquillizers, little really changed. Mind-altering drugs have always been a useful tool for Canadian physicians.

NOTES

There are many good sources of information about the health and social consequences of pharmaceutical use. For a general discussion and description, see E. Brecher and the Editors of Consumer

Reports, *Licit and Illicit Drugs* (Boston: Little, Brown, 1972). See also A. Weil and W. Rosen, *Chocolate to Morphine: Understanding Mind-Active Drugs* (Boston: Houghton Mifflin, 1983), pp. 28–113. For a more specific discussion of the problems of tranquillizers, see M.A. Cormack et al., *Reducing Benzodiazepine Consumption: Psychological Contributions to General Practice* (London: Springer Verlag, 1989) and H. Petursson and M. Lader, *Dependence on Tranquillizers* (Oxford: Oxford University Press, 1984).

For an early history of pharmacy in Canada, see A.V. Raison, ed., *A Brief History of Pharmacy in Canada* (Ottawa: Canadian Pharmaceutical Association, 1969), and Glenn Murray, "Cocaine Use in the Era of Social Reform: The Natural History of a Social Problem in Canada, 1880-1911," 2 *Canadian Journal of Law and Society* (1987): 29–43. For a history of the patent medicine industry in the United States, see James Young, *The Toadstool Millionaires* (Princeton: Princeton University Press, 1961). For a good conceptual history of medicine and pharmacy, see Paul Starr, *The Social Transformation of American Medicine* (New York: Basic Books, 1982).

A good indication of the current extent of licit drug use in Canada can be gleaned from M. Eliany, ed., *Licit and Illicit Drugs in Canada* (Ottawa: Health and Welfare Canada, 1989). And a good indication of the problems for law enforcement can be found in Royal Canadian Mounted Police, *National Drug Intelligence Estimate, 1988–1989* (Ottawa: Supply and Services, 1990), Chapter 5. See also Joel Lexchin, *The Real Pushers: A Critical Analysis of the Canadian Drug Industry* (Vancouver: New Star Books, 1984). For a current diagnosis of the pharmaceutical industry, see *Prescriptions for Health: Report of the Pharmaceutical Inquiry of Ontario* (Toronto, Minister of Health: 1990).

This chapter was also informed by a series of interviews, by newspaper and magazine articles, and by archival retrieval from the National Archives of Canada.

OUR FAVOURITE DRUG

*In the emergency department in some hospitals it
varies to some extent, but in the one that I work
in now, and the one I used to work at, from
midnight until eight in the morning a good two-
thirds of everything we see is related to alcohol in
some way. There's drunk falls down and hits
head, drunk gets into fight, drunk found lying in
street, and drunk driver. . . . Alcohol is the
major drug problem in the emergency
department.*

— JOEL LEXCHIN, M.D.

Every weekday morning, "Paul Jones" puts on the uniform
that identifies him as one of British Columbia's "major"
drug dealers: the pinstriped shirt and its BCL insignia. He
earns a little more than $30,000 annually, stocking shelves,
advising customers, and working the cash. He agrees that
he's a drug dealer, but says that his work brings more joy
than grief to most people's lives.

There are many different roles in the distribution of
alcohol, from growing grapes, brewing sprouted grains, and
distilling various fermented fruits and grains, to serving
these drugs at home, and in licensed facilities. There are
importers of beer, wine, and spirits, and domestic producers
of the same products. There are state and private retail
outlets for alcohol, employing street-level dealers. And
there are pubs, bars, and restaurants, each again employing
street-level dealers.

In all Canadian provinces, the state is either the major or
the only trafficker in alcohol, employing citizens to sell the

drug: to stock shelves, operate cash registers, and complete the necessary paperwork. Purchasers of the product are usually confined to specific retail outlets, but there are exceptions. Ontario allows the sale of wine in certain grocery stores, Newfoundland allows the sale of beer in all grocery stores, and Quebec allows the sale of beer and wine in all grocery stores. Rates of alcohol consumption in Newfoundland and Quebec are currently below the national average, their less restrictive forms of access notwithstanding.

Most provinces also operate specialty liquor stores, usually located near the homes or businesses of the affluent. This is the high end of the alcohol market, stocking a French bordeaux that might cost the consumer hundreds of dollars. The cost of an equivalent amount of the finest Colombian cocaine or the most resinous sinsemillan marijuana is, in comparison, insignificant. Alcohol is the most valued of psychoactive drugs in Western culture. In Canada's specialty stores, employees advise interested shoppers of the characteristics of some of the particularly expensive chemistry. There is talk of the "overpowering oak from the Chardonnay" and "the unbelievable butter of the Krug champagne."

There is very little talk in the elegant wine stores or in other licensed facilities, of alcohol's more unpleasant effects. But Ontario's Addiction Research Foundation notes: "At low to moderate doses, alcohol usually produces a general feeling of well-being and mild relaxation of inhibitions. As the dose is increased per unit time, the drinker experiences . . . increasing degrees of cognitive, perceptual and motor impairment. Greater relaxation of emotional controls under these circumstances often results in actions and attitudes that are socially unacceptable, frequently taking the form of aggressive or hostile behaviour. On the other hand, some intoxicated persons become so depressed that they make serious suicide attempts."

Alcohol in low doses resembles a stimulant, but increasing the dose of the drug dramatically changes its effects; as most users have discovered, it is quite easy to move from a moderate and mildly pleasant dose to one causing unpleasant effects. It is the most toxic of mind-active drugs, and yet most Western cultures have made alcohol their drug of choice. Physician Andrew Weil has written of this paradox: "In certain groups liquor is so much the required social lubricant that non-drinkers feel uncomfortable and out of place. . . . Airlines sell drinks in flight and placate passengers with free drinks if planes are subject to undue delays. On billboards and in magazines, the pleasures of drinking are everywhere extolled. . . . Unless you are a Muslim or a Mormon or belong to some other group that prohibits its use altogether, you will have to learn how to refuse alcohol . . . or how to drink it intelligently and not let your use get out of control."

Heavy drinking makes more drinking more likely. The cycle of drinking, waking up with a hangover, and then drinking to kill the pain can quickly create physical dependence. When a drinker becomes dependent on substantial daily doses to achieve inebriation, a medical crisis is created. Withdrawal from chronic alcoholism is typically more dangerous and more severe than withdrawal from any other drug. In the first phase of withdrawal, symptoms include tremulousness, profuse perspiration, a general weakness, abdominal cramps, and hallucinations. The second phase usually begins twenty-four hours after drinking has stopped: *grand mal* seizures and continuing hallucinations. And the third phase of alcohol withdrawal, *delirium tremens*, typically lasts about three days and includes severe agitation, high temperature and rapid heartbeat, disorientation, hallucinations, and delusions. Deaths number in the hundreds annually, caused by high fever, cardiovascular collapse, or traumatic injury.

While federal and provincial revenues from alcohol

amount to about $4 billion annually, the costs of alcohol abuse to Canada are estimated by Health and Welfare Canada at more than $5 billion annually. The $5 billion figure is an amalgam of $2.2 billion in health care costs, $1.2 billion in reduced productivity, 1.4 billion in social welfare costs, and a little over $500 million in law-enforcement costs. It appears that Canada's drinkers are not paying fully for the damage that they inflict upon themselves and others.

Alcohol can be both a direct cause of death, and more commonly, a contributing factor. We have about 4,000 deaths annually in Canada directly attributable to its consumption — about 3,500 from cirrhosis of the liver, and about 500 from other symptoms of alcoholism. But it is not only alcoholics who create social problems. Alcoholics place a chronic stress upon themselves and their families, but single instances of alcohol abuse can be as fatal or disabling. Canada's homicides, suicides, motor-vehicle accidents, and domestic disputes involve not only alcohol and alcoholics, but also alcohol and "ordinary" Canadians.

In about 300 of Canada's 600 to 700 homicides police cite alcohol, on the part of the victim or offender, or both, as a significant factor. More important, at least in numerical terms, are the number of Canadians who die in accidents and in other forms of alcohol-related violent deaths. In a 1985 report to the federal Department of Justice, Ottawa's Traffic Injury Research Foundation found that, each year, about 2,000 fatally injured drivers in Canada were legally impaired at the time of death. The researchers concluded that, between 1974 and 1982, about 9,000 Canadians were killed in auto accidents as a direct consequence of impairment by alcohol. (Had there been no drinking in these cases, there would have been no death.)

The annual number of fatalities on Canadian highways doubled between 1960 and 1975, from about 2,800 to about 5,600. From 1975 to the early 1980s the number of fatalities dropped by about one-third, to about 4,000 per year. But the percentage of fatally injured drivers who were legally impaired did not change. Canadians keep drinking and driving, while automobile manufacturers provide improvements in safety technology, the medical profession betters its delivery of emergency services, and various governments work to build safer highways.

Roadside surveys in both the 1970s and 1980s have indicated no significant differences in the percentage of Canadians who drive while impaired. Canada's rate of injury per 100,000 drivers has not changed signficantly in the thirty years between 1960 and 1990. The Canadian most likely to die on the road is young, male, intoxicated, and involved in a single-car accident between midnight and 6:00 a.m. on a summer weekend.

Social scientist Manuella Adrian has estimated that about 20 per cent of all visits to Canada's emergency rooms are alcohol-related casualties: road accidents, assaults, poisonings, falls, suicides, and other injuries. Alcohol-driven violence creates about 300,000 annual visits to emergency wards and about 60,000 cases of hospitalization. Men are more than twice as likely as women to be treated for alcohol-related violence.

Toronto physician Joel Lexchin confirms the prevalence of alcohol in Canada's emergency wards. Asked about the drug most dangerous to public health, he responds, "It's alcohol. In the emergency department in some hospitals it varies to some extent, but in the one that I work in now, and the one I used to work at, from midnight until eight in the morning, a good two-thirds of everything we see is related to alcohol in some way. There's drunk falls down and hits head, drunk gets into fight, drunk found lying in street, and drunk driver."

In 1972 Western cultures became aware of a further direct effect of alcohol consumption. Estimates of the number of Canadian children born each year with foetal alcohol syndrome range from nearly 100 to just under 500.

The characteristics of foetal alcohol syndrome are slow growth, a small head, facial deformities, heart irregularities, and mental retardation. Pregnant women who drink can create significant disabilities for their offspring; there is no safe level of consumption.

The first human use of alcohol seems to have coincided with the discovery of agriculture; the first record of consumption dates from 5,000-year-old Sumerian cuneiform symbols. And for most of these 5,000 years we have been debating the moral choices of abstinence, moderation, and indulgence. About 3,000 years ago, the nomadic Reschabites became the first prohibitionists, rejecting wine as an acceptable drug for their lifestyle in the Middle East. Growing grapes for wine was seen as a cultural refinement that would lead to a more settled life, which would remove them from communion with God.

For much of the past 5,000 years people have been concerned about those who were constantly inebriated. Much of this history, like that of the Reschabites, had political agendas, but there have also been thousands of years of concern with the health and social consequences of overindulgence. In the Book of Proverbs there is the admonition, "Who has woe? Who has sorrow? Who has strife? Who has complaining? Who has wounds without cause? Who has redness of eyes? Those who tarry long over wine. . . . Do not look at wine when it is red, when it sparkles in the cup and goes down smoothly. At the last it bites like a serpent and stings like an adder. Your eyes will see strange things and your mind utter perverse things."

Until the middle of the nineteenth century, however, drunkenness was a pervasive part of social life in most Western cultures. In Upper Canada during the early 1800s settlers often attended neighbours' land-clearing and barn-raising bees. The settler who was the beneficiary of free labour was expected to supply ample amounts of food, beer, and whisky. The bee would have a "grog boss" who would keep the alcohol flowing. Though some precautions were taken, there were apparently a large number of Ontario men killed each year in drunken falls.

Over the past 150 years, however, the development of the modern industrial order and its mandate of productivity have combined with public-health concerns and a social gospel ideology to subject alcohol indulgence to continuing scrutiny, and, at some points, to increasing control. Social scientists have estimated that settlers in Canada prior to Confederation drank about 30 per cent per capita more than Canadians drink in the 1990s. In Upper Canada in 1850, there was one tavern for about every 500 people, compared to the current norm of about one tavern or licensed restaurant for every 900 Ontarians. London, then a town of 1,300, had seven licensed taverns to alter its citizens' consciousness.

The critical link between Canada in 1850 and Canada today is the movement for prohibition. This was a late nineteenth- and early twentieth-century crusade for a more productive and efficient workplace, and a more tranquil home life. Sociologist John Rumbarger has argued that prohibition in North America is rooted in rapid industrialization and its improvements in material well-being: "workers [were] satisfied to subordinate their values of comradeship, conviviality, and political solidarity to those of the emerging consumer society: acquisition of automobiles, radios, washing machines, and vacuum cleaners; cultivation of the nuclear family and development of hobbies and pastimes, to attain mythic levels of individual fulfillment that industrial capitalism now promised."

Between 1915 and 1917 Canada's three prairie provinces held plebiscites; all advocated prohibition by a margin of two to one. Manitoba, Saskatchewan, and Alberta closed down their bars and abolished the retail sale of liquor. And in 1918, as a part of the war effort, the federal government announced a national prohibition, outlawing the interprovincial shipment of alcohol.

For the temperance movement in Canada, this was a

significant victory, and with the United States about to proclaim national prohibition in its Volstead Act, it seemed that alcohol might be banished from North America. Support for temperance as a moral and political value was widespread. In the prairie provinces, the cauldron of prohibitionist sentiment, support united the Women's Christian Temperance Union, the United Farmers, most Boards of Trade, most major newspapers, and the overwhelming majority of merchants and bankers.

Women were more likely to be in favour of prohibition than men, only too aware of the consequences of their husbands' and fathers' alcohol abuse. And the temperance movement was often allied with calls for better protection of factory workers, for improvements in child-labour legislation, and for the right of women to vote in political elections. Those with the power of ownership of industry generally supported the temperance movement, if not the other initiatives. They had seen the effects of alcohol abuse on the productivity of their workers. Improvements in working conditions might lessen profitability, but prohibition was likely to enhance the profit that could be extracted from labour.

Canadian support for prohibition was, however, not unanimous; those living in Quebec were least receptive to the concept, and no government edict, provincial or federal, took away the power to market alcohol. Possession of the drug was never criminalized in Canada, and it was never the intention of the federal government to stop its production for the export market.

Prohibition was, in theory, an attack on alcohol and the altered state that it produces. In practice, it was an attack on the drinking habits of the working class, perceived as a threat to the nuclear family and the emerging industrial order, with its values of thrift and sobriety. Legal loopholes ensured that more affluent Canadians could obtain their drug of choice by mail order, or by prescription. It was the bar, its drunkenness, its camaraderie and social solidarity that were ultimately feared and attacked through prohibitive legislation.

Harry Bronfman's response to the Saskatchewan legislation prohibiting bars and retail liquor sales was to move from the hotel trade into alcohol, its most profitable derivative, and to exercise his legal right to export liquor interprovincially. The 1918 national prohibition of interprovincial distribution of alcohol was, if effective, short-lived. In November 1919 the Liberal government of Mackenzie King announced that such export of alcohol would no longer be prohibited. Prohibition of the drug would become a provincial matter, and all provinces wishing to confirm adherence to prohibition could do so in referenda to be held in the fall of 1920.

The Bronfmans had been given a one-year window of opportunity within Canada and, with the declaration of prohibition in the United States, an opportunity to extend product sales in the larger market to the south, regardless of the results of provincial votes. It was clearly understood, by King's government, and by the Bronfmans, that production of spirits for export would be encouraged, and by the late 1920s the brothers were living in mansions in the more receptive climate of Montreal's Westmount.

Through the 1920s and 1930s, however, the alcohol traffic sparked a number of incidents, not all that different from those in today's unregulated market of illegal drugs: violence, the allegation of fraud, and criminal charges of tax evasion. In 1922, in Bienfait, Saskatchewan, Sam Bronfman's brother-in-law Paul Matoff was killed by a shotgun blast. Matoff was in charge of the local liquor warehouse, and was taking care of business when he was killed. The murder was not resolved: it was either a simple robbery with violence, or a reprisal by American rum runners.

The traffic in alcohol, like the traffic in illegal drugs today, was much more dangerous to those engaging in the

business than the drug itself. In 1929 Harry Bronfman was
snatched from his mansion in Westmount and brought to
Regina by two RCMP officers to face trial on charges of
attempting to bribe a customs officer, and attempting to
tamper with witnesses in a criminal proceeding. In 1928, the
Royal Commission on Customs had recommended that
Bronfman be prosecuted for attempted bribery.

The Conservative government had been elected in Saskatchewan in June 1929, at least in part because of their
election promise to prosecute Harry Bronfman for what
they saw as his flouting of Customs law. There was, of
course, moral opposition to the product that he sold and
ongoing anti-Semitism. Bronfman assembled an impressive
legal team for his defence, and he was acquitted of both
charges.

In 1934, with R.B. Bennett's Conservative government
installed in Ottawa, the four Bronfman brothers and their
associates were charged with conspiracy to smuggle alcohol;
the Crown prosecutor alleged that the accused had evaded
more than $5 million in Customs duties. The four brothers
went to RCMP headquarters for photographing and fin-
gerprinting and were released on bail. The defence team
this time resembled what one commentator called "a minor
Bar convention." The prosecution's case depended on linking the Bronfmans to Atlas Shipping, a company allegedly
involved in the smuggling of alcohol into Canada and the
United States. The company's documents were never found
by police, and the case could not be convincingly made. All
charges were dismissed.

The documents had been in the charge of David Costley,
the company's secretary-treasurer. Costley apparently
drank heavily after the 1935 trials and later suffered a head
injury in a traffic accident. His body was found floating in
the St. Lawrence River in 1942. His wife reportedly told a
friend that she had not been permitted to view the body and

that "I still think it has something to do with David burning those papers in the basement."

At the close of prohibition, Seagrams, then controlled by Sam Bronfman, set out to soothe the fears and concerns of prohibitionists. In the fall of 1934 the company launched a lavish advertising campaign with the headline, "We Who Make Whisky Say: Drink Moderately." The advertisement went on to say that "the pleasures of gracious living" would only be possible if quality drink was taken in moderation, and that "The House of Seagram does not want a dollar that should be spent for the necessities of life." The company received more than 100,000 telegrams and letters of support from both drinkers and abstainers.

It was a socially responsible and remarkably successful marketing initiative. In the post-war era Seagrams diversified from domestically produced spirits to the purchase of wineries and distilleries abroad. The company now owns Paul Masson Wines in the United States, Mumm's and Barton & Guestier in France, and Glenlivet and Chivas Regal in Scotland. Seagrams produces about three times more wine than spirits today and the company operates in more than a hundred countries.

Today, Seagrams represents less than a quarter of Bronfman family holdings, which include real estate and real estate firms, fast-food operations, and supermarkets, among other things. CEMP Investments, an acronym for the names of Sam Bronfman's four children, controlled over $38 billion in assets in 1984. Another branch of the Bronfman family remains involved in the alcohol business. Edward and Peter Bronfman, the sons of Allan Bronfman, control Edper Enterprises, and Edper has the largest group of shares in John Labatt Ltd., owning over 39 per cent of the common stock. Peter Bronfman is also a member of the board of directors of Labatt.

The structure of alcohol-distribution has changed markedly from the days in which Harry Bronfman produced the product for sale. Sociologist Eric Single has noted: "the owners of the alcohol industry are best represented as a highly complex set of corporate interests which transcend national boundaries and are highly diversified in their investments. Like other industries, the alcohol industry has been transformed from a set of small firms owned by entrepreneurs into a smaller set of large international corporations with complex intercorporate connections."

From the late 1920s to the present, the size of the alcohol distribution industry and the consumption of alcohol in Canada have accelerated significantly. We now drink five times as much beer, wine, and spirits per person as we did at the end of prohibition, and about twice as much as we did in the late nineteenth century. About 80 per cent of adult Canadians consume the drug, with rates of consumption highest in British Columbia, Alberta, and the Yukon and Northwest Territories. Those who consume relatively large amounts are likely to be male, young, affluent, and agnostic. Abstainers or those who consume relatively low levels of alcohol tend to be female, elderly, low-income, fundamentalist in religious outlook, with little education. Canadians with post-secondary education are least likely to abstain or to be daily users.

In terms of the industrialized world, Canada, like the United States, consumes a moderate amount of alcohol per capita, placing 18th of 29 countries between 1970 and 1985. If we add the developing countries, however, Canada places about 20th among 130 countries. Germany, Italy, Spain, Switzerland, Argentina, and France consume from 50 to 100 per cent more alcohol than we do. In Asia there is much less use of the substance, except in Japan. In Islamic countries alcohol is generally prohibited, and in most of Africa, except for South Africa and Uganda, there is very little use of the drug. Like marijuana, coca, and opium, alcohol has specific cultural contexts, denounced in some social settings and accepted in others.

Global rates of alcohol consumption are a reflection of these varying degrees of cultural support. In most instances a nation's rate of alcohol consumption is also highly correlated with its rates of alcoholism, cirrhosis of the liver, and cancer of the esophagus. Italy and Ireland are the notable exception; Italy has a higher per-capita alcohol-consumption rate than Ireland, but fewer alcohol-related health consequences. The difference flows from differences in consumption patterns and from family histories of drinking to excess. Such findings have suggested to some researchers that there may be a genetic basis for alcoholism: that some cultures and some individuals may be predisposed to this "disease." At the turn of the century one physician claimed that "the heredity of inebriety is established beyond all possible doubt."

How and why a person becomes an alcoholic or an alcohol abuser are the subject of considerable social and academic controversy. One theory holds that certain individuals become alcoholics because of peculiarities of biochemistry, metabolism, or genetic structure. In a second formulation, it is argued that alcoholism is a learned behaviour, flowing from a complex history of social relationships. Key variables include the presence or absence of good role models in the family and community, and cultural support for responsible consumption.

Research has determined that alcoholics have common identifiable characteristics before they begin to drink: hyperactivity, social aggressiveness, emotionality, and a short attention span. "Although these traits are sometimes viewed as specific temperamental antecedents of alcoholism," writes psychologist Bruce Alexander, "people with these traits are also prone to other behavioural problems, including hysteria, borderline personality, bulimia, anorexia nervosa, other forms of drug abuse, gambling, and anti-social personality.''

The notion that alcoholism is a disease first arose in America in the middle of the eighteenth century. The claim became part of the logic of prohibition, and was then popularized and elaborated by the formation of Alcoholics Anonymous in 1935. New York stockbroker William Wilson and Ohio doctor Robert Smith developed a support group for men and women with alcohol problems, bound by the common goal of abstinence.

The need for abstinence was explained in a series of articles by New England doctor E.M. Jellinek. In his 1960 book, *The Disease Concept of Alcoholism*, Jellinek argued that alcoholics could be defined as alpha, beta, gamma, or delta alcoholics. Jellinek suggested that alcoholism wasn't so much a species of disease as a genus of disease; he likened alcoholism to the hibiscus, which appears in the form of a shrub or a tree. He was essentially arguing that there was substantial breadth in this disease; symptoms and diagnosis could vary considerably.

In Jellinek's view, some kinds of alcoholism were due to disease, some revealed only symptoms of disease, and some were simply habits. His research had led him to believe that there is a genetic predisposition to alcoholism in certain individuals, but he rejected the notion that the disease could flow from an allergic reaction to the drug.

The subjects of Jellinek's research were members of Alcoholics Anonymous, men and women who generally believed that their problem was a form of structural defect. As sociologist Harry Levine noted in a 1984 article, Jellinek was translating the life experiences and views of AA members into medical and scientific terminology and categories, rather than really testing whether alcoholism flows from a genetic predisposition.

In the 1970s and 1980s there was more systematic research. Social scientist George Vaillant compared a large sample of young men with alcoholic relatives to a large sample of young men with no alcoholic relatives. Vaillant found that, while 10 per cent of those with no alcoholic relatives went on to become alcohol dependent at some point in their lives, over 30 per cent of those with alcoholic relatives became alcohol dependent. He concluded that this was support for a genetic predisposition.

But the research could not separate the effects of alcoholic environments from genetic predisposition. One would expect children raised in an alcoholic environment to be more likely to be alcoholic, regardless of genetic structure.

Vaillant's findings have, nonetheless, generated considerable cultural support for the belief that alcoholism is a disease or genetic weakness. More compelling, however, are said to be studies of adopted children, most notably those conducted in Denmark by American psychologist Donald Goodwin. Goodwin found that while 4 per cent of adopted male children with non-alcoholic biological parents went on to become alcoholics, about 15 per cent of adopted male children with alcoholic biological parents went on to become alcoholics. (For adopted females there were no significant differences, though another unrelated study suggested that, while 2 per cent of adopted daughters with a non-alcoholic biology will become alcoholic, almost 7 per cent of those adopted from alcoholic parents will become abusers.) Unaccounted for is the finding that human beings exposed to alcohol in utero have increased preferences for alcohol in later life, as well as learning difficulties and hyperactivity.

Children raised by alcoholic parents, whether biological or adoptive, are more than twice as likely to become alcoholics than those raised by non-alcoholics. Environment is typically more important in the shaping of alcoholism than any sort of genetic predisposition. The overwhelming majority of the adopted children of alcoholics do not go on to become alcoholics, and the adopted children of non-alcoholics do occasionally go on to become alcoholics. There may well be some kind of genetic transmission occurring here, but more significant seem to be forces of cultural support, ethnicity, and the absence or presence of positive role models in the family and community.

We continue, nonetheless, to define alcoholism as a metabolic or biochemical disorder that originates in the structure of human beings. In 1985, the *New York Times* enthused, "Many experts see the dawn of a new age of enlightenment, wherein alcohol will be proved to have a tapestry of subtle biological causes. Though the disease may be set in motion by environmental and/or psychological factors, alcoholics fall prey to their illness because their metabolisms, due to either genetic predisposition or to the effects of heavy drinking, differ distinctively from those of nonalcoholics."

But the best and most recent academic literature does not support this view. Clinical psychologist Christopher Clarke and physician John Saunders conclude in their recent book, *Alcoholism and Problem Drinking: Theories and Treatment*: "There is evidence for a genetic influence on normal and abnormal drinking behaviour. In some families the degree of familial aggregation is very marked, to the extent that a majority of the male members have a drinking problem. A highly heritable 'subtype' of alcoholism has been described. More important reasons for the familial association are the modelling of drinking behaviour on that of older members of the family, and pathological family dynamics."

Ron Cooney is a little over forty-five, and he has not been drinking for two years. His life experiences are somewhat different from those of most Canadian alcoholics: he has spent more than a decade in jail for murder and other offences. But his story of alcohol abuse and its relationship to crime is not atypical. In the face of conflict and violence, alcohol can do little but accelerate social tensions.

Ron Cooney was raised in the St. Henri district of Montreal, and was drawn to the economically marginal bars and clubs of Montreal at an early age. He was first served a beer in a bar at the age of fourteen, "It was *the* bar around my neighbourhood . . . the Atwater Tavern. We used to refer to it as the 'Bucket of Blood.'

"I asked the waiter for a big bottle of Molson," Cooney continued. "And he turned to the barman and he said, '*Un grand Mo*, a big Molson for the big man' . . . and that was the first time I ever drank beer in a bar. . . . I had this little baby face. And I ended up hanging around that bar up until I was twenty-seven years old. I actually became manager."

As an adolescent Ron Cooney was, at first, a weekend drinker. "We would take a couple of flasks of rye with us to Saturday night dances. And the whole thing was to go to these Saturday night dances, get sloshed, and end up in these fights. . . . After I was thirteen, most of my crimes were basically committed under the influence of alcohol. By the time I was fifteen, I had been in juvenile detention centre over forty times."

A string of convictions followed Cooney into his twenties: break, entry, and theft; theft auto; armed robbery; and assault. He was drinking a twenty-six-ounce bottle of spirits daily. He was also involved with an organized criminal network. "I would go to the Atwater Tavern about 9:30 in the morning, in and out all day long, going out and taking care of business, coming back. All the day, drinking beer or hard stuff and shooting pool."

His crimes were a mixture of property offences and offences against people, and he spent about five years in Quebec jails between the ages of seventeen and twenty-seven. He continued drinking in jail on the weekends. "Money was a common commodity inside. It was basically pretty open in Bordeaux jail in the 1960s. The guards were really underpaid. You could buy phone calls, you could actually buy steak dinners, and you could buy booze."

During his time on the streets, Cooney continued his pattern of heavy drinking, aggression, and anti-social behaviour. "There was always physical abuse going on. I was either getting beaten up or beating somebody up. I mean, I did things during that period of my life that when I look back on it, it makes me shudder. But we drank. Everybody drank."

In 1973 Ron Cooney shot a man to death on a Montreal street. The man was a member of a rival organized-crime group, and his death was a reprisal. "I was drinking the day that I did it. I had fifteen years of consumption of alcohol behind me. There was really no judgment. It was a cold, calculated thing that I did. I was totally aware of what was happening, but I spent that day, just like the day before, and the day before, drinking in bars, playing pool, planning scores, ripping people off. It was like always, my whole social life was around consuming."

At twenty-seven he was convicted of non-capital murder and sentenced to life imprisonment. After his sentencing he returned to his twelfth-floor cell in Montreal's Parthenais Detention Centre, and was served a glass of cognac and a Cuban cigar by a fellow prisoner. "A big water glass," Cooney said. "When I got back he gave me a Cuban cigar and he had cognac, and we shared this cognac. And it was a very common thing in Parthenais."

Ron Cooney spent eleven years in federal penitentiaries in Ontario and Quebec; he was released from Kingston's Collins Bay Institution in 1984. In those eleven years he would encounter more alcohol and illegal drugs than he had ever seen on the street. "When I was doing time I never had a weekend where there wasn't something. When I was inside I smoked grass, hash; I did mescaline; I did speed; I did cocaine." Cooney would never inject any drugs, but he would smoke, sniff, and drink.

He found that the most dangerous drugs inside Canadian prisons were the legal ones: a combination of tranquillizers and alcohol. "Downers and alcohol are actually really scary inside . . . Valiums. I've seen guys popping thirty, forty . . . I mean, Valium's unbelievable, how many Valiums you can take."

During his time in jail, Ron Cooney's health improved. If he was drinking, it was only on weekends. He developed a more positive outlook, trying to assemble a life for himself on release. He read widely, ran marathons, learned to meditate, and met a woman from the local community. The story of their relationship became the subject of a CBC documentary, *The Lifer and the Lady.*

When he was released in 1984, alcohol was still his drug of choice, but now he could enjoy it in more comfortable surroundings. "I would go down to the classier places, to the fifth-story hotel thing, and we'd sit up there and look out. That kind of made me feel good because I could get dressed up a little bit and be cool and sit down and order . . . and have a nice waitress bringing me a nice mixed drink. And I would go with straight friends, they weren't criminals, and sit down in these luxury places and drink."

Within a few months Ron Cooney was going to both the better class of bars and the economically and socially marginal bars of Kingston. He was leading what he calls "a secret life," maintaining the image that he was just a social drinker. "I had friends that I would get together with once a week and have a good time with, and that was the only time that they would drink. And they'd think that was the only time that I would drink, but the reality is that I was drinking quite often, at least five out of seven days.

"I wouldn't drink with people who were really close to me," he continued. "I had my drinking buddies, and I had my buddies that were social drinkers who could control it. And I couldn't control it, so I wouldn't drink around them."

He went on to take a cooking course, while continuing his life as a secret drinker. In 1988 he checked himself into a detoxification centre, but within a few weeks he was drinking again. Trouble finally arrived at the graduation party for his cooking course. Before coming to the bar and the celebration, he had cleaned out his locker, putting all of his kitchen knives in his gym bag. At the bar he drank heavily and became very drunk. "I met this gal and I was trying to get her phone number and I was digging through my bag to get out my pen and paper, and while I was emptying out the bag, what I put on the table were my knives . . . they were all in their cases and everything.

"I had my foot up on the table," he continued. "A waitress came by and told me to take my foot off the table, and by this time I was so drunk I could hardly walk. I got up and told her to fuck off and I picked up my knives. I was scooping my stuff back into the bag . . . she ran and called the cops."

Cooney finished packing his knives and left the bar, but the police arrested him outside. "They broke my ribs, they choked me, took me out to the cop shop. When they searched me, and found my i.d., they proceeded to charge me with five charges of possession of dangerous weapons."

Ron Cooney's parole was suspended and he was back in federal penitentiary for the first time in about six years. He spent three months in jail, receiving a thirty-day sentence for possession of dangerous weapons. Though he maintains the weapons conviction was "harassment," he also feels that the criminal-justice system probably did him a favour.

When he was released from jail he went to Alcoholics Anonymous. "It made me want to drink more, because all I kept hearing was how people were addicted to the stuff. But I got a lot out of it because I started understanding alcohol . . . to an alcoholic, you're allergic to it. You react to it. When I heard that, this little light went on. And then I kind of like reviewed my whole life, and realized that, yeah, every time I drank, I reacted."

But Alcoholics Anonymous was ultimately not a method that Ron Cooney found useful. "AA wasn't doing it for me. Every time I went to a meeting I'd come out shaking, because I really wanted to go out and get fucking drunk. . . . When I hear people talking about how addictive it is, it makes my body want it. It's a mind thing, it just fucks your mind. . . . There are people smoking cigarettes, and talking and drinking coffee.

"I took a radical approach," he continued. "I decided that if I really wanted to cure myself of drinking, I had to put myself in a position where there was nothing but alcohol and drugs and I wouldn't touch it."

He went to Alberta to work as a cook in a lumber camp, a camp in which the bar was open and well patronized about nineteen hours a day, "And all the time I was in this camp, I saw more drugs and more booze. I smoked dope, but I didn't touch alcohol. And I stayed in Alberta for about six months. I was in Yellowknife, I laid carpets, and all the people I worked with were hard boozing, fighting, you know, like these real tough dudes. After work they'd down a couple of bottles of beer, they'd go home and beat up their old ladies.

"Now, I wouldn't drink alcohol if my life depended on it," he continued. "You have to recognize you have a problem, and you've gotta deal with it. I heard a comedian one time . . . and he was telling a joke, and basically he said, 'Every weekend I would go out and get drunk and my mother would tell me that I was an alcoholic. And one day I said to her, 'No, Mom, I'm not an alcoholic. I'm a drunk.'

"So if you want me to define an alcoholic," Ron Cooney concluded, "an alcoholic is someone who doesn't drink."

Ron Cooney is working in Vancouver now and living in a suburban community. "I have something that replaces alcohol," he says, "I have drive now. I have ambition now. As long as I was consuming alcohol, I wasn't doing nothing with my life. I was always dependent on someone else to make me happy. Now, I make myself happy."

Abstinence is probably best for Ron Cooney, but it is not clear that abstinence is the best approach for all those with alcohol problems or all alcoholics. It is, however, the dominant therapeutic approach in response to problem drinkers.

In 1962, physician D.L. Davies noted, in an academic journal, that seven of ninety-three alcoholic patients had become successful moderate drinkers over a ten-year period. He was censured for his remarks, and an entire edition of the journal was later devoted to articles attacking his observation.

Later research with control groups has also suggested that controlled drinking is a possible outcome for many problem drinkers. And other work with skid-row alcoholics has cast doubt on the conventional wisdom that alcoholism is inevitably characterized by a constant loss of control and craving. Yet, for long-term hospitalized alcoholics, neither abstinence nor controlled drinking seems to have significant impact. Regardless of what form of therapy is employed, return to alcohol is highly probable.

The failure rate of Alcoholics Anonymous and its commitment to abstinence has been estimated at between 70 and 95 per cent. And yet, alternative possibilities of controlled drinking are rarely explored by physicians, or others in the health-care system. It may be that many or even most alcoholics will be best served by abstinence, but it also seems empirically undeniable that some percentage will be best served by a move towards controlled drinking.

The greatest difficulty for clinicians comes in defining alcohol problems. Are there many stages of alcoholism, as Jellinek first implied? Is "alcoholism" itself a useful concept? Should we speak instead of "problem drinkers" of various types, or individuals with varying degrees of an "alcohol dependence syndrome"? Psychologist Christopher Clarke and physician John Saunders have concluded: "The most serious mistake of all would be to present excessive drinking and alcohol-related problems as disorders whose causes, as before, are located within the drinker, but which are now called his 'dependence syndrome' instead of his alcoholism.

Drinkers, whether of low, moderate, or high dependence, have to contend with relationships, obligations and stressors in a real world."

In this real world of the 1990s Canadians fifteen years of age and older are averaging about two drinks per person per day. For the 80 per cent of the population who are drinkers, average daily consumption is, then, slightly in excess of two drinks per day. Health and Welfare Canada reports that an average of more than two drinks per day or more than four drinks at a time, three days a week, is correlated with various health problems.

There has been no signficant change in the total amount of alcohol consumed per capita in Canada since 1970, when the forty-year upward trend in consumption levelled off. The most popular alcoholic beverage, in terms of absolute alcohol per capita, is beer, accounting for about half the market. Spirits account for a further 35 per cent, and wine 15 per cent. (Since 1975, the consumption of spirits has dropped by 20 per cent and the consumption of wine has almost doubled; beer consumption has been relatively constant.) However, the economics of alcohol distribution tell a different story: spirits account for more than 50 per cent of total revenues, beer a little less than 40 per cent, and wine a little more than 10 per cent.

Canadians are more likely to drink at home than in a bar or restaurant; about 70 per cent of all alcohol is purchased for off-premise use. We are also reasonably patriotic, buying more than 80 per cent of our purchases from home industries. We spend more than 90 per cent of our beer money on local brew, mostly Molson's and Labatt's. With spirits, our interest tends to wander a little; we buy about 20 per cent of our liquors from distributors outside the country. And with wine, we are not very patriotic at all, spending equal amounts on domestic and imported products.

Beer consumption is particularly high in Quebec and Newfoundland, and low in Alberta. Wine is most popular in the producing provinces of Quebec, Ontario, and British Columbia. Spirits are most popular in Alberta and Saskatchewan, and least popular in Quebec. There are also regional differences in drinking itself. While about 85 per cent of British Columbians drink alcohol, less than 70 per cent of Atlantic Canadians indulge in the drug. About 80 per cent of those who live in Ontario, Quebec, and on the prairies are drinkers. Canadians between the ages of eighteen and twenty-nine are those most likely to be consumers of alcohol, and to consume the largest amounts. Drinking between the ages of thirty and forty-nine is almost as common, but after the age of fifty the number of drinkers falls to about 60 per cent. Alcohol is used by 85 per cent of Canadian men, and 75 per cent of Canadian women.

There has been no systematic study of drinking in the family home, its most common location, but there have been a number of Canadian studies of drinking in bars and taverns. Most patrons, mainly men, tend to drink in groups of three to five. Group drinkers stay longer than single drinkers, and drink more. On average, patrons drink one drink every twenty-three minutes.

Those who work in the alcohol industry in Canada are generally reluctant to consider alcohol a drug. They usually describe their product as a "beverage."

"Frankly, we have some problems with the drug-alcohol link," Molson's Cal Bricker said, adding that the company was also wary of comparisons with tobacco. Bricker is Molson's manager of government relations. He explained that he and others were tied up in meetings for next year's product line, but offered to respond, in writing, to written questions. Lorne Stephenson, Bricker's equivalent with Labatt's, made a similar offer, after pointing out that, in order to answer my questions properly, he would have to call in executives from marketing, public affairs, and other areas of the company. And just as I had a financial interest in writing a book, Labatt's had a financial interest in minimizing their costs.

Sandy Morrison, president of the Canadian Brewers Association, did agree to be interviewed. Asked if alcohol was a drug, he replied, "Clearly, in any kind of specific description, it is a drug," quickly adding the caveat that there is "a clear and significant difference" between legal and illegal drugs. "Beverage alcohol is produced and manufactured under very close scrutiny. It is defined in our case as a food product, beer. Its ingredients and its method of manufacture insures, I think, a high degree of consumer confidence in its safety and reliability, when used in an appropriate fashion. Illicit street drugs bring all sorts of hazards."

Tim Woods, Sandy Morrison's counterpart at the Distillers' Association, was equally uncomfortable with the concept of alcohol as a drug. The Distillers' Association represents the interests of Seagrams and other Canadian-based distillers. (The domestic wineries are not represented by an association. They account for only about 5 per cent of total alcohol sales, and a number of them are owned by the major breweries or distilleries.)

"It seems a long way from the history of beverage alcohol to reposition it as another drug," Tim Woods said. "Alcohol is a naturally occurring phenomenon. It's been part of virtually every culture around the world for thousands of years. . . . I guess the beverage alcohol industry finds it not instructive, in terms of social-policy issues, to lump together the consumption or availability of their industry's products with illicit products such as cocaine, marijuana, or whatever."

Tim Woods and Sandy Morrison prefer to think about pricing, taxation, and advertising, and the regulatory network that applies to the drugs they help to distribute. Tim Woods is a former press secretary to Ed Broadbent, and Sandy Morrison a former executive assistant to Jack Pickersgill during his time as minister of transport. They are both trained in the art of reasoned diplomacy, veterans in the game of government relations. They represent their alcohol interests on Parliament Hill and across the country, working with a wide range of government agencies and academics in the ongoing formulation of alcohol-control policy.

Spirits are the cheapest liquor to produce, yet the most expensive to consume. The federal and provincial taxes applied to a bottle of domestic beer or wine virtually double the producer's price. The taxes applied to imported beer and wine more than triple the import price. And the taxes applied to spirits, whether domestic or imported, are about five times the cost of manufacture.

The slogan "A drink is a drink is a drink" is meant to address this disparity. An ounce and a half of spirits is, in terms of absolute alcohol, no different from five ounces of wine or twelve ounces of beer. (Spirits are about 40 per cent absolute alcohol, wine about 10 to 13 per cent, and beer about 4 to 6 per cent.) But Sandy Morrison argues that there is a difference between beer and spirits that justifies the preferential tax. "Beer has a different role in society. It's consumed in different environments. It is still subject to abuse, but not to the same degree as higher-concentrated beverages. I relate beer more closely to wine, consumed with food frequently, and in a social atmosphere. Not that hard liquor isn't, but . . . normally, if you look at the abusers, the beverage alcohol product of choice tends to be the harder liquor."

If we look at alcohol's damage to health, however, the type of beverage used does not appear to be relevant. Cirrhosis of the liver and cancers of the upper digestive and respiratory tract are as likely to occur in drinkers of beer as drinkers of wine or spirits. And research attempting to relate the type of beverage consumed to various kinds of accidents has produced inconclusive results.

Dependence on beer is as likely as dependence on wine or spirits. And while it may generally be wiser to use drugs in their least potent forms, it is not clear that there is any social benefit that flows from taxing an ounce and a half of domestic liquor at more than twice the rate of its equivalent, twelve ounces of beer. The issue, for those of us who drink, is not the form in which we take our drug, but the social and cultural context in which our use takes place. For example, while beer is the drink that is most strongly associated with impaired driving and fatal accidents, "type of beverage" does not explain the correlation. Beer is simply consumed by more Canadians than any other drink and is the drink of choice among young men in North America, who are the population least able to afford wine and spirits and most likely to drive while impaired.

Sandy Morrison does not believe that, given current demographics and lifestyles, beer consumption will increase in the near future. In North America, alcohol has generally become what economists call a mature market: virtually all potential consumers are aware of the product and the product is easily accessible.

"The market size is a given," agrees Tim Woods. "With advertising, the distillers want to expand their share of the pie, or retain their share of the pie within it. You don't see ads for Shell, telling people to consume more gas. They might say use more of *this* product. . . .

"The distillers don't have to go out there and say, 'Hey, buddy, have you ever tried a vodka?" Woods continued. "There's two thousand years of history to demonstrate that people have already come to understand what role alcohol has in their life experience — cultural, religious, et cetera, et cetera."

Both Tim Woods and Sandy Morrison accept that their product is not like other commodities in the marketplace, "The distillers have never had the view," Tim Woods said, "that their product was a product that should be viewed as per toaster ovens, or hairspray, or whatever. They've always recognized, in the post-prohibition period, that their product has a special place, in the way that the community allowed it to be marketed, and sold and distributed.

"Sam Bronfman," he continued, "Seagrams founder . . . he used to take his workers out in Kitchener and give them lectures on the role of the products they manufactured, and how important it was for them to convey that role: that it was not a substitute for food, it was not something that you do until you're inebriated. It was a luxury that was there to improve the social amiability of people, and they had a responsibility to make sure it wasn't seen as just another thing you can consume, like so many candy bars."

The concept that government should tax alcohol as a commodity separate from other commodities has been described as a "sin" tax. Similarly applied to tobacco, the sin tax is often perceived as a cash cow for government, generating billions of dollars annually. In fact, annual revenues from alcohol form a very tiny part of the total federal or provincial government revenues: about 2 per cent of all federal funds and about 3 per cent of all provincial funds.   For the last decade Canadians, from Halifax to Vancouver, have been driving across the border to purchase cheaper legal drugs. The less substantial taxes that the Americans impose on alcohol and tobacco make their products more attractive. The American Congress seems less willing to acknowledge the social costs of alcohol and tobacco in their pricing of these drugs.

"We've had a threefold increase over ten years in the single day trips to the United States," Sandy Morrison said. "The Customs people we talk to will tell you there's a tremendous flow of repeat traffic going. And they don't perceive their job is to nail the guy bringing milk or chickens back, or even a case of beer. . . . The Royal Bank guesstimated that this trade represented $7.5 billion dollars. That's a chunk out of our GNP."

"I think you can argue that the free-trade deal sent a signal to Canadians," said Tim Woods. "It basically told them that the border was different. Now things go back and forth duty-free. And at the consumer level, then, that should mean that they would be able to go the States and take advantage of lower prices. And clearly, the evidence suggests that's exactly what they're doing.

"There are two possible solutions," he suggested. "One is that we try to change Canadians' view of the border, so that it's an impenetrable border. The other is to equalize the laws and taxes in each jurisdiction, so that the desire of Canadians to get equal access, equal price is met. In other words, we're caught between a rock and a hard place."

If government increases the current federal and provincial taxes on alcohol, it creates the risk of diverting even more Canadian consumption to the cheaper American market. And if we reduce our federal and provincial taxes to correspond to American policies, we decrease government revenues, surrender some of our autonomy, and give Canadians the opportunity to purchase cheaper and more potent alcohol, at a time when Health and Welfare reports indicate that national alcohol consumption levels are right on the line between use and abuse. Pricing policy in the 1990s will require a subtle blending of the problems of international commerce and politics with a better appreciation of the critical impact of alcohol on Canada's health-care, social-welfare, and law-enforcement costs.

The appropriateness of what is called lifestyle advertising will be a key part of this debate. Lifestyle advertising is defined as an attempt to lure consumers to a potentially dangerous product by linking it to attractive young people, typically featured in glamorous or exciting social settings.

Asked about this connection between beer, a glamorous, exciting lifestyle, and a sexually attractive partner, Sandy Morrison responded. "And if you drive a Firebird Car, or if you wash your hair with Halo. That is the classic challenge of lifestyle advertising. People don't go out and spend tens or hundreds of millions of dollars to cast their product in an uncomfortable or negative light. If you look at the group we're advertising to, they *are* young people, they do enjoy going out to bars, they do enjoy going to the beach, they do enjoy going to the cottage for the weekend. It reflects what your market is.

"If these commercials were not found to be acceptable and attractive to the target consumers," he continued, "they'd be pulled, or never hit air in the first place. . . . Look at the rules now — you can't talk about price; you can't talk about product quality, other than to say it's cool and refreshing. You can't use celebrities who would influence young people, you can't show people drinking."

While beer and wine may be advertised on television and radio, advertising for spirits in Canada is limited to newspapers and magazines. The Distillers' Association is challenging this limitation, arguing for a change in CRTC regulations, and the right to advertise their products on an equal footing with other forms of beverage alcohol.

Tim Woods argues that the industry does not have a direct interest in placing ads on television or radio, but wants to raise the issue as a matter of general principle. In the United States, where distillers have the right to advertise on television, they have chosen not to do so. "The industry, themselves, agreed that it was not in their interest, that it was not in anybody's best interest . . . and they, among their own collectivity, agreed that they would not advertise their brands on television."

The appropriateness of advertising alcohol is not straightforward. The current rules permit brewers to suggest to their target youth audience that, if they use their product, they are likely to have an exciting and sexually rewarding lifestyle. When Canada has at least 5,000 deaths annually directly attributable to alcohol — cancers and heart disease, cirrhosis of the liver, suicides, homicides, and motor-vehicle accidents — how can we condone such cavalier treatment of an important social issue?

However, the alcohol industry and its advertising have brought us low-alcohol beer, now apparently entrenched at 20 per cent of market share. With 20 per cent of beer consumers consuming 20 per cent less in absolute alcohol, the advertised message can only be seen as positive for public health. "Responsible drinking," the holy grail of 1980s alcohol-control policy, echoed the "drink moderately" campaign initiated in 1934 by Sam Bronfman and Seagrams.

The role of alcohol in our culture has changed during the last sixty years, particularly since the Second World War. Changes to provincial laws and regulations have made alcohol more easy to obtain in a greater range of social settings. In the late 1940s, lounges and bars were given permission to sell spirits and wine, in addition to beer. In the early 1960s, the hours of sale for on-premise consumption were extended to twelve hours a day. Other new regulations permitted the sale of alcoholic beverages on airplanes and in live theatres. In the late 1960s, self-service stores were introduced in most Canadian provinces, and the prohibition against drinking on the patios and in the backyards of private homes was eliminated. (Although this prohibition had seldom been enforced, it remained on the books for about forty years, a vestige of the anti-alcohol sentiments of the 1920s.)

In the early 1970s, the drinking age in most provinces was lowered from twenty-one to nineteen or eighteen. Licences were granted to establish bars or lounges on college campuses and universities, permit requirements were relaxed for community events such as fairs, festivals, or winter carnivals; and serving children alcohol in the family home became legally permissible.

Between 1945 and 1970, we moved to integrate alcohol into our culture more extensively, expanding the social and institutional contexts in which drinking could be seen as legitimate and supportable. In the wake of this deregulation, we increased our intake by about 60 per cent per capita. Our death rate from cirrhosis of the liver increased more quickly, however, more than doubling in the thirty years after the war. Our rate of admission to hospital for "alcoholism and alcohol psychosis" more than quadrupled between 1950 and 1975. On a brighter note, arrests and convictions for public drunkenness declined markedly, an indication that, at least in some sense, alcohol was being better managed.

Canadian alcohol policies are now being debated in terms of a trilogy of product availability, price, and the right to advertise. For forty years we have increased product availability, reduced price relative to disposable income, and permitted increasingly sophisticated advertising on television and radio, and in magazines. In the last twenty years, in the face of stable prices and advertising efforts, we have not changed our absolute levels of consumption.

There is no simple relationship between this trio of advertising, availability, and price, and our incidence of alcohol-related problems in Canadian society. It does not follow that, when alcohol is cheap, accessible, and stimulated by industry advertising, its use inevitably increases. Evidently, Canadians are not the automatons that those advocating restrictive policies might suppose.

In Manitoba and British Columbia changes were made in the 1970s to restrict the ability to advertise alcohol: there was no observable impact on patterns of consumption. And in Owen Sound, Ontario, liquor law changed in 1973 to permit the opening of bars and lounges: there were no changes in the number of alcohol-involved traffic accidents or impaired driving charges. In three northern Canadian communities, the consequences of reducing availability were somewhat mixed. Frobisher Bay on Baffin Island and Rae Edzo and Fort Resolute on Great Slave Lake all closed down local retail liquor outlets during the 1970s in order to reduce alcohol abuse and assault. Only Frobisher Bay had any success in reducing alcohol abuse, apparently because the two communites on Great Slave Lake had road access to the liquor stores of nearby communities. Frobisher Bay was accessible only by air.

The chequered prohibition of the 1920s and these more recent skirmishes show us that it is possible to use the law, criminal and otherwise, to reduce dramatically the incidence of alcohol consumption in Canada, and the incidence of alcohol abuse. At the same time, however, sixty years of increasing availability, diminishing price relative to income, and product advertising have not produced an invariably upward trend in consumption.

Alcohol differs from tobacco, our second most popular recreational drug, in that it can be used moderately. While over 90 per cent of tobacco users become dependent on their drug, and hence subjected to the health risks of their habit, less than 10 per cent of alcohol users become dependent on alcohol and at risk because of their consumption. Alcohol is like tobacco, however, in that it is a very toxic drug, implicated in cardiovascular and neurological disease.

In the creation of alcohol advertising policies, do we advocate for the majority of responsible users of the product, or for those who abuse the drug? Drug dependence and consequent health risks are the overwhelming response to any initial use of tobacco, so restrictions on advertising seem more than reasonable. But for most people alcohol brings far more pleasure than pain, a reality that must have a place in alcohol-control policy.

"My dad told me," Tim Woods said, " 'When I look back at my life, I'm happier that I drank and that alcohol was available. It made my life better.' And it's like, say no more. He remembers good times that he associates with the fact that there was drinking, as well as whatever else they were doing. And for him, this is his measure of things."

But, as Tim Woods and Sandy Morrison would acknowledge, there is a downside to alcohol, which social and legislative policy must stress. This is a drug in the same way that cocaine, heroin, and marijuana are drugs. In our culture and in virtually every other culture in the world, alcohol is, for the consumer, the most dangerous of these drugs. Yet the media typically fail to make this obvious empirical connection because of the powerful presence of alcohol in all aspects of social life. In the language of our culture, beer, wine and spirits are "beverages," not "drugs."

Our attitudes towards drinking, if not our collective habits, have shifted during the past twenty years. Drunks are no longer funny and endearing, and alcohol-free celebrations are somewhat more common. We have begun to recognize, at least in theory, the need for moderate use of this drug. But there are obstacles. The men who control this industry are not called drug dealers. They are manufacturers who can promote their product in the media and on the street. Yet their product kills thousands every year. A cold beer on a warm summer day is a highly pleasant experience, but like its relatives cocaine, opium, and marijuana, it is not without its risks.

NOTES

There are many good sources of information about the health and social consequences of alcohol use. See, for example T.C. Cox et al., *Drugs and Drug Abuse: A Reference Text* (Toronto: Addiction Research Foundation, 1983), pp. 249–62, and A. Weil and W. Rosen, *Chocolate to Morphine: Understanding Mind-Active Drugs* (Boston: Houghton Mifflin, 1983), pp. 60–67.

For more specific elaboration of these issues, see R.G. Smart and A.C. Ogborne, *Northern Spirits: Drinking in Canada Then and Now* (Toronto: Addiction Research Foundation, 1986), and E.

Single et al., eds., *Alcohol, Society and the State*, Volumes 1 and 2 (Toronto: Addiction Research Foundation, 1981).

For a colourful history of prohibition in Canada, see J. Gray, *Booze* (Toronto: Macmillan, 1972), and J. Gray, *Bacchanalia Revisited* (Saskatoon: Western Producer Prairie Books, 1982). See also P.C. Newman, *The Bronfman Dynasty* (Toronto: McClelland and Stewart, 1979). On the notion of a genetic predisposition to alcohol, see J.C. Clarke and J.B. Saunders, *Alcoholism and Problem Drinking: Theories and Treatment* (Sydney: Pergamon Press, 1988). See also B.K. Alexander, *Peaceful Measures: Canada's Way Out of the War on Drugs* (Toronto: University of Toronto Press, 1990) pp. 250–80; D.W. Goodwin et al., "Drinking Problems in Adopted and Nonadopted Sons of Alcoholics," 31 *Archives of General Psychiatry* (1974): 164–69; and G.E. Vaillant, *Adaptation to Life* (Boston: Little, Brown, 1977). For a good description of the relationship between alcohol and casualties, see N. Giesbrecht et al., eds., *Drinking and Casualties* (London: Routledge, 1989).

For a comprehensive look at impaired driving, see Department of Justice, *Impaired Driving, Reports 1–5* (Ottawa: Policy, Programs and Research Branch, Research and Statistics Section, 1985). For the most current description of alcohol in Canada, see M. Eliany, ed., *Alcohol in Canada* (Ottawa: Health and Welfare Canada, 1989).

This chapter was also informed by a series of interviews, by newspaper and magazine articles, by archival retrieval from the National Archives of Canada, and by a number of specific requests for government correspondence, pursuant to the Access to Information Act.

THE UNKINDEST DRUG

*Our King likes snuff no more than I do, but all
his children and grandchildren take to it. . . . It
is better to take no snuff at all than a little; for it
is certain that he who takes a little will soon take
much, and that is why they call it the enchanted
herb, for those who take it are so taken by it that
they cannot go without it.*

— PRINCESS ELIZABETH CHARLOTTE OF
ORLEANS, 1710

Bill Neville was sitting in the corner of the lounge at the
Camberley Club, smoking a Salem Light cigarette. The
Camberley is a Toronto hotel, described in promotional
material as "an exclusive enclave of 58 suites, on the 28th
and 29th floors of Scotia Plaza." Neville has been the president of the Canadian Tobacco Manufacturers' Council
since 1987 and is an "unrepentant" smoker. He was chief of
staff in the Clark government and a member of Brian
Mulroney's election campaign committee for 1988.

Asked if tobacco companies are drug dealers, he responded, "Well, I guess, depending on how far you want to
reach for a colourful phrase. . . . Well, no I wouldn't. Again,
I think that's the sort of pejorative language that gets in the
way. They try to wrap the word 'addiction' around tobacco.
Credible international health organizations have stopped
using the word 'addiction' because of the kind of emotive
quality surrounding it, and I don't think it takes debate over
tobacco anywhere to attach those kind of labels."

Tobacco is a central-nervous-system stimulant that alternately stimulates and tranquillizes the user. The active drug

in tobacco is nicotine; it can be chewed, sniffed as snuff, or smoked. Smoking the drug for the first time often results in nausea, gagging, vomiting, coughing, sweating, abdominal cramps, dizziness, and diarrhoea. But a tolerance for these effects typically develops within a few days. It has been estimated that of those who smoke more than a few cigarettes as a teenager, more than 70 per cent will remain committed to daily consumption for about forty years.

Physician Andrew Weil has written of these empirical realities. "In the form of cigarettes, tobacco is the most addictive drug known. It is harder to break the habit of smoking cigarettes than it is to stop using heroin or alcohol. Moreover, many people learn to use alcohol and heroin in non-addictive ways, whereas very few cigarette smokers can avoid becoming addicts. Occasionally you will meet someone who smokes two or three cigarettes a day or even two or three a week, but such people are rare. Interestingly enough, these occasional users get high from smoking and like the effect, while most addicted smokers do not experience major changes in consciousness."

Unlike other drugs of dependence, tobacco is individually and socially intrusive, requiring about 75 per cent of users to give themselves a "fix" every thirty minutes of the waking day. The typical user smokes between twenty and forty cigarettes daily, between 7,000 and 15,000 cigarettes annually. "Smokers respiratory syndrome" is described by the Addiction Research Foundation. "With regular heavy smoking, the following syndrome often occurs: laboured breathing, shortness of breath, wheezing, constriction of the pharynx, and frequent upper respiratory infections. The syndrome clears when smoking is discontinued."

More troubling are smoking's strong correlations with lung cancer; emphysema; heart disease; cancer of the larynx, mouth, and esophagus; pneumonia; bronchitis; and stomach ulcers. The Addiction Research Foundation and countless research studies have indicated that tobacco is responsible for more than twice as many premature deaths in Canada as all other drugs combined.

Mike McLellan is lucky; he survived his heart attack and subsequent surgery. Now in his early forties, he began smoking at the age of twenty while working as a trucker; he wanted something to do during long drives, and cigarettes met that need. Within a few months he found himself smoking two packs a day and enjoying the experience immensely. During the next twenty years, working as a blacksmith and then as a union and labour representative, he kept up his habit.

In the summer of 1990, while out of town on a business trip, he was hitting baseballs at a batting range with a friend, preparing for an upcoming tournament. "I was in the batting cage, swinging at the ball, and I noticed a funny feeling in my elbow. And I'd just shake my arm and keep hitting, and then it went higher in my arm."

Mike began to sweat, and his arms were hurting, "a pins-and-needles type of thing, right in the bone, not in the meat, but in the bone." His friend was driving him back to his hotel, but when Mike began rolling around in agony, they went directly to the local hospital. Mike walked into emergency hunched over, and told the receptionist that he was in a lot of pain. He thought he was having a heart attack. He was right.

Some months later he underwent bypass surgery, which was successful. Mike McLellan returned to work early in 1991; he is no longer smoking.

He was told by physicians that smoking was a critical factor in his heart attack; he was also told that the surgeon who performed his bypass operation is a two-pack-a-day smoker. "I think smoking was a player in my heart attack. I don't think it was the sole cause — both my parents died from heart problems, and as good a shape as I thought I was in, I'm not in good shape. I've been told that if I'm going to smoke I might as well shoot myself. It would kill me.

"I think quitting smoking is a lot like anyone on the wagon. It's a day-by-day thing. You could go back and start smoking tomorrow and be a pack- or two-pack-a-day smoker immediately.

"I don't think it can be compared to making love or anything like that. But I'm not so sure that if I'd thought about smoking while I was making love, I wouldn't have tried it." He laughed. "If you could do both at the same time, it might be real good." He laughed again. "From the moment I got out of bed in the morning I lit a cigarette before I did anything. . . . Life has been good, life has been smoking."

He had known that smoking had its risks, but he had not known of their extent. "I've always thought that smoking caused cancer. Somewhere along the line I was convinced that, if you were susceptible to cancer, you would probably get it anyway, whether you smoked or not. . . . It never entered my mind that smoking could do anything else to you. I find out today that smoking can cause heart attacks."

Many smokers are not as fortunate as Mike McLellan; they are unable to stop inhaling tobacco smoke, even when they know that it is killing them. Buerger's disease, a nicotine-induced constriction of the blood vessels, can lead to gangrene and necessitate amputation of the limbs, usually the legs. If patients stop smoking, the condition almost always disappears. But despite these realities, many patients continue to smoke after their second or third amputation. Social scientist Edwin Brecher noted, "Surgeons report that it is not at all uncommon to find a patient with Buerger's disease puffing away in his hospital bed. . . . Much the same is true of patients who suffer a heart attack or stroke, or the onset of high blood pressure. These patients have a life-and-death incentive to abstain — yet many go right on smoking."

Tobacco is grown in southwestern Ontario and to a very limited extent in Quebec and the Maritimes. There are about 1,200 farms in Ontario's tobacco belt, clustered around the small towns of Tillsonburg, Delhi, and Simcoe. Like the coca growers of South America, the tobacco growers and pickers of Ontario are not paid well relative to the street price of their drug. The government and three major dealers, Imperial, RJR-Macdonald, and Rothmans, share most of the proceeds. The grower receives less than three cents of every dollar spent on tobacco, the government a little more than sixty-three cents, and the manufacturers and street-level distributors about thirty-four cents. Domestically produced filter-tipped cigarettes account for more than 97 per cent of total sales; imported cigarettes, and domestic and imported cigars and pipe tobaccos have a negligible share of the market.

Once the tobacco leaf has been picked, it is heat-dried in curing barns and aged for up to a year; it is then sold to one of the major distributors, who transform it into one of their many products: Player's, du Maurier, Craven A, Viscount, and so on. About half of Canadian-grown tobacco is consumed in our country, the rest is sold to one of around fifty export markets in the United States, Europe, and Asia.

During the past decade, consumption of tobacco in Canada has dropped by about 30 per cent. Tobacco growers have taken the brunt of these changes. While the labour force of the three major manufacturers and distributors has shrunk by about 30 per cent, there are fewer than half the number of tobacco farmers in 1991 that there were in 1981. Meanwhile, the government's share of the take has increased from about 53 per cent of the retail price to about 63 per cent.

Mike Downing grows tobacco on his family farm near Simcoe, Ontario. He figures that he grossed about $4,500 last year for each acre of his tobacco and about $1,000 for each acre of apples. The price that he receives for his tobacco is a blend: a higher price for the domestic market and a lower price for the export market. If he had to sell his crop at the current export price, "it wouldn't be worth putting the seeds in the ground."

Even with a subsidy for the domestic market, most of Canada's tobacco growers are not doing well financially; only a few large organizations are profitable. Mike Downing believes that those who remain on family farms — those who have not been forced out by reductions in domestic consumption and by poor export prices — are making little more than $25,000 income from their annual crop. Diversification into fruits and herbs requires substantial capital expenditures, and years before any profits can be realized. Moreover, given the current global oversupply of food, the market in these substituted commodities is unlikely to be any stronger than the market in tobacco. Asked if marijuana could be a valuable crop if legalized, Mike Downing laughed. "It wouldn't take long before there'd be no money in it, just like apples or potatoes or beef."

While Ontario's farmers struggle to maintain their presence as growers of food and drugs, the profits of the three major tobacco corporations have increased. Rothmans' most recent annual report to its shareholders begins: "The Company's financial results for the year ended March 31, 1989 are a concrete reflection of the year's achievements, and continue to reflect the positive earnings trend enjoyed in recent years. The fiscal year saw both profits and earnings per share increase for Rothmans Inc. After-tax income rose 10.9 per cent to $33.7 million from 30.4 million last year, resulting in earnings per share of $5.82, up from $5.21 in fiscal 1988. Return on shareholders' equity improved from 16.8 per cent to 20.9 per cent."

The use of tobacco began among the natives of the Americas and spread to Europe in the sixteenth century, shortly after the discovery of the New World. Columbus was given tobacco leaves by American Indians as a gesture of friendship. His men quickly became dependent on the drug, taking seeds and leaves with them to Europe. Within about fifty years tobacco seeds and tobacco leaves had spread around the world. The Spanish left seeds in the Phillipines and other ports of call, the Portuguese brought the drug to Polynesia, and the Dutch to the Hottentots.

Within a few decades it became clear that users were becoming physically dependent on the drug experience. Francis Bacon wrote in 1623 of the pharmacological properties of tobacco, "The use of tobacco is growing greatly and conquers men with a certain secret pleasure, so that those who have once become accustomed thereto can later hardly be restrained therefrom." In Malaysia, at about the same time, sailors approaching the island of Nias were greeted with the cries, "Faniso toca" and "Faniso sabe": "Tobacco, sir, strong tobacco," and "We die, sir, if we have no tobacco."

There were some attempts to prohibit the drug. Pope Urban VIII denounced tobacco in 1642, and Pope Innocent IX issued another denunciation in 1650. During that decade, tobacco was prohibited in Bavaria, Saxony, and Zurich. In Moscow, in 1634, the first of the Romanoff czars, Michael Feodorovitch, prohibited tobacco; those convicted of possession typically had their nostrils split open with a knife. Within the Ottoman Empire, at about the same time, tobacco users were executed. Sultan Murad IV was said to be fond of surprising his men on the battlefront when in the act of smoking. His response to such indiscretions was beheading, hanging, or drawing and quartering. If in a lenient mood, he would simply crush the offender's hands and feet.

In Japan edicts against smoking were issued in 1603 and 1607, and in 1609 cultivation of the drug was made a criminal offence. In 1612, the war against the drug escalated with the goal of zero tolerance. Any person found transporting tobacco would have their pack horse seized, along with any other valuables found to be in transit. In spite of these measures, tobacco consumption persisted and ultimately flourished, even in the Ottoman Empire.

In these early years the New World form of consciousness alteration was demonized, cast as immoral but not generally considered to be a threat to health. Tobacco's addictive qualities had also been recognized, and the combination of its mind-active properties and its pharmacology were frequently censured, at least initially.

In a time in which the life expectancy of human beings was about forty years, tobacco was perceived more as a comfort than a risk. The playwright Christopher Marlowe noted that tobacco was a kind of sacrament in these times, remarking that "Holy Communion would have been much better served in a tobacco pipe." In spite of the spectre of criminal law, use gradually increased across Eastern and Western Europe. In England, between 1700 and 1800, the drug became an accepted product of commerce, the per-capita annual consumption increasing more than thirtyfold. Tobaccos that could be more easily inhaled were being developed in the Americas; in Europe the drug was smoked in pipes, chewed, and sniffed as snuff. Hand-rolled cigarettes had also begun to appear.

The social meaning of tobacco was beginning to change. The early form of the drug was too harsh to be ingested continuously and was appreciated for its mind-altering properties, which were more effective with occasional use. But, as more Europeans and Americans began to smoke milder blends more regularly, they were no longer smoking for the purpose of altering consciousness in some kind of ceremonial context. They were smoking because of physiological dependence.

In the late nineteenth and early twentieth centuries, tobacco and tobacco dependence became an object of some scorn, subject to the scrutiny of the social gospel movement. The Womens' Christian Temperance Union campaigned to suppress the vice of cigarette smoking in Canada, along with the vices of alcohol, opium, and cocaine. Though they were not prepared to advocate a criminal prohibition of the drug, they were motivated to urge criminalization of the sale of cigarettes to minors. Legislation providing greater penalties for such transactions was introduced in Ontario just after the turn of the century.

By the 1920s, however, prohibitionist sentiments were in decline, at least with respect to alcohol and tobacco, and the multinational cigarette industries were taking shape. The sparks for this development were two American inventions — a machine capable of producing 120,000 cigarettes a day, and the introduction and mass manufacture of safe portable matches. In 1916, U.S. general John Pershing decreed that cigarettes were to be a part of every soldier's daily ration; cigarettes had come to be seen as a positive accompaniment to social life. They were thought to focus concentration and to provide relaxation when necessary.

The tobacco companies embraced these initiatives and launched advertising campaigns, pushing their drug into new markets, extolling glamour and success as the benefits of smoking. Through the 1950s, tobacco was not generally considered to be a social or medical problem.

Between 1920 and 1970 the per-capita consumption of tobacco in Canada and the United States increased by over 800 per cent. The waves of tobacco-related drug dependence and premature death in this century are unprecedented. Of 1,000 young smokers in 1990, scientists estimate that 1 will be murdered, 6 will die on the roads, and 250 will die from tobacco consumption. It is only in the past ten to twenty years that consumption trends have been in decline. While half of Canadian adults smoked during the 1960s, less than 30 per cent are currently indulging in the drug.

Asked if his product leads to premature death for a certain percentage of users, Bill Neville replied, "There are plenty of epidemiological studies around on the subject. . . . I don't think the industry, at this point in time at least, spends an inordinate amount of effort arguing with them. Certainly, at the very least, the industry's never tried, certainly not in the last twenty years, to make any counter-claims in terms of health."

The last twenty years have been difficult for the industry; the link between lung cancer and smoking was made public as early as 1964, and tobacconists have been under attack ever since. The opposition has generally included the federal ministry of health and welfare, the Canadian Cancer Society, the Canadian Medical Association, and since the mid-70s, the Toronto-based Non-Smokers' Rights Association. Bill Neville's most formidable adversary has been this organization and its long-serving executive director, Garfield Mahood. Mahood is a fifty-year-old university-trained political lobbyist. He works in an unspectacular third-floor office in an older building and is often described as an impoverished David in his battle against the moneyed Goliaths, Bill Neville and the tobacco companies. Asked if he regards his adversaries as unethical, he responded, "To be frank, I have far more respect for the women who stand out on street corners and hustle their bodies. I mean, these sons of bitches have choices. I'm not talking about the guy who works in the plant, who works in the field. I'm talking about the people at the senior levels. I think they have choices about what they do with their lives. . . . They have access to the research studies. They know what they're doing. Look up the definition of sociopath," Mahood added, his voice rising. "That's the stuff."

Bill Neville expressed his sentiments about Garfield Mahood and the Non-Smokers' Rights Association. "I might, in a cynical way, acknowledge they've been very clever in some of the things they do. That doesn't mean I applaud or agree with their tactics. I find them thoroughly dishonest, in everything they do."

These men do not like each other. They have never met to try to talk through their differences, but neither seems particularly interested. "Not with those guys," Mahood snapped. "There is nothing you can negotiate. Everything

you negotiate away has ten or twenty thousand deaths attached to it or more. . . . Are you prepared to have a mini
epidemic? Do you just want a smaller epidemic? There are
some of us who say 'no epidemic.' "

Neville is also reluctant to begin any discussions with his
adversary. "I've spent a large part of my life in the government relations business. . . . I've tried to keep some reasonable lines of communication open to other people. The most
effective kind of lobbying is when you can try to find some
commonality. . . . And I would normally — even acknowl-
edging some disagreement — at least keep some lines of
communication open to people who have a different view.
But it's impossible with these guys."

The focus of the clash between the tobacco industry and
the Non-Smokers' Rights Association has been the right to
advertise. Until the 1960s there were virtually no restrictions on the rights of tobacco companies to promote or push
their product. A full-page advertisement in *Life* magazine
during this era featured a doctor in tie and white lab coat
smoking. The copy read: "More Doctors Smoke Camels
Than Any Other Cigarette."

In 1987 the Mulroney government announced its intention to prohibit all forms of tobacco advertising. Bill C-51
was introduced in the House of Commons by then Conservative health minister Jake Epp. (The Tobacco Products
Control Act, Canada's attempt to ban all forms of tobacco
advertising, ultimately became law on January 1, 1989.)

In December 1987 the Canadian Tobacco Manufacturers' Council presented its fifty-one-page brief on Bill
C-51 to the Legislative Committee of the House of Commons. They made essentially four arguments: the legislation
would not achieve its objectives; it would have serious economic consequences; it would impose a significant restriction on freedom of expression; and, finally, other more
workable and realistic solutions were possible and should be
pursued.

The council began with their first argument — that the

legislation simply would not work. They noted that cigarette consumption has been declining in Canada for almost a
decade, at about 4 per cent per year. Tobacco is a commodity in what economists call a "mature market." Like
gasoline or soap, virtually all consumers are aware of the
product and its basic qualities. And in these mature or
saturated markets, advertisers compete not to expand public demand for the product, but to increase their market
share. The tobacco companies were telling government that
they wanted only to compete among themselves, not to
attract the undecided to the consumption of their drug.

Furthermore, they suggested, the decision to begin smoking has very little to do with advertising. Most reputable
studies point to peer pressure, family influence, and curiosity as the principal reasons for development of the habit.
And patterns of youth smoking do not appear to change as
one moves from countries with advertising bans to countries
that permit advertising. Finally, the legislation would affect
only a small part of what Canadians see; about two-thirds of
all print advertising originates in publications from the
United States and elsewhere.

The response of the Non-Smokers' Rights Association to
these claims was contained in a forty-one-page package distributed to all members of Parliament and called "An
Attempt to Outmuscle Parliament." Companion pieces,
entitled "Give Kids a Chance" and "How to Cut through
Tobacco Industry Deception" had already been sent to
every MP.

The association called the industry's claim that it is only
after a larger share of the already saturated market "a
fantasy." "These mature markets seem to exist whether the
proportion of cigarette smokers in a population is 20 per
cent or 80 per cent," they wrote, and continued, "If indeed,
advertising has no impact on consumption, one might won-
der why manufacturers with a tobacco monopoly in other
countries still continue to advertise."

Mahood's association did not dispute the tobacco industry's claim that the bulk of cigarette advertising, originating outside Canada, would be unaffected by Bill C-51. Nor did they really dispute the industry's claim that peer pressure, family influence, and curiosity are more important than advertising in the decison to begin smoking. The Non-Smokers' Rights Association suggested that tobacco ads are of "critical importance," in that they link the drug with fitness, health, sexuality, and social success; but they also conceded that "no health organization would dispute the importance of peer pressure and parental guidance in the process of initiating children to the tobacco market."

They argue that the decision to smoke does not take place with informed consent: Canadian children don't really know what they are doing when they begin this form of drug use. Gallup polls indicate that about 30 per cent of those who smoke begin smoking daily before the age of fifteen, and that another 40 per cent begin smoking daily before the age of seventeen. Gallup polls also indicate that less than 25 per cent of all Canadians between the ages of twelve and twenty-nine are aware that lung cancer is one of the possible effects of tobacco consumption. Young Canadians fare even less well with their knowledge of tobacco's relation to other forms of disease.

Bill Neville seemed irritated by the suggestion that to-bacco companies are luring uninformed young people into drug addiction. "The charge that's made," he said, "that most people start to smoke when they're teenagers, is one of those wonderful pieces of rhetoric that's meaningless. (a) The legal smoking age in eight provinces is sixteen; and (b) That's when we start to do everything. That's like saying the beer companies get most of their people when they're young.

"Tobacco companies are interested in building a mar-ket," he continued, "and competing for brand shares within that. . . . I'm saying that the *impact* of advertising is not in terms of overall consumption. You cannot produce a single, credible study to make the point . . . look at the profitability of this business. Brand points or market share points are very profitable, as they are in the beer industry. Why do they spend a lot of money? Because there's a lot of profit to be made."

Asked about Project Viking and its product, the Tempo cigarette, Neville remained unrepentant. Project Viking was a tobacco-industry initiative to build market share by attracting teenage smokers. The ads portrayed young people smoking in very attractive settings.

"The Tempo campaign," Neville replied, "the entire file is now in the public record. It was aimed at the eighteen-to-twenty-four market. It's all right there. Again, why wouldn't you? It fell on its ass, but I mean, what was, quote, *wrong* with that?"

Project Viking and its Tempo cigarette were 1986 initiatives from Imperial Tobacco, disclosed in one of the recent and ongoing civil suits brought by damaged smokers against tobacco companies for their failure to make consumers aware of the damages produced by their product. Project Viking had two important components: Project Pearl and Project Day. As summarized by Imperial Tobacco's Creative Research Group, "Project Pearl is directed at expanding the market, or at the very least, forestalling its decline. Project Day represents the tactical end by which Imperial Tobacco Limited may achieve competitive gains within the market of today, and in the future. Unmet needs of smokers could be satisfied by new or modified products. Products which could delay the quitting process are pursued."

Other documents obtained during civil trials demonstrate how tobacco companies are targeting particular types of consumers. The research unit employed by RJR-Macdonald developed five "tobaccographic" clusters in 1985: "experimenters," "quitters," "guilty, unselective habituated," "selective habituated," and "ostriches." Their description of "ostriches" is particularly unflattering. "The main characteristic of people in this group is their lack of health concern and lack of non-smoker consciousness. They enjoy smoking and are not experimental. They have a relatively strong commitment to their regular brand. Half are in Quebec and relatively few live in Ontario or in the Prairie provinces. This group is the most male and only half of its members have a paid job (blue collar rather than white). They are the least well educated and have relatively low household incomes."

The ostriches are counterparts to the "virile females," the market envisioned for the Dakota cigarette, test marketed in the United States in early 1990. *Harper's* revealed the confidentially commissioned proposal in its May 1990 issue. The target customer was an eighteen-year-old white female with no more than high-school education. "Occupation: Entry level service or factory job. Attitude toward work: Work is a job, not a career; a way to make money. Aspirations: To have an ongoing relationship with a man, to get married in her early twenties and have a family, to have fun with her boyfriend and party with her friends. How she spends her free time: With her boyfriend, doing whatever he is doing. Events: Drag races, motorcross and motorcycle races; hot rod shows; tractor pulls and monster trucks; wrestling."

The tobacco industry in Canada and the United States continues to recruit new smokers; brand share is only a part of their strategy. Bill Neville's comments and projects Pearl and Day confirm that tobacco companies are interested in attracting new consumers and in delaying "the quitting process." Advertising is probably less important than peer pressure and family influence in attracting new customers, but the industry's well-publicized depictions of healthy young people in pristine settings provide at least cultural support for this kind of drug use.

The tobacco industry has a twenty-year record of arguing

against the need for prominent display of health risks, and of violating its own rules of advertising. In legal terms, it is often alleged that they have omitted to do that which the reasonable manufacturer would do: to inform the user of the nature of the risk of the product, in terms that are commensurate with the gravity of the hazard. Their liability to ongoing civil suits, in light of the lack of adequate health warnings prior to 1970, is, understandably, a matter of corporate concern.

In one well-publicized violation of advertising regulations, it was revealed that Rule 13 of the Code — a rule requiring that health warnings be "prominently displayed" on all billboard advertising for cigarettes — was being consistently ignored.

In 1985 the Non-Smokers' Rights Association launched a complaint against Mediacom, the billboard company, and its president and chief executive officer, Thomas J.P. Saso. After discovering that the lettering of the health warning was only two inches in height, the association wrote to Saso and the tobacco industry in 1985, pointing to the need for more visibility. Mediacom's own manual made clear that the warning's height would be inadequate. "Size is important. Lettering of 4 inches or less becomes a smudge at 200 feet. Unimportant statements can be printed at 4 inches or less. This guarantees that no one will be able to read them." Mediacom did not respond to the association's request for information until the association was able to interest Jake Epp, then minister of health, in their correspondence on the issue.

The tobacco industry generally believes that government-control policies are jeopardizing the use of their drug, its 60,000 Canadian jobs and its billions of dollars annually in public revenues. The Non-Smokers' Rights Association argues that tobacco is a drain on the economy, rather than a benefit. They suggest that, if tobacco jobs disappeared, the smoker's available income would be spent on other consumer goods and services, creating new employment. "The tobacco industry argument reduced to its essential absurdity is simply this: we should all encourage smoking as a make-work project. Such leadership would increase tobacco taxation and create greater demand for those who service the epidemic — doctors, nurses and florists."

The tobacco industry is expected to ring up close to $9 billion in sales this year; a little more than $5.5 billion of this amount will go into government revenue. In a 1984 article, Health and Welfare Canada researchers N. Collishaw and G. Myers calculated, in 1984 dollars, that the public expenses of tobacco amount to about $7 billion annually, comprising income forgone as a consequence of premature death ($4.6 billion), the direct costs of hospitalization ($1.5 billion), disability ($.8 billion), and fire damage traced to smoking ($.1 billion). In the same year federal and provincial governments realized only $3 billion in taxes, for a net loss of $4 billion.

This study and its $7 billion price tag have often been used to justify increased government intervention in tobacco distribution. Our current Tobacco Products Control Regulations mention the amount under the heading "Allocative Impacts." The regulations note that the $7 billion in "total adverse consequences" is "$2 billion higher than the total consumer expenditure on tobacco, including all taxes." It is suggested that a decline in tobacco use, aided by regulatory law, will lead to a reduction in the "long term costs incurred by society."

The implication is that, if smokers were to pay their way in Canada, compensating the public for the damage that they cause, a package of twenty cigarettes would now cost more than $10. But the $7 billion figure is an exaggeration. About $4.6 of the $7 billion is to be found in "forgone income due to premature mortality." The money that a man or woman loses because of his or her premature tobacco death is not a social cost; it is more appropriately described as a missed opportunity. Premature death imposes no direct economic toll on the general public.

Non-smokers also receive direct economic benefits from our current patterns of tobacco dependence. Kenneth Warner notes in the *Journal of the American Medical Association*, "Use of tobacco claims most of its victims toward the end of their working lives or early into their retirements . . . the age distribution of smoking's victims is such that smokers are currently subsidizing nonsmokers' retirement incomes."

Even the direct social costs of tobacco consumption — physician services, hospitalization, and disability — would not disappear entirely in a tobacco-free society. Warner suggests that "precisely because smoking tends to kill smokers at an earlier age, nonsmokers have more years during which to incur health-care bills; in particular, nonsmokers have more years of old age, years often plagued by chronic illness and large medical bills." In sum, those of us who argue against tobacco dependence are probably taking a position that runs contrary to our own economic interests. Smokers subsidize our pension plans, and current tax revenues from cigarettes probably have smokers paying for a little more damage than they cause themselves and others. In 1991 smokers will provide us with more than $5 billion; they will probably cost us about $4 billion. Further tax increases, such as those in the Ontario and federal governments' 1991 budgets, can be fairly described either as revenue grabs or as moral tolls, penalties for the socially inappropriate practice of imposing a serious risk on one's health.

The policy of price increases is also not without its risks. With the real cost of manufacturing twenty cigarettes only thirty-seven cents, high Canadian prices have already created a black market in this drug, not unlike the market in marijuana, cocaine, or heroin. Million-dollar loads of cheaper American cigarettes are now being smuggled into Canada. And as long as Canada, the United States, and other tobacco-growing countries maintain different pricing structures for the drug, the incentives to smuggle, to steal, and to rob will exist.

As Warner and others have argued, the benefits of reducing tobacco dependence are to be found in health, not in tangible economic returns or in the economic manipulations of the marketplace. A tobacco-free society would increase life expectancy by close to two years, and partially collapse the differences in longevity now existing between men and women.

Popular culture has told us that men die early because of the stresses of employment and the responsibility of providing for their families. Yet at least half of our present seven-year gap between men and women can be accounted for by a more mundane and less flattering reality: the three-to-one ratio in male to female tobacco consumption that existed before 1970. With the growing equality of male and female rates of smoking during the past generation, we can expect a narrowing of the seven-year difference over the next forty years. If Canadians stop smoking, men will live longer. If we continue current patterns of use, women will die sooner.

Garfield Mahood and the Non-Smokers' Rights Association favour a complete ban on advertising and the prohibition of smoking in places in which non-smokers are affected. "If the product causes 30 per cent of all cancer deaths, 30 per cent of all heart-disease deaths, and 90 per cent of all chronic obstructive lung-disease deaths, then you don't market the product in sexy, glamorous, sophisticated packaging. You recognize that the addicts still need the product, but you take the glamour away, and put it in plain black and white packages with nothing but the brand name and health risk warning information, and content additive information. And so you strip the product and the industry of its allure."

During 1987 and 1988 the Non-Smokers' Rights Association and the tobacco industry lobbied the Mulroney govern-

ment with letters, briefs, and phone calls, for and against Bill
C-51. In July 1987 the Canadian Tobacco Manufacturers'
Council wrote to the prime minister, claiming that the legislation was jeopardizing tens of thousands of jobs. They
argued that they would be "entirely at the mercy of American cigarette manufacturers and without any means of
defending ourselves."

The letter was answered by Minister of Health and Welfare Jake Epp, about four months later. He rejected the
fears of the council, suggesting that with only 1 per cent of
market share, American cigarettes could not constitute an
economic threat to the Canadian industry. "Accordingly,"
he concluded, "I find the line of argument that you have
espoused concerning the feared detrimental marketing impact of Bill C-51 to be less than convincing. . . . Thank you
for keeping the prime minister and me apprised of your
views."

When Mac Harrison wrote to the prime minister about
Bill C-51, he also received his response from Jake Epp. "My
name is Mac Harrison," his letter began. "I am a proud
Canadian and the father of six children that my wife and I
are raising to be productive, contributing human beings and
citizens."

Harrison was the regional sales director, Ontario Region,
for Imperial Tobacco, and he was angry. "I protest vehe-
mently the proposals. . . . I further protest the irresponsible
statistics I see published in all of our still 'Free' press. Your
Minister quotes '32,000 deaths annually caused by smoking,' where does that number come from?" Harrison argued that abortion, not smoking, was "the most preventable
cause" of premature death in Canada. He concluded his
letter, "I don't wish to go on and on, I simply urge you, Sir,
to counsel your Minister and your caucus, lest you rush
the NDP to power — then Heaven help us all . . . Humbly
yours . . ."

A little over a year later Jake Epp responded to Harrison's

letter; there was no apology for the delay, and no support for Harrison's arguments. Epp's detailed three-page reply set out the rationale for Bill C-51. "I appreciate hearing your views on these dificult public health issues," he concluded. "These matters are receiving the most serious attention from myself and others in the government and Parliament."

The correspondence between Jake Epp and the Non-Smokers' Rights Association was a little less guarded and a little more prompt (about six weeks for a response). In May 1987, Epp wrote to Garfield Mahood, "pleased" to tell him that the federal government had decided to prohibit tobacco advertising and promotion. "Through concerted effort," he concluded, "I am confident that we can make real progress towards ensuring that all Canadians have the opportunity to grow up, live and work in a healthy smoke-free society."

Bill C-51 became law in late June 1988, and the regulations were registered in late December of the same year. One other piece of legislation, Bill C-204, was also passed, a private member's initiative from NDP MP Lynn McDonald, prohibiting smoking in federal buildings and federally regulated transportation facilities, except in designated smoking areas. Known to her less fervent admirers as "Willard," after the rodent of screen fame, Ms. McDonald was tenacious and ultimately successful in pursuit of her proposals. "A victory for all caucuses, and not just the NDP," was her comment when the legislation was passed by the Senate. Now, even on bleak February days, the drug-dependent masses huddle outside office buildings across the country, their time-consuming discomfort a penalty for their habit.

Section 4 (1) of Bill C-51, now the Tobacco Products Control Act, reads, "No person shall advertise any tobacco product offered for sale in Canada." It is a ban on advertising, with a number of important qualifications; other sections of the act and regulations diminish the force of this declaration.

Publications and radio and television broadcasts originating outside of Canada are, as expected, exempted from control. Billboard advertising and retail displays are to be phased out over three- and five-year periods, respectively, in order to "reduce any impact on jobs in the advertising and retail sectors." There are specifications about the size and shape of the warnings on packages, and minimum percentages of the "principal display surface" that must be given over to a warning. And tobacco companies may continue to use their names in the promotion of cultural and sporting events.

However, Bill C-51 is a global precedent. Though diminished by Cabinet compromises, the act demands the most substantial cigarette health warnings in the world. It was a significant victory for the Non-Smokers' Rights Association and for public health groups. As we began the 1990s, the correspondence between health minister Perrin Beatty and the association remains supportive.

In March 1990 Health and Welfare announced proposed amendments to the Regulations of the Tobacco Products Control Act. Four new warnings were to be added to the existing four: "Smoking is addictive," "Tobacco smoke can harm non-smokers," "Smoking is a major cause of stroke," and "Smoking is the major cause of fatal lung disease."

More significantly, the regulations require black and white warnings on cigarette packages as of January 1991 and insert warnings as of June 1991. Further, the eight warnings are to be alternated on the tops of packages, above the product trademark, and to cover no less than 25 per cent of the "principal display surface."

Canada has become a world leader in the control of tobacco advertising. David Sweanor, legal counsel for the Non-Smokers' Rights Association, has been asked to testify before a committee of the House of Representatives in the United States, and before another government panel in New Zealand. In 1989 and 1990, the first two years of the Tobacco Products Control Act, Canada experienced unprecedented annual declines in tobacco consumption — almost 7 per cent in 1989 and more than 10 per cent in 1990. The social acceptability of smoking has been undermined by more effective communication of the risks of consumption and by the growing belief among non-smokers that they are morally entitled to breathe smoke-free air. Restrictions have followed, limiting the number of public places in which tobacco can be used.

Canada appears to have had some modest success in this regulatory war against this drug, and it is not surprising that other jurisdictions are interested. It is not as much of a news story, however, as the successive wars on illegal drugs. Richard Nixon's declaration against "public enemy number one" and Nancy Reagan's much parodied "Just say no" campaign received more coverage in a week than tobacco control has ever received. In 1986, when Brian Mulroney declared that there was a "drug epidemic" in Canada, he was, like Nixon and Reagan, contradicted and, in some more cynical quarters, ridiculed. The prime minister, like most politicians, tends to exclude tobacco from the "drug epidemic." Tobacco is rarely seen as our "public enemy number one," though deaths from tobacco outstrip deaths from all illegal drugs combined, by more than ten to one.

For Wally Elliott, tobacco is not fairly cast as "public enemy number one" and Bill C-51 is not really a success story. Elliott spent thirty-three years of his life on the road as a salesman for Imperial Tobacco. He views his employer as a "very responsible" company, which has treated its employees well and been active in community affairs.

In the early years Elliott would go to his customers with a sample tray. "It had all the brands that didn't move that quickly . . . a pack of each. When you went in the store you'd check their stock, and while you were checking the stock you'd see, well, maybe this guy could use some Colombian cigars or Lord Tennyson . . . so then you took out your tray and you'd ask, 'Would you like to try a carton of these?' "

During the 1960s, illuminated signs were developed to promote the drug. "Much better, more expensive, but as the competition came out with different things, our advertising department came up with new facilities . . . to bring the message to the people." The structure of sales also changed, becoming increasingly specialized, and advertising and marketing budgets more lavish.

Voluntary promotion of tobacco products has been replaced by contracts for the rental of display space. In the 1980s contracts were drawn up between tobacco companies and chain stores. "We'd sign contracts with individual stores, depending on their volume, for a counter display. We'd sign a contract for a year . . . to buy four feet of space up on top, which we call a 'pop' display, which is popularity."

Wally Elliott suggests that displays of tobacco products are unlikely to disappear after all other forms of advertising have been prohibited. The tobacco industry will have large advertising budgets to spend on more subtle forms of product placement within the market. "You can still have a sign saying, 'Cigarettes,' without any advertising. You can buy more space in the guy's store. As long as there's no advertising piece on it, you can have a whole wall of Player's . . . they'll have more money for that. They'll have more money for package lineups — for visibility, when people walk in."

It is ultimately the economy of tobacco that most concerns Wally Elliott. The price increases of the past decade are not without their social costs — tobacco has begun to inhabit the netherworld of marijuana, cocaine, and heroin. There are even allegations of drugs-for-guns scenarios: like smuggled cocaine, smuggled cigarettes can be used to purchase guns, in order to further the politics of armed confrontation. The

drug is increasingly a target in break and entries, and robberies; a travelling tobacco salesman might have more than
$10,000 worth of the product in the trunk of his car. To-
bacco salesmen have had meetings and discussions about the
threats of theft and robbery. There is now no advertising on
their vans, the windows are smoked glass, and only minimal
stock is kept on board, wherever possible. There is a sense in
which travelling tobacco salesmen have become like those
who drive around with a few pounds of marijuana in their
trunk, confederates in the risky business of bringing drugs
to market.

Violence has driven Vancouver smoke-shop operator
William O'Neill out of business. He has been robbed eight
times in the last two years, beaten, stabbed, and hospitalized.
In the spring of 1991 he told the press, "I'm getting out
October 9, and I hope and pray I'll last that long. . . . I'm
really afraid of being killed. I'm expecting another two or
three robberies before I go. And I'm just praying no one
comes in here with a shotgun."

Is this where we are heading with tobacco, towards an
armed dispute over distribution rights and a culture in
which only the rich can afford to devour and be devoured by
the drug? In the 1990s the top 20 per cent of income earners
in Canada smoke as much as the bottom 20 per cent of
income earners. (However, those with post-secondary education are about half as likely to smoke as the rest of
Canadians.)

The use of tobacco is remarkably idiotic, at least in terms
of public health — an act of self-flagellation that provides
little of the euphoria associated with alcohol, marijuana, and
cocaine. Tobacco is a drug that is almost impossible to use
wisely; instead of minimizing physical risks and maximizing
mind-active experiences, cigarettes typically maximize
physical risks and minimize mind-active experiences.

It is also the most socially intrusive of drugs, affecting
non-users in a wide range of settings and circumstances. It is

this intrusiveness — second-hand smoke — that has galvanized public opinion and ultimately shaped public policy, tilting the political balance in favour of non-smokers' rights. In the early 1980s a number of research reports, most notably two by medical researchers Hirayama and Trichopoulous, claimed a significant relationship between the passive inhalation of tobacco smoke and lung cancer. And in 1986 U.S. Surgeon General C. Everett Koop released a 359-page report, *The Health Consequences of Involuntary Smoking*, citing an impressive breadth of empirical research in support of the same proposition.

Koop's appointment as surgeon general was initially unpopular and bitterly contested, given his history of advocacy for the "pro-life" movement. The perception was that the Reagan government was trying to impose its moral dogma on public health. But Koop surprised the American public, and the Reagan government, in his eight years as surgeon general, by attacking the tobacco industry and its wave of premature death, in five reports. He issued a report on AIDS, speaking out against discrimination and urging more effective communication of information about the disease. Moreover, when asked by the Reagan government to prepare a report on the health consequences of abortion, Koop declined, in spite of his personal convictions. His dogma as surgeon general was ultimately public health: he had to respect the overwhelming evidence that women do not suffer adverse consequences from safe abortions.

Everett Koop was not reappointed by the Bush administration in 1988, despite his obvious interest in continuing in the job. In 1990 he spoke on American television of the hypocrisy of America complaining about cocaine exported from Colombia, while exporting tobacco, at least as dangerous a drug, to third world countries. (Indeed, export is emerging as the strategy of tobacco multinationals in the 1990s. They are taking their drug to the poor and often illiterate of the third world, even if it means supplanting the indigenous tobacco industries of these countries. The third world is a more comfortable haven for their capital: there are no advertising restrictions and little consciousness of the rights of non-smokers. Health is a less valued commodity.)

Everett Koop's 1986 report placed the issue of "involuntary smoking" before the public with unprecedented publicity. There were three major conclusions: that involuntary smoking can cause lung cancer; that children of parents who smoke are more likely to suffer respiratory infections than children of parents who do not smoke; and that separating smokers and non-smokers within the same air space may reduce involuntary smoking, but will not eliminate it.

"The environmental tobacco smoke issue is the vehicle for the social change," said Garfield Mahood. "It's the vehicle for undermining the social acceptability of smoking."

In Bill Neville's view, "the second-hand smoke issue was almost invented by political necessity to pull non-smokers into the debate and mobilize them. And whatever one says about the scientific literature on the so-called primary issue," he continued, his tone one of exasperation, "I think you can look and find a lot of very credible scientists, including those who don't dispute the primary case, who have serious reservations about the secondary-smoke issue."

Mahood disagrees. "When environmental tobacco smoke is responsible for more lung-cancer deaths than lung-cancer deaths caused by over-the-fence sources of pollution, related to industrial production of coke, arsenic, benzene, vinyl chloride, and radio nucleids all combined? When there are more environmental tobacco-smoke deaths from lung-cancer than the aggregate of all of those other lung cancer deaths, and by a factor of one hundred times? At that point you say, we've got to get it out of the indoor environment, at the very least."

Neville wisely concedes the issue of tobacco's harm upon its intended consumers. But the issue of tobacco's harm upon its unintended consumers is much more complex, and Neville is probably right to have reservations about the strength of the connection. There is a mix of propaganda and science here, and it is not easy to separate grim truth from moral posturing.

The Koop report of 1986 cites thirteen studies that have examined the relationship between involuntary smoking and lung cancer, concluding, "most (11 of 13) have shown a positive association with exposure, and in 6 the association reached statistical significance. Given the difficulty in identifying groups with different environmental tobacco-smoke exposure, the low-dose range of exposure examined, and the small numbers of subjects in some series, it is not surprising that some studies have found no association, and that in others the association did not reach a conventional level of statistical significance."

There is another way of characterizing these research results: fewer than half the studies were able to establish that environmental tobacco smoke is related to lung cancer. Like the seven inconclusive studies, the six that were able to claim something other than a random relationship are weakened by the difficulties in accurately measuring second-hand exposure to tobacco smoke, and in accurately classifying its rate of consumption.

The most widely cited studies of the connection between lung cancer and environmental tobacco smoke are those of Japan's Hirayama, published through the early 1980s. The work began in 1965, with a survey of over 90,000 Japanese women over the age of forty. The women were asked about their smoking or drinking habits, their diet, and their occupation. In 1979 Hirayama returned to the pool of 90,000 aging Japanese women, and found 240 cases of lung cancer among the non-smoking married women. He classified the women into five categories, on the basis of their relationship to their husbands: married to a non-smoker, to an ex-smoker of more than five years, to a smoker of between one and fourteen cigarettes daily, of fifteen to nineteen, or over a pack.

Women married to smokers were about 50 per cent more likely to die from lung cancer than women married to non-smokers; the relationship was statistically significant. The general trend was particularly significant, again in statistical terms: with each increase in the level of exposure the likelihood of lung cancer increased. Hirayama also reported that daily intake of green or yellow vegetables decreased the risk of lung cancer among all groups by about 30 per cent.

Hirayama's results run contrary to those of the American Cancer Society. These researchers surveyed about one million Americans in twenty-five states, asking questions about smoking, education, occupational exposure, and medical history. The initial questionnaire was conducted in 1960, and the follow-up in 1972. Among the one million Americans were more than 176,000 non-smoking married women; during the twelve years between 1960 and 1972, 564 of these women died from lung cancer. Information about their husbands' smoking habits was available in 153 of these deaths. The research team divided the husbands into three categories: non-smoking, smoking less than one pack per day, and smoking more than one pack per day.

Women married to smokers were slightly more likely to die from lung cancer than women married to non-smokers, but the differences were so small that they could have occurred by chance. The general trend was also not in the expected direction: women married to smokers of more than one pack per day were less likely to die from lung cancer than those married to smokers of less than one pack per day. This lack of significance between lung cancer and exposure persisted after eliminating age, race, education, residence, and occupational exposure as potentially confounding variables.

There probably is some connection between environmental tobacco smoke and lung cancer, but as the Koop report notes, exposure to environmental tobacco smoke varies substantially, depending on living arrangements, the presence of the drug in the workplace, and population density. The type of cigarette, the rate of smoking, ventilation, and duration of exposure are also critical, not easily measureable variables. Individual response to environmental tobacco smoke will be further affected by nutrition, lifestyle, exercise, and genetic predisposition.

Passive inhalation of tobacco smoke at relatively low levels cannot be scientifically linked to disease. The cumulative weight of the research does suggest, however, that passive inhalation can cause disease in extreme circumstances — at the least, for genetically susceptible men and women with compromised health and poor nutrition, exposed to heavy smokers over many years, and in places with little ventilation. Everett Koop is probably correct in his claim that environmental tobacco smoke can trigger cancer, but a coherent understanding of how this might happen is not yet within our grasp.

However, there is much stronger evidence in support of Koop's claim that infants exposed to cigarette smoke have a greater susceptibility to respiratory infection. Researchers have consistently found that the children of smokers have significantly more respiratory illnesses (principally bronchitis and pneumonia) than those of non-smokers. These findings apply only to children under two years of age, and evidence of any permanently compromised lung function is not clear; nonetheless, it does seem that parents who smoke around their newborns are imposing a significant risk of disease on their babies. Different studies have measured different variables — rates of hospitalization for bronchitis or pneumonia, physician diagnoses, and rates of tonsillectomy; but the results have been consistent. The parent who smokes around his or her infant is, quite literally, pushing drugs upon a defenceless child, increasing that baby's risk of hospitalization and surgery.

These results have been consistent across cultures. In 1974 Harlap and Davies published "Infant Admissions to Hospital and Maternal Smoking" in the prestigious British medical journal, *Lancet*. The researchers followed more than 10,000 newborns in Israel for a period of two years, finding that infants with mothers who smoke are 30 per cent more likely to be hospitalized for a respiratory illness. They also found that the more the mother smoked, the more likely hospitalization became. In another article published in the same year, researchers obtained similar results in a study of British infants.

In 1978 a team of French researchers published an article titled, "Parental Smoking Related to Adenoidectomy and Tonsillectomy in Children." Said and his colleagues interviewed about 4,000 French children between the ages of ten and twenty, asking them about adenoidectomies, tonsillectomies, and their parents' smoking. Children with parents who smoked were almost twice as likely to have had this surgery, and typically before the age of five.

The separation of smokers and non-smokers in the same airspace seems a reasonable response to such findings; there is some degree of harm in exposure to second-hand smoke, and the rights of non-smokers are fairly protected. But evidence is very strong that separation within the same airspace will not eliminate exposure to tobacco smoke. Environmental tobacco smoke takes the form of what physical scientists have labelled "respirable suspended particulates." Within these particulates a number of carcinogens can be identified and measured, carcinogens that typically increase in their concentration in enclosed and smoky spaces — cars, closed rooms, airplanes, and taverns.

Respirable suspended particulates are submicron particles that follow air streams, quickly diffusing through the air of a room. Some exposure to tobacco smoke is virtually assured within urban industrial culture. In rooms or buildings where air is recirculated, tobacco smoke is diffused. In the enclosed space of the commercial jet, for example, those in the non-smoking section are exposed to almost as great a volume of respirable suspended particulates as those in the smoking section.

What emerges from all of this is a sense that tobacco, like marijuana, should be consumed in private by consenting adults. For Bill Neville, increasing restrictions on the right to smoke are worrying. "I have lots of friends who don't accept smoking in their house," he began, "and I take that as part of the ground rules, and I'm quite comfortable to sit on the airplane for five hours, if that's the rule. Those aren't issues for the tobacco industry, or any reasonable smoker.

"Our position on workplaces," Neville continued, "is one that accepts that you have a right to work in a smoke-free environment. But if 35 per cent of the people still choose to smoke, whether you think they're smart, dumb, or whatever, can't we accommodate them? Do we have to send them out on the front step? Come on. Mahood is at least being semi-honest with you when he says he's at war with the tobacco industry. . . . He'd like generic packs, sold out of government liquor stores, with a law written on them that says you can smoke them in the privacy of your own bathroom, as long as it's separately ventilated."

How far should we take the battle against these re-calcitrants? For twenty years we have been negotiating new terms for the use of tobacco, and in the late 1980s, we have made remarkable progress, banning any direct promotion of the drug, and increasingly restricting its use in public buildings. This tighter regulation appears to have drama-tically reduced consumption, at least in the short term. We are working towards a new understanding of drug use, coming close to a society in which smoking takes place in private, among consenting adults.

But what we mean by private is not clear. In many bars and restaurants tobacco remains a prominent part of social life, and management retains the right to create its own standards of tolerance. And tolerance is a consideration. As we increase the economic costs of cigarette addiction and increasingly ostracize the afflicted, we run the risk of violence related to distribution and social division. Tobacco is the most destructive psychoactive in global circulation, but any war on drugs, whether military or economic, always has its casualties.

NOTES

There are a great number of good sources of information about the health and social consequences of tobacco consumption. See, for example, T.C. Cox et al., *Drugs and Drug Abuse: A Reference Text* (Toronto: Addiction Research Foundation, 1983), pp. 378–86; E.M. Brecher et al., *Licit and Illicit Drugs* (Boston: Little, Brown, 1972), pp. 209–14; and A. Weil and W. Rosen, *Chocolate to Morphine: Understanding Mind-Active Drugs* (Boston: Houghton Mifflin, 1983), pp. 50–54.

For a broader sense of tobacco's historical relevance, and its relation to other drugs, see T. Szasz, *Ceremonial Chemistry* (Garden City, NJ: Anchor Books, 1975). For a thorough (albeit somewhat alarmist) social and pharmacological accounting of tobacco, see J. Wilkinson, *Tobacco, The Truth Behind the Smokescreen* (Harmondsworth: Penguin, 1986). For a thorough review of the issues surrounding environmental tobacco smoke, see A Report of the Surgeon General, *The Health Consequences of Involuntary Smoking* (Washington: U.S. Government Printing Office, 1986).

For good annual summaries of tobacco growing, consumption, and taxation, see *Tobacco in Canada, 1981-89*, A Report prepared by the Canadian Tobacco Manufacturers' Council. For a thorough analysis of tobacco pricing in Canada see Neil Collishaw, "Tobacco Pricing," *Working Paper #12* (Ottawa: Bureau of Tobacco Control and Biometrics, Department of National Health and Welfare, 1984). On the issue of tobacco's costs and economic benefits, see N. Collishaw and G. Myers, "Dollar Estimates of the

Consequences of Tobacco Use in Canada," 75 *Canadian Journal of Public Health* (1984): 192–99. See also, in this context, K. E. Warner, "Health and Economic Implications of a Tobacco-Free Society," 258 *Journal of the American Medical Association* (1987): 2080–86.

This chapter was also informed by a series of interviews, by newspaper and magazine articles, by archival retrieval from the National Archives of Canada, and by a number of specific requests for government correspondence, made pursuant to the Access to Information Act.

WHERE CAN WE GO FROM HERE?

Drugs are not likely to disappear from Canadian life. Alcohol seems well entrenched; tobacco retains considerable popularity, and pharmaceuticals, marijuana, cocaine, and heroin are also billion-dollar markets.

Popular culture tells us that cigarette smoking is bad for your health, that alcohol is acceptable in moderation, and that tranquillizers are to be left to the discretion of physicians. Marijuana, cocaine, and heroin are said to be of a morally different character, typically associated with young, violent, and/or dissolute males.

If we strip away cultural deceptions, this is what emerges: Tobacco is probably our most dangerous drug. It kills more of us than all the others combined and doubled. If there were a free market in all psychoactives, it is unlikely that tobacco's morbidity would be surpassed. Alcohol is our second most dangerous drug, at least in terms of premature death. Cocaine, if it was encouraged in the way that alcohol is, could probably exact a similar toll. Heroin can, like alcohol and cocaine, kill a user at a single sitting. Marijuana and the tranquillizers are less dangerous, but the sedation they provide is not without its risks.

There is an irony in our policies of control: we place costly criminal prohibitions on drugs that are less dangerous to us and we permit the promotion of drugs that are killing us. Canada's Narcotic Control Act dictates that the use of marijuana in private by consenting adults can be punishable by up to seven years in jail. The sale of tobacco in public to children is punishable under the Tobacco Restraint Act by a maximum fine of $10 for a first offence, $100 for repeat offenders.

These differences have nothing to do with public health, and everything to do with our moral, social, economic, and political history. Drugs are not inextricably bound to the left or the right. They are neither a threat nor an agent of capitalism or communism, nor an inevitable consequence of either political theory. The only useful issue in drug control is public health, and on this ground, the legal drugs are the greater threat to social order.

Psychoactives occupy a more important role in our day-to-day life than is typically acknowledged; tobacco, alcohol, tranquillizers, marijuana, and the others are tied to routines, beliefs, and values. Tolerance of different methods of consciousness alteration is a significant social priority. The U.S. government believes that a military attack on cocaine is good social, political, and economic policy, while tobacco producers are friends and allies. In the fall of 1990, during his last days as America's drug czar, William Bennett flew around North Carolina with Senator Jesse Helms, helping to boost Helms's candidacy. The plane was paid for by the Philip Morris tobacco company; Helms is an ardent supporter of the tobacco industry and its government subsidies. For his part, Bennett did not release the report of the National Commission on Drug Free Schools. That report, submitted in September 1990 and leaked to the press after Bennett resigned, concluded that alcohol and tobacco present a greater threat than illicit drugs to American youth.

We should be wary of our hypocrisy and of wars against drugs. We do not need an economic war on tobacco; smokers are already paying more than their share for the damage that they inflict on themselves and others. And we do not need a military war against cocaine; for most users this drug is much less dangerous than tobacco. Given an agenda of public health, it seems incongruous for the state to profit from tobacco distribution while insisting that its police risk their lives to prohibit the distribution of cocaine.

The smuggling of tobacco from the United States to Quebec is no different, in economic terms, from the smuggling of cocaine from Colombia to New Brunswick. Because of the artificially inflated price of these drugs at the street level, there is occasional violence and an incentive to avoid government control. With tobacco it is government taxation that is avoided; with cocaine, it is prohibition.

Drugs provide us with slippery slopes; their use provides pleasure and their abuse provides pain. In low doses, alcohol and cocaine can be pleasant stimulants; high doses can result in paranoia, violence, and the possibility of overdose. Heroin and tobacco are difficult to use without creating physical dependence, and marijuana and tranquillizer consumption can lead, in some circumstances, to psychological dependence.

These "circumstances" are critical for all mind-active substances. What ultimately counts in taking drugs are mental set and social setting. The mental attitude that a person has towards the experience of drug taking combines with the social and physical circumstances of drug use to produce either desirable or undesirable effects.

And in drug taking, less is usually more effective. The person who drinks alcohol or smokes marijuana all day doesn't get the high of the occasional user. The pharmacological properties of drugs are only triggers for achieving altered states of consciousness. If we press these triggers repeatedly, they simply wear out. The best example of this phenomenon is the typical cigarette smoker, no longer feeling tobacco's intoxicating effects, but rather ingesting the drug when the nicotine in the brain falls to an uncomfortable level.

Drug control requires a blend of methods: prohibition, medical prescription, taxation, and education. Tobacco is prohibited in certain settings and circumstances, taxed by provincial and federal governments, offered by prescription in the form of Nicorettes, and the subject of many aggressive education campaigns. Alcohol is prohibited in certain settings and circumstances, taxed by provincial and federal governments, and the subject of a reasonable amount of public education. It is no longer available as a prescription drug.

Tranquillizers are prohibited in certain settings and circumstances, offered for sale only by prescription; physicians act as society's gatekeepers. Tranquillizers are usually the drugs of the socially or economically disempowered and they are rarely the subject of public-education campaigns. They are taxed lightly, relative to tobacco and alcohol. Marijuana is offered by prescription in very limited circumstances: for the treatment of glaucoma or as an anti-nausea agent during chemotherapy. Its recreational use generates no tax revenue and is the subject of many aggressive education campaigns. Cocaine is also offered only by prescription in limited circumstances. Its recreational use generates no tax revenue and is the subject of many aggressive education campaigns. Opiates are widely prescribed for their painkilling properties; their recreational use generates no tax revenue and is the subject of many aggressive education campaigns.

Prohibition is our present strategy for marijuana, cocaine, and heroin, and pharmaceuticals not obtained through a physician. The problems with such selective prohibition are its arbitrariness and the glamour that it inadvertently brings to certain forms of drug use. If prohibition was applied to the recreational use of all drugs, it could be sustained only by means of an extremely costly and intrusive form of social control.

This does not mean, however, that all strategies of prohibition are to be avoided. The prohibition of the public use, production, and sale of drugs can be very effective when enforced through economic sanctions. And prohibition of the giving or selling of drugs to children is also sound social policy, given a child's lack of informed consent.

Medical prescription is the strategy of drug control currently employed with minor tranquillizers and other sedatives. Again, the problem with medical prescription is its arbitrariness. During the past century, Canada's physicians have prescribed opiates, cocaine, alcohol, and amphetamines; the latest entry in the catalogue, the minor tranquillizers, are not easily separable from past practice.

Taxation is the favoured strategy for tobacco and alcohol, providing billions of dollars annually in service of the public interest. The consumers of tobacco are overtaxed, relative to the damage inflicted by their drug. The consumers of alcohol are undertaxed. And the consumers of marijuana, cocaine, and heroin are not taxed at all. Rather than deriving revenues from these industries and regulating their production and distribution, we have chosen a military solution to the problems of use and abuse.

By denying legitimacy in the market to these commodities we have increased their economic value, and, accordingly, their social importance. We spend billions of dollars annually to prohibit certain drugs; as a result, billions of dollars of investment and sales remain in private hands. This is the last frontier of *laissez-faire* capitalism, an unregulated industry in which the corporate exercise of military force is the final authority on social relations. In the international context, this creates the irony observed by Princeton political scientist Ethan Nadelmann, "The illicit drug business has been described — not entirely in jest — as the best means ever devised by the United States for exporting the capitalist ethic to potentially revolutionary Third World peasants. By contrast, U.S. sponsored eradication efforts risk depriving those same peasants of their livelihoods, thereby stimulating support for communist insurgencies."

Nadelmann advocates some form of drug legalization as

an alternative to criminal prohibition: "The middle ground combines legal availability of some or all illicit drugs with vigorous efforts to restrict consumption by means other than resorting to criminal sanctions."

The middle ground is what we have lost. We declare wars on certain drugs, while promoting others. The removal of the criminal apparatus from the desire to alter consciousness is not a surrender to addiction and death. Correspondingly, the elimination of the right to advertise mind-active drugs on radio and television seems a reasonable restriction on the Charter's guarantee of a right to free expression. If we are criminalizing marijuana, we should at least be willing to restrict the pushing of other drugs — the messages that link alcohol and tobacco consumption to attractive models in attractive and glamorous settings.

The two charts at the end of this chapter compare legal and illegal drugs; they demonstrate that even when rates of use are taken into account the legal drugs exact a greater toll on Canadians. Marijuana is simply a less destructive drug than tobacco; alcohol is more likely to kill than all illegal drugs combined.

Alcohol is and has been the drug of choice in most societies, even when other substances are available. It quenches thirst, lessens inhibitions, and is a relaxing accompaniment to an evening meal. There is little reason to believe that alcohol's pre-eminence would be eclipsed by the decriminalization of other drugs.

There are some risks, but ultimately there is little to fear from a careful realignment of government policy with respect to psychoactive drugs. It is not helpful to think of saying yes or no to drugs; these are not the choices that most Canadians make. The better answer is maybe, depending on the drug and its dose, the purpose in taking it, and the social circumstance in which it is taken.

What will happen if drug distribution and use are decriminalized? On the negative side, the use and abuse of illegal drugs may increase. It is unlikely that many Canadians will become interested in injecting any drugs, but there may be some increase in the use of cocaine, opium, and marijuana and some realignment of our cultural drugs of choice. If the experience of the Netherlands and marijuana is repeated, there may actually be a reduction in rates of consumption. On the positive side of decriminalization we will remove the stigma of criminalization from millions of users, remove violence from the business of drug distribution, reduce law enforcement, court and prison costs, enhance consumer protection through government regulation and aggressive education campaigns, and produce revenue through taxation.

This is what we have been doing during the past decade with tobacco, and we have made significant progress; there has been a 10 per cent decline in per-capita consumption, and tobacco is gradually disappearing from the workplace. The drug is finally being recognized as highly addictive and socially intrusive; our policy has been to restrict its public consumption and to increase its cost. There is, of course, still room for improvement. There are many public indoor spaces and many job sites in which non-smokers are still exposed to tobacco smoke. And in recent years tobacco has become overtaxed. This has inadvertently created significant increases in robberies and other violence, and potentially diverts the economically disadvantaged smoker's income from the more important necessities of life.

The keys to thoughtful management of tobacco are to allow its price to reflect tobacco's true costs, to eliminate advertising, to minimize the intrusion of public consumption, and to provide consumers with detailed information about health effects in every package. (This is not to say that the price of tobacco should be lowered immediately. A tax freeze, with price increases subject to inflation, seems more prudent.) Tobacco has created an economic surplus for government, but there are some tobacco-related costs to which these funds could be directed. If smokers and non-smokers are to live in harmony, smokers will have to pay for the construction of better ventilation systems in public buildings. Given the potentially devastating consequences of tobacco, moreover, it seems reasonable for tobacco-tax revenues to subsidize Nicorette maintenance and other treatment programs for interested addicts.

The consumer should probably pay a little more for indulgence in alcohol, particularly beer, which is undertaxed in relation to wine and spirits. There is an apparent shortfall of about $1 billion in government revenues, relative to the health-care and law-enforcement costs generated by this drug. These inequalities could be addressed by modest tax increases and adjustments over several years, for a glass of wine, a bottle of beer, and a shot of spirits have equivalent alcohol content; it seems reasonable that there should be equivalent taxation.

Given the health consequences of alcohol abuse, advertisements that tie consumption to things exciting, glamorous, and attractive seem frivolous and deceptive. There is a value in permitting the manufacturer of a product to communicate information about its utility and desirability, particularly in the launching of less potent new products. But giving alcohol corporations the right to spend hundreds of thousands of dollars on one thirty-second commercial virtually guarantees a slick, seductive appeal to consumption. We already know that alcohol can be fun; we don't need to be told, in vivid and quickly moving collages, that it can also be exciting, glamorous, and sexy.

What we do need to be told, on every bottle or can of alcohol, is of the risks of alcohol abuse and the possibility of foetal alcohol syndrome. There is an obligation on the manufacturer of all potentially dangerous commodities to inform the consumers of their possible risks.

Not all aspects of alcohol policy merit greater control. During the past twenty years we have liberalized our policies towards alcohol consumption, reducing the age of majority and permitting consumption in a greater range of social situations. Yet our rates of alcohol consumption have remained unchanged.

Alcohol is a Jekyll-and-Hyde drug, a social lubricant without peer, and a potentially fatal addiction. When alcohol is mixed with tranquillizers, it can become particularly incapacitating. The tranquillizers are inexpensive drugs, the late-twentieth century mind-altering sedatives. The recipients are usually elderly or female, taking the drug not so much for enjoyment as for relief. Access through prescription generally serves to make these drugs available to those who feel they need them; the criminal process is rarely invoked. If anything, we might want to consider better controls on physicians, in order to limit open-ended prescriptions to those who have developed a dependence on tranquillizers.

Marijuana is the drug most maligned by our present methods of control. We might take a lesson from Sam Bronfman in the days of alcohol prohibition by constructing a government-regulated mail-order business: the production of marijuana and hashish in factories for interprovincial shipment. The public consumption of marijuana would remain prohibited, as would advertising, and taxation revenues could be collected at source. Growers and distributors could be required to place insert warnings with all cigarettes, and taxation would be based on annual estimates of marijuana's individual and social costs. Increases in rates of use could be followed by increases in rates of taxation. Tax revenues could also be used to fund public-education initiatives to provide young people with useful health information about the drug.

Cocaine presents us with difficult choices, particularly when in its most potent or injected forms. To the extent that people enjoy stimulant experiences occasionally, the drug can be a pleasant form of recreation. But cocaine, like alcohol, has a very slippery slope for a small minority of users. It is likely that if the drug were freely available and subject to cultural encouragement, the slippery slope could attract increasing numbers.

The least potent forms of the coca leaf could be economically encouraged: the sale of coca leaf and *bazuco* would be taxed less heavily than cocaine in crystalline form. There could be provisions restricting public consumption and distribution, and aggressive public-education campaigns discouraging intravenous use and heavy consumption, paid for by the tax dollars of consumers. Every amount of coca or cocaine would be accompanied by detailed information about the risks of use and abuse. Licences to distribute from a factory source could be issued, subject to government health regulations. Advertising would not be permitted.

Heroin and other opiates require a combination of medical prescription and — if this does not cover all users — some tolerance of the recreational use and distribution of opiates. Again, economic encouragement could be given to the drug in its least potent forms. There could be provisions restricting public consumption and distribution, and aggressive public-education campaigns discouraging intravenous use and heavy consumption. Every quantity of opiates sold would be accompanied by detailed information about the risks of use and abuse. Opiates create physical dependence or addiction, and this must be stressed in all transactions involving the drug. Licences to distribute from a factory source could be issued, subject to government health regulations. Advertising would not be permitted.

It is wishful thinking to believe that drugs are going to go away; moreover, it is not clear that this would be desirable, in any event. We can all become dependent on alcohol, marijuana, cocaine, tobacco, opiates, and tranquillizers, LSD, and the amphetamines. But we can also find pleasure and relief from pain in these substances.

Drug dependence is not a function of exposure to a given

drug. While it is clear that heroin, tobacco, cocaine, and alcohol are all pharmacologically risky, it is also clear that even with tobacco and heroin there is a range of use that cannot be explained by the availability of the given drug. Psychologist Bruce Alexander argues that we take a drug because of the way it allows us to cope with or adapt to the flow of social life. Alexander differentiates dependence and addiction, suggesting that dependence becomes addiction when the drug interferes with our objectives and the things that are important to us. A person might be dependent on two bottles of beer every evening, but would not necessarily be addicted. It might even be argued that this is a positive dependence, posing minimal health risks for most users and providing a pleasant taste on the palate and a mild alteration of mood.

When we have difficulties in adapting to life around us, we may involve ourselves in drug abuse. Yet, like heroin-dependent soldiers returning from Vietnam, most of us will stop the abuse when we change our social circumstances. People take drugs; drugs don't take people. Dependence and addiction are better understood as flowing from social circumstances than from pharmacology. After all, we permit the sale and promotion of tobacco, the globe's most pharmacologically addictive drug. The flood gates of chemical dependence have already been opened.

When we take drugs we do so to alter ordinary waking consciousness. The criminal control of a citizen's desire to alter consciousness is unnecessary. We have other at least equally useful and less punitive measures available for control: taxation, education, prescription, and the prohibition of public consumption.

But most important, we should confront our own hypocrisy. We can no longer afford the illusion that the alcohol drinkers and tobacco smokers of Canada are engaging in methods of consciousness alteration that are more safe or more socially desirable than the sniffing of cocaine, the smoking or drinking of opiates, or the smoking of marijuana. The answer is not to usher in a new wave of prohibitionist sentiment against all drugs, nor is the answer to allow the free-market promotion of any psychoactive. The middle ground is carefully regulated access to drugs by consenting adults, with no advertising, fully informed consumers, and taxation based on the extent and harm produced by use. There is a need for tolerance, for both tobacco addicts and heroin addicts. And there is a need for control of the settings and social circumstances of drug use. There are no good or bad drugs, though some are more toxic, some are more likely to produce dependence, and some are very difficult to use without significant risks.

Canadians would probably be wise to use less destructive means to alter ordinary waking consciousness — exercise and sexual relations are two of the more popular possibilities — but the advantage of chemical stimulation of the brain is that it works quickly and with most drugs of choice, quite predictably. This process may be lamentable in that the brain forsakes the possibility of stimulating itself for a cheap chemical high. But does this really merit application of criminal sanction, particularly when illegal drugs seem, in a worst-case scenario, no more dangerous than legal drugs?

It would be better if the brain was its own engine for the alteration of consciousness. But the average human being has only seventy-five years on the planet and taking drugs can add to life experiences. A bottle of French champagne, a joint of Hawaiian sinsemilla, a hand-rolled Turkish cigarette, or a line of Peruvian cocaine: we cannot distinguish these drugs of quality in terms of their risks to health, their morality, or the pleasure they provide to their consumers. Yet tolerance is taking a back seat to military and police action against certain drugs. The task is to dismantle the costly and violent criminal apparatus that we have built around drug use and distribution, mindful that our overriding concern should be public health, not the self-interested morality of Western industrial culture.

APPENDICES

CANADA'S DRUG TAKERS: Users, Costs, and Attributable Deaths

	Annual Number of Users	Cost per Week for Average User	Possibility of Overdose Death	Drug Related Deaths per Year
Alcohol	16,000,000	$10 – $100	YES	3,000 – 15,000
Amphetamines	<100,000	$100 – $500	YES	<100
Cocaine	300,000 – 500,000	$10 – $5,000	YES	<100
Heroin	<100,000	$50 – $5,000	YES	<100
LSD	<100,000	<$20	NO	<10
Marijuana	1,500,000 – 2,500,000	$10 – $100	NO	<10
Tobacco	6,000,000 – 8,000,000	$30 – $100	NO	35,000
Tranquillizers	1,500,000 – 2,500,000	$0 – $20	NO	<10

DRUG USE AND ABUSE:
The Consequences

	Short-term Effects *Long-term Risks*
Alcohol	Impairment of motor and perceptual skills, gastric stimulation, relaxation of inhibitions Risks of cirrhosis with abuse, acute gastritis, neurologic damage, hepatitis, heart disease, overdose
Amphetamines	Increased heart rate, restlessness, euphoria, irregular breathing, risk of convulsions, overdose High blood pressure, anxiety, tension, insomnia, skin rash, overdose, paranoia
Cocaine	Increased blood pressure, respiration, reflexes: risk of nausea, vomiting, and convulsions in overdose High blood pressure, paranoia, anxiety, risk of overdose
Heroin	Pain relief, decreased respiration, constipation, nausea, itching, sweating Mood instability, reduced libido, constipation, overdose
LSD	Perceptual distortion, heightened sensory experiences, increased blood pressure, nausea Possible flashbacks, tolerance to effects, some psychological difficulties for a few
Marijuana	Increased heart rate, reddening of eyes, some impairment of motor skills, euphoria Risks of lung damage in extreme cases, sedative effects

PCP   Time and space distorted, dissociative
                         state, risk of overdose
                         Unpredictable, risk of overdose

Tobacco   Increased heart rate and respiration,
                         mild arousal, increased adrenaline
                         production
                         Risks of pneumonia, lung cancer,
                         chronic bronchitis, emphysema

Tranquillizers   Impaired motor skills, anxiety relief,
                         nausea
                         Sedation emotional instability

BIBLIOGRAPHY

Abel, E.L. 1980. *Marihuana: The First Twelve Thousand Years.* New York: Plenum

Abel, E.L., and R.J. Sokol. 1987. "Incidence of Fetal Alcohol Syndrome and Economic Impact of FAS-related Anomalies." *Drug and Alcohol Dependence* 19: 51–70

Addiction Research Foundation. 1990. *Drugs in Ontario.* Toronto: Addiction Research Foundation

Adlaf, E.M., and R.G. Smart. 1982. "Risk-taking and Drug-use Behaviour: An Examination." *Drug and Alcohol Dependence* 11: 287–95

Alexander, B.K. 1990. *Peaceful Measures: Canada's Way Out of the "War on Drugs."* Toronto: University of Toronto Press

Alexander, B.K. 1985. "Drug Use, Dependence, and Addiction at a British Columbia University: Good News and Bad News." *Canadian Journal of Higher Education* 15: 13–29

Alexander, B.K., R.B. Coambs, and P.F. Hadaway. 1978. "The Effect of Housing and Gender on Morphine Self-administration in Rats." *Psychopharmacology* 58: 175–79

Alexander, B.K., and P.F. Hadaway. 1982. "Opiate Addiction: The Case for an Adaptive Orientation." *Psychological Bulletin* 92: 367–81

Alexander, B.K., P.F. Hadaway, and R.B. Coambs. 1988. "Rat

Pack Chronicle." In J.S. Blackwell and P.G. Erickson, eds., *Illicit Drugs in Canada: Risky Business*. Scarborough, ON: Nelson Canada

Amato v. R. 1982. *Criminal Reports* (scc), 3rd Ser., Vol. 29. Toronto: Carswell

Appleton, P., and A. Sweeny. 1987. "Canada's Monstrous Drug Problem." *Globe and Mail*, 24 February

Becker, H.S. 1963. *Outsiders: Studies in the Sociology of Deviance*. Glencoe, IL: Free Press

Beecher, H.K. 1959. *The Measurement of Subjective Responses: Quantitative Effects of Drugs*. New York: Oxford University Press

Berridge, V., and G. Edwards. 1981. *Opium and the People: Opiate Use in Nineteenth Century England*. London: Allan Lane

Blackwell, J.S., and P.G. Erickson, eds., *Illicit Drugs in Canada: A Risky Business*. Scarborough, ON: Nelson Canada

Blum, R.H., and Associates. 1969. *Society and Drugs*. San Francisco: Jossey-Bass

Boyd, N. 1983b. "The Supreme Court on Drugs: The Masters of Reason in Disarray?" *Canadian Lawyer* March: 6–10

————. 1983a. "Canadian Punishment of Illegal Drug Use: Theory and Practice." *Journal of Drug Issues* 13: 445–59

————. 1984. "The Origins of Canadian Narcotics Legislation: The Process of Criminalization in Historical Context." *Dalhousie Law Journal* 8: 102–36

————. 1986. *The Social Dimensions of Law*, Scarborough, ON: Prentice-Hall

————. 1988. *The Last Dance: Murder in Canada*, Scarborough, ON: Prentice-Hall

Brecher, E.M. 1972. *Licit and Illicit Drugs*. Boston: Little, Brown

British Columbia Alcohol and Drug Programs. 1986. *Methadone Policy and Procedure*. Victoria, BC: Ministry of Health

Bureau of Dangerous Drugs. 1968–88. *Narcotic, Controlled and Restricted Drug Statistics.* Ottawa: Department of National Health and Welfare

Burroughs, W.S. 1959. *Naked Lunch.* New York: Grove Press

Canadian Tobacco Manufacturers' Council. 1980/88, *Tobacco in Canada.* Montreal, CTMC

———. 1987a. *Brief to the Legislative Committee of the House of Commons on Bill C-51.* December 11

———. 1987b. *Brief to the Legislative Committee of the House of Commons on Bill C-204.* October 29

Clarke, J.C., and J.B. Saunders. 1988. *Alcoholism and Problem Drinking: Theories and Treatment.* Sydney: Pergamon Press.

Clarke, R.C. 1979. *Marijuana Botany.* Berkeley: And/Or Press

Collishaw, N. 1984. "Tobacco Pricing," *Working Paper #12/84.* Ottawa: Bureau of Tobacco Control and Biometrics, Department of National Health and Welfare

Collishaw, N., and G. Myers. 1984. "Dollar Estimates of the Consequences of Tobacco Use in Canada, 1979." *Canadian Journal of Public Health* 75: 192–99

Collishaw, N., et al. 1988. "Mortality Attributable to Tobacco Use in Canada." *Canadian Journal of Public Health* 79: 166

Cook, S.J. 1969. "Canadian Narcotics Legislation 1908–1923: A Conflict Model Interpretation." *Canadian Review of Sociology and Anthropology* 6: 36–46

Cormack, M.A., et al. 1989. *Reducing Benzodiazepine Consumption: Psychological Contributions to General Practice.* London: Springer Verlag

Cox, T.C., et al. 1983. *Drugs and Drug Abuse: A Reference Text.* Toronto: Addiction Research Foundation

Department of Justice, Canada, 1985. *Impaired Driving, Reports 1–5.* Ottawa: Policy, Programs and Research Branch, Research and Statistics Section

Dole, V.P. 1972. "Narcotic Addiction, Physical Dependence and Relapse." *New England Journal of Medicine* 286: 988–92

Dole, V.P., and M.E. Nyswander. 1983. "Behavioral Pharmacology and Treatment of Human Drug Abuse — Methadone Maintenance of Narcotic Addicts." In J.E. Smith and J.D. Lane, eds., *The Neurobiology of Opiate Reward Processes*. Amsterdam: Elsevier

DuPont, R.L., Jr. 1984. *Getting Tough on Gateway Drugs: A Guide for the Family*. Washington: American Psychiatric Press

Eliany, M., ed. 1989a. *Alcohol in Canada*. Ottawa: Health and Welfare Canada

———. 1989b. *Licit and Illicit Drugs in Canada*. Ottawa, Health and Welfare Canada

Ericson, R.V., P.M. Baranek, and J.B.L. Chan. 1987. *Visualizing Deviance: A Study of News Organization*. Toronto: University of Toronto Press

Erickson, P.G., and B.K. Alexander. 1989. "Cocaine and Addictive Liability." *Social Pharmacology* 3: 249–70

Erickson, R.V., P.M. Baranek, and J.B.L. Chan. 1987. *Visualizing Deviance: A Study of News Organization*. Toronto: University of Toronto Press

Fielding, J.E., and K.J. Phenow. 1988. "Health Effects of Involuntary Smoking." *New England Journal of Medicine* 319: 1452–60

Fingarette, H. 1988. *Heavy Drinking: The Myth of Alcoholism as a Disease*. Berkeley: University of California Press

The Food and Drugs Act, Revised Statutes of Canada 1985, Chapter F-27

Foucault, M. 1979. *Discipline and Punish: The Birth of the Prison*. New York: Vintage Books

Frank. 1990. Issue 73, October 2. Halifax: Great Central Publishing

Freud, S. 1884/1974. "Uber Coca." Translated in R. Byck, ed., *Cocaine Papers by Sigmund Freud*. New York: Stonehill

————. 1929. *Civilization and Its Discontents*. Chicago: Great Books

Giffen, P.J., and S. Lambert. 1988. "What Happened on the Way to Law Reform?" In J.S. Blackwell and P.G. Erickson, eds., *Illicit Drugs in Canada: A Risky Business*. Scarborough, ON: Nelson Canada

Gold, M.S. 1984. *800-COCAINE*. Toronto: Bantam Books

Goldstein, P.J. 1985. "The Drugs/Violence Nexus: A Tripartite Conceptual Framework." *Journal of Drug Issues* 15: 493–506

Goldstein, P.J., et al. 1989. "Crack and Homicide in New York City, 1988: A Conceptually Based Event Analysis." *Contemporary Drug Problems* Winter: 651–87

Goodwin, D.W. 1979. "Alcoholism and Heredity: A Review and Hypothesis." *Archives of General Psychiatry* 36: 57–61

————. 1985. "Alcoholism and Genetics: The Sins of the Fathers." *Archives of General Psychiatry* 42: 171–74

Goodwin, D.W., F. Schulsinger, N. Moller, L. Hermansen, G. Winokur, and S.B. Guze. 1974. "Drinking Problems in Adopted and Nonadopted Sons of Alcoholics." *Archives of General Psychiatry* 31: 164–69

Gray, J.H. 1972. *Booze: The Impact of Whiskey on the Prairie West*. Toronto: Macmillan of Canada

————. 1982. *Bacchanalia Revisited: Western Canada's Boozy Skid to Social Disorder*. Saskatoon: Western Producer Prairie Books

Grinspoon, L., and J.B. Bakalar. 1976. *Cocaine: A Drug and Its Social Evolution*. New York: Basic Books

Gusfield, J.R. 1963. *Symbolic Crusade: Status Politics and the American Temperance Movement*. Urbana, IL: University of Illinois Press

Hadaway, P.F., and B.L. Beyerstein. 1987. "Then They Came for the Smokers But I Didn't Speak Up Because I Wasn't a Smoker: Legislation and Tobacco Use." *Canadian Psychology* 28: 259–65

Harlap, S. and A.M. Davies. 1974. "Infant Admissions to Hospital and Maternal Smoking." *Lancet* 529–32

Health and Welfare Canada. 1988. *Canada's Health Promotion Survey: Technical Report*, Ottawa: Ministry of Supply and Services

Helzer, J.E., L.N. Robins, and D.H. Davis. 1975/76. "Antecedents of Narcotic Use and Addiction. A Study of 898 Vietnam Veterans." *Drug and Alcohol Dependence* 1: 183–90

Hirayama, T. 1981. "Non-smoking Wives of Heavy Smokers Have a Higher Risk of Lung Cancer: Study From Japan." *British Medical Journal* 282: 183–85

Huxley, A. 1963. *The Doors of Perception and Heaven and Hell*. New York: Harper

Illich, I. 1973. *Tools for Conviviality*. New York: Harper & Row

Inciardi, James. 1986. *The War on Drugs: Heroin, Cocaine Crime, and Public Policy*. Palo Alto, CA: Mayfield

Jaffe, J.H. 1985. "Drug Addiction and Drug Abuse." In A.G. Gilman et al., eds., *Goodman and Gilman's The Pharmacological Basis of Therapeutics*. 7th Edition. New York: Macmillan

Jellinek, E.M. 1960. *The Disease Concept in Alcoholism*. New Brunswick, NJ: Hill House

Johnston, L.D., P.M. O'Malley, and J.G. Bachman. 1986. *Illicit Drug Use, Smoking, and Drinking by America's High School Students, College Students, and Young Adults, National Trends through 1985*. Rockville, MD: National Institute of Mental Health

Judson, H.F. 1973. *Heroin Addiction in Britain: What Americans Can Learn from the English Experience*. London: Harcourt, Brace, Jovanovich

King, William Lyon Mackenzie. "Mission to the Orient, 1907–09." *Dairies*. Public Archives of Canada, 85–86

Le Dain, G. 1972. *Cannabis: A Report of the Commission of Inquiry into the Non-Medical Use of Drugs*. Ottawa: Information Canada

————. 1973. *Final Report of the Commission of Inquiry into the Non-Medical Use of Drugs*. Ottawa: Information Canada

Levine, H.G. 1978. "The Discovery of Addiction: Changing Conceptions of Habitual Drunkenness in America." *British Journal of Addiction* 79: 109–19

Lexchin, J. 1984. *The Real Pushers: A Critical Analysis of the Canadian Drug Industry*. Vancouver: New Star Books

McCoy, A.W. 1972. *The Politics of Heroin in Southeast Asia*. New York: Harper & Row

MacFarlane, B. 1986. *Drug Offences in Canada*, 2nd ed. Aurora: Canada Law Book

Malarek, V. 1989. *Merchants of Misery: Inside Canada's Illegal Drug Scene*. Toronto: Macmillan

Manning, P.K. 1980. *The Narcs' Game: Organization and Informational Limits on Drug Law Enforcement*. Cambridge, MA: The MIT Press

Maugham, W.S. 1922. *On a Chinese Screen*. London: William Heinemann

Mitchell, C.N. 1986. "A Justice-Based Argument for the Uniform Regulation of Psychoactive Drugs." *McGill Law Journal* 31: 221–63

————. 1990. *The Drug Solution*. Ottawa: Carleton University Press

Murphy, E. 1922/73. *The Black Candle*. Toronto: Coles

Murray, G.F. 1988. "The Road to Regulation: Patent Medicines in Canada in Historical Perspective." In J.C. Blackwell and P.G. Erickson, eds., *Illicit Drugs in Canada: A Risky Business*. Scarborough, ON: Nelson Canada

Murray, G.F. 1987. "Cocaine Use in the Era of Social Reform: The Natural History of a Social Problem in Canada, 1880–1911." *Canadian Journal of Law and Society* 2: 29–43

Musto, D.F. 1973. *The American Disease: Origins of Narcotic Control.* New Haven: Yale University Press

Nadelmann, E.A. 1989. "Drug Prohibition in the United States: Costs, Consequences, and Alternatives." *Science* 245: 939–47

The Narcotic Control Act, Revised Statutes of Canada, 1985, Chapter N-1

Newman, P.C. 1979. *The Bronfman Dynasty.* Toronto: McClelland and Stewart

Nicholl, C. 1985. *The Fruit Palace.* London: Heinemann

Novak, W. *High Culture: Marijuana in the Lives of Americans.* New York: Knopf

O'Malley, P.M., L.D. Johnston, and J.G. Bachman. 1985. "Cocaine Use among American Adolescents and Young Adults." In Kozel and Adams, eds., *Cocaine Use in America.* Rockville, MD: National Institute on Drug Abuse

Peele, S. 1985. *The Meaning of Addiction: Compulsive Experience and Its Interpretation.* Lexington, MA: D.C. Heath

Peele, S., and A. Brodsky. 1975. *Love and Addiction.* Scarborough, ON: New American Library of Canada

Petursson, H., and M. Lader. 1984. *Dependence on Tranquillizers.* Oxford: Oxford University Press

Pfohl, S.J. 1985. *Images of Deviance and Social Control: A Sociological History.* Glencoe, IL: Free Press

Raison, A.V., ed. 1969. *A Brief History of Pharmacy in Canada.* Ottawa: Canadian Pharmaceutical Association

Report of the Surgeon-General, 1986. *The Health Consequences of Involuntary Smoking.* Washington, DC: U.S. Government Printing Office

Robins, L.N., J.E. Helzer, and D.H. Davis. 1975. "Narcotic Use in

Southeast Asia and Afterwards." *Archives of General Psychiatry* 32: 955–61

Rootman, I. 1988. "Epidemiologic Methods and Indicators." In J.C. Blackwell and P.G. Erickson, eds., *Illicit Drugs in Canada.* Scarborough, ON: Nelson Canada

Rothmans Inc. 1989. *Annual Report.* Toronto, pp. 1–18

Royal Canadian Mounted Police. 1988/89. *National Drug Intelligence Estimate 1988/1989.* Ottawa: Ministry of Supply and Services Canada

Rumbarger, J.J. 1989. *Prohibition, Power and Profits.* Albany: State University of New York Press

Said, G., et al. 1978. "Parental Smoking Related to Adenoidectomy and Tonsillectomy in Children." *Journal of Epidemiology and Community Health.* 32: 97–101

Schneider v. The Queen. 1982. *Canadian Criminal Cases* (scc) 2nd Ser., Vol. 68. Aurora, ON: Canada Law Book

Siegel, S., R. Hinson, M.D. Krank, and J. McCully. 1982. "Heroin 'Overdose' Death: Contribution of Drug Associated Environmental Cues," *Science* 216: 436–37

Single, E.W. 1982. "Intercorporate Connections of the Alcohol Industry in Canada," *Contemporary Drug Problems.* Winter: 545–67

———. 1987. "The Structure of the Alcohol Industry as It Relates to Transportation Issues." *Accident Analysis and Prevention* 19: 419–31

Single, E.W., et al., eds. 1981. *Alcohol, Society, and the State.* Volumes 1 and 2. Toronto: Addiction Research Foundation

Smart, R.G. 1983. *Forbidden Highs: The Nature, Treatment and Prevention of Illicit Drug Abuse.* Toronto: Addiction Research Foundation

Smart, R.G., and E.M. Adlaf. 1987. *Alcohol and Other Drug Use among Ontario Students in 1987, and Trends since 1977.* Toronto: Addiction Research Foundation

————. 1988. "Alcohol, Cannabis, Cocaine, and Other Substance Use among Ontario Adults, 1977–1987." *Canadian Journal of Public Health* 79: 206–7

Smart, R.G., and A.C. Ogborne. 1986. *Northern Spirits: Drinking in Canada Then and Now.* Toronto: Addiction Research Foundation

Solomon, R.R. 1988a. "Canada's Federal Drug Legislation." In J.C. Blackwell and P.G. Erickson, eds., *Illicit Drugs in Canada: A Risky Business.* Scarborough, ON: Nelson Canada

————. 1988b. "The Noble Pursuit of Evil: Arrest, Search, and Seizure in Canadian Drug Law." In J.C. Blackwell and P.G. Erickson, eds., *Illicit Drugs in Canada: A Risky Business.* Scarborough, ON: Nelson Canada

Solomon, R.R., and M. Green. 1982. "The First Century: The History of Non-medical Opiate Use and Control Policies in Canada, 1870–1970." *University of Western Ontario Law Review* 20: 307–36

Solomon, R.R., E. Single, and P.G. Erickson. 1988. "Legal Considerations in Canadian Cannabis Policy." In J.C. Blackwell and P.G. Erickson, eds., *Illicit Drug Use in Canada: A Risky Business.* Scarborough, ON: Nelson Canada

Spear, H.B., and M.M. Glatt. 1971. "The Influence of Canadian Addicts on Heroin Addiction in the United Kingdom." *British Journal of Addiction* 66: 141–49

Starr, P. 1982. *The Social Transformation of American Medicine.* New York: Basic Books

Stoddart, K. 1982. "The Enforcement of Narcotics Violations in a Canadian City: Heroin Users' Perspectives on the Production of Official Statistics." *Canadian Journal of Criminology* 24: 425–38

Stoffman, D. 1987. "Where There's Smoke." *Report on Business Magazine, Globe and Mail,* September 29, pp. 20–28

Szasz, T. 1975. *Ceremonial Chemistry: The Ritual Persecution of Drugs, Addicts, and Pushers.* Garden City, NJ: Anchor Press

Taylor, A. 1969. *American Diplomacy and the Narcotics Traffic.* Durham: Duke University Press

The Tobacco Products Control Act, Statutes of Canada 1988, c. 20

The Tobacco Products Control Regulations, 1989, Canada Gazette, Part II, Volume 123, January 18

The Tobacco Restraint Act, 1985. R.S. c. T-9, section 2

Trebach, A.S. 1982. *The Heroin Solution.* New Haven: Yale University Press

————. 1987. *The Great Drug War: And Radical Proposals That Could Make America Safe Again.* New York: Macmillan

Trichopoulous, D., et al. 1981. "Lung Cancer and Passive Smoking." *International Journal of Cancer.* 23: 803–07

Vaillant, G.E. 1977. *Adaptation to Life.* Boston: Little, Brown

Warner, K.E. 1987. "Health and Economic Implications of a Tobacco Free Society." *Journal of the American Medical Association* 258: 2080–86

Weil, A. 1972. *The Natural Mind: A New Way of Looking at Drugs and the Higher Consciousness.* Boston: Houghton Mifflin

Weil, A., and W. Rosen. 1983. *Chocolate to Morphine: Understanding Mind-Active Drugs.* Boston: Houghton Mifflin

Westermeyer, J. 1982. *Poppies, Pipes, and People: Opium and Its Use in Laos.* Berkeley: University of California Press

Wilkinson, J. 1986. *Tobacco: The Truth Behind the Smokescreen,* Harmondsworth: Penguin

Wisotsky, S. 1983. "Exposing the War on Cocaine: The Futility and Destructiveness of Prohibition." *Wisconsin Law Review* 6: 1305–1426

Zinberg, N.E. 1984. *Drug, Set, and Setting: The Basis for Controlled Intoxicant Use.* New Haven: Yale University Press

INDEX